GLOWING
Embers

PAOLA SANTANA

PSantana ♡

PS.

Paola Santana Books
(Formerly P.S. So Bookish)
www.paolasantanabooks.com
Liverpool, UK

First published worldwide by Paola Santana Books
1st EDITION – March 2026

Cover design and illustration by Ivanna Nashkolna

A CIP catalogue record for this book is available from the British Library.

Paperback ISBN: 978-1-0684670-2-8

Printed and bound worldwide by: IngramSpark, Lightning Source LLC and Kindle Direct Publishing,Amazon.com, Inc.
18+ content – not suitable for young readers.

NOTE TO READERS

Dear Reader,

Thank you so much for reading *Glowing Embers,* and for continuing to support my debut series *Playing with Fire*. This means the world to me.

There are phrases in Brazilian Portuguese throughout this novel, intended to make you feel as alienated as our main character does when she struggles with the language. But don't worry, if you want to know what they mean, you can check their translation in the 'Portuguese Translations' section at the end of the book.

TRIGGER WARNINGS

Please note that, although less spicy than *Playing With Fire,* this novel is still classed as a spicy romance with mentions of trauma, depression, and deteriorating mental health. As such, it's not recommended for readers younger than eighteen.

I hope *Glowing Embers* takes you on a trip to London and makes you laugh and cry with Paige and Marcelo. May you love it as much as—or even more than—you loved *Playing with Fire*.

Happy reading!
Paola 🤍

To Natalha—my daughter, my sunshine, my greatest challenge, and greatest achievement. I'm so proud of the woman you have become. Love you always, to the moon and back.

"Hatred stirs up conflict, but love erases all sins."

PROVERBS 10:12

PROLOGUE

Marcelo

"SO, AFTER ALL THAT, AFTER SHE GOT YOUR ASS BEAT AND CAUSED a rift in your family, she's leaving?" Both of Angie's eyebrows lifted, her eyes wide open. The expression adding to the sting, twisting the knife in my wound, and making me feel all the more like the fool in the punchline of a bad cosmic joke.

I nodded. Spent, empty, and running on fumes.

"That sucks, babe." She pretended to be surprised and supportive, but we both knew she'd always thought this was doomed. Angie was never sold on the idea that I could be monogamous long-term. "Was she at least worth it? All the drama she caused, I mean?"

I turned my back to her to lean against the kitchen island. I had no answer to give. Because Paige was worth it, yes. That's why I'd bought into the fight in the first place. But right now, with my life in shreds and her leaving, it sure as hell didn't feel like it.

Angie got off her bar stool and walked around the unit—a hand dragging along the countertop, heels creating muffled thumps against the ceramic floor until she was standing right in front of me.

"Don't you miss it?" She leaned in, eyes trying to pull me, fingers playing with my T-shirt. "When things were simpler, before she got here?" She stepped closer, toe to toe with me. "You and I used to have so much fun and none of this drama."

The puffs of air from every single one of her words hit my face. Her perfume oriental and fruity.

I placed my hands on her shoulders, leaned away a little. "What are you doing, Angie? We talked about this already."

"We did." She moved a strand of hair away from my face. Nails scraping at my temple, behind my ear, and along my jaw line, sending shivers down one of my arms. "But that was before she was leaving." She looked at me for a moment, gaze and lips flirting with me. "What difference would it make? She's leaving anyway." She pressed closer still, whispering, "And I know you. I know what you like." Her arms wrapped around my neck.

"Angie…" My tone was a warning, hands pushing against her forearms to keep a level of distance. But she tangled her hands in my hair, nails running at the back of my head, soothing and sexy all at the same time.

"I know what you need to feel better. And after she's gone, it's me you're going to come to anyway. So why wait?" She kissed me. Fast and furtive, then leaned away ever so slightly —nose centimeters from mine, waiting for a response, checking my temperature.

I didn't reciprocate, but I didn't push her away either. Just stared at her thinking about what she'd said. She wasn't wrong. After Paige left, I would probably end up in her bed at some point. Not because we had any feelings for each other, but because that was what we always did.

Angie kissed me a second time. Her lips more assertive, staying on mine a little longer. And a third time, lingering, nose touching mine. For another minute I did nothing, but on the fourth kiss I returned the favor.

In the back of my mind, I knew it was a mistake. Paige was leaving, but she hadn't told me. For all intents and purposes, we were still dating. Messed up, distant, sexless dating, but dating, nonetheless. I knew I shouldn't be doing this. But man, I was so tired. Tired of overthinking, of waiting for the death sentence. And I wanted, needed, to get some of the tension and frustration out of my body. The moment I acknowledged that, my brain shut off any lingering vestige of a conscience I had left.

I knotted my fingers in the hair at the back of her head. If I got rough with her, Angie wouldn't care. She would enjoy it. I knew what she liked too. And what she liked was fucking. Fast, furious, and intense. Right now, that suited me just fine. It required no thinking, no self-control. Most importantly, it required no feelings.

So I made the kiss deeper, hungrier, grabbed at pieces of her like I owned them. She turned us, pushed me toward the lounge. Nails scratching my skin, my T-shirt came off, teeth biting my shoulder, my nipples, like she wanted to mark me.

She smiled, her lips on mine. "Didn't you miss this?"

I grabbed at her ass and hoisted her up; she was only petite, light as a feather. Her legs wrapped around my waist, and I carried her upstairs.

Somewhere along the way she lost her top, her shoes, and when we got to my room, I threw her on the bed. Held her by the neck while I got rid of her shorts. She smiled all the way, like she always did.

I unbuttoned and unzipped my jeans. She kneeled on the bed, ready and willing, and I let her do the rest. Her hands found their way inside my denim, circling my hips from the front to the back, squeezing handfuls of my ass, scratching my skin, and pulling everything I was wearing down my legs. Palm closing around me, pumping me up before she laid her mouth on me. And fuck me, that felt incredible. Dopamine and endorphins rushed through my body, making everything disappear. It had been a while since I'd felt like this.

She worked me like a machine, sucking, licking, beating the meat, and hitting all the spots she knew damn well I liked. And I kneaded her ass, smacked it, grabbed handfuls of her hair every time I wanted her to work me harder.

While her mouth was busy, I reached for the bedside table, pulled a condom out of the drawer, and placed it in her hand. She dressed me up, then flipped over onto her all-fours—face on the mattress, hips high above her knees, and I knew I didn't have to worry. This kind of shit lit her up like a Christmas tree.

Without ceremony, I pulled her thong to the side and gave her exactly what she wanted. I held on to her hair, riding her fast and loud, until she changed position—shimmying sideways down the bed, getting rid of her panties, and making me step out of my jeans to follow suit.

"Look at me," she whispered, trying to hold on to my face and look me in the eyes as I went back inside her.

But I didn't. Instead, I kissed her, pulled her bra down, sucked at her nipple, kissed and licked my way across to her other shoulder.

My ribs complained. They were halfway through healing, and the muscles were stiff, complacent, accustomed to taking it easy while my bones rebuilt themselves after the fight with Felipe. But the rest of me was riding into oblivion. Working myself into physical exhaustion and the mental release of a brain that had stopped overthinking.

Angie had started to moan louder when something banged on the other side of me. I moved my head from the groove of her neck to look at the source.

Paige was standing by the door—eyes wide, eyebrows screwed together, one hand on her stomach, the other over her mouth as if to keep herself from throwing up.

Time stopped.

My heartbeat thundered in my ears. Mouth instantly dry. Stress rising up my back and freezing my muscles into place.

Then the bungee jump cord snapped—after I jumped.

I said her name, but the word didn't make it out of my throat. I looked at Angie. Looked down at where I was—naked, in between her bare legs—realization hitting home like a high-speed head-on collision on the highway. That split second when you realize there is minimal chance of survival. Panic fizzed in my stomach like acid.

Paige turned her back to us and walked out, one hand dragging along the wall, body bent over, the other still clutching her stomach.

"Cacete! Merda! Porra! Desgraça!" The colorful words I used all meant the same thing—that I was screwed beyond saving. I jumped off the bed, the mattress shaking under my weight and frenzy. Scanned the floor, found my jeans, and put them on, hopping and tripping over my own damn feet. The condom snapped off me like an elastic band.

Then I heard the smashing.

Glass breaking, things hitting the floor, her screaming. It paralyzed me from the neck down. Frozen, halfway through fastening my jeans. This was catastrophically bad. Real, real bad. Paige was leaving me, but I hadn't meant for things to end this way. I was mad, sure. Upset with her for leaving, sure. But I didn't want to break things off; I didn't want to hurt her, even if she was hurting me. Not like this. Not this way.

Dread sank its teeth into me, my whole body feeling out if it like I was on some bad trip. Slowly, I moved toward the door and stopped in the doorway, staring at the staircase.

"Stay here," I said to Angie without looking at her, one arm stretched behind me in warning.

I was vaguely aware of her getting up and moving around until she tried to push past me. I slammed the wall, blocking her way with my arm. My eyes focused on her then, my temper starting to show.

"I said stay here," I barked through my teeth. "If you try to walk past her now… Just… Just stay here."

I walked down the corridor, down the stairs—each step ripping a piece of my gut, telling me the consequences of my actions would make me regret living. And what was I going to say? I had never in my life been in this situation. What *could* I say? What could explain or justify what I'd just done?

Nothing.

Whether she was leaving or not, we were still together. I hadn't broken it off with her, neither she with me. And this? This was cheating. Caught red-handed, butt naked, dick in hand, *undeniable* ugly-ass cheating. How could I even begin to explain *that*?

I stopped at the bottom of the stairs, overlooking the open plan front room. Paige had my baseball bat, the one from the signed memorabilia, and she was smashing everything—the bookcase on the floor together with all its contents, the plates and glasses from the cupboards broken, the countertops wiped clean of everything that was once on them. Did she just try to throw a frying pan through the window? Good fucking job it was tempered glass.

And I couldn't move. It's not that I didn't see what she was doing or couldn't stop her. I deserved it. I deserved every bit of it. She was breaking my stuff because I had broken her heart.

She spotted me and walked toward the lounge dragging the bat behind her. Tears streamed down her cheeks in sobs she made no effort to control. Eyes full of questions—why? Why had I done this to her? I had been the one to put a label on it. I had wrapped silver around her wrist and called her mine. How could I do this?

I didn't say a thing. There was nothing I *could* say. And looking at her like this—red face, messy hair, tears streaming down her face like a river—shattered something in me that was already broken. I wanted to scream, pull the hair out of my head, knock myself unconscious. Instead, I did nothing. Just stood there, looking at her, wishing I could rewind the clock and erase the last hour of my life.

Paige looked down—her hair falling over her face, one hand over her eyes, shoulders hunched, the bat held loose to one side of her—and she sobbed like she was in physical pain. Guilt clawed at me, ripping chunks of my flesh like a hungry lion. As she raised her gaze back to me, she stopped.

Her breath caught, the sobbing stopped instantly, her eyes blinked repeatedly, but her eyelids didn't quite touch. And my blood ran cold because something behind me moved.

Angela. She had not stayed in the room like I'd told her. She had come down here, to make herself seen. To kick the chair I was standing on, while my neck hung in a noose and I balanced on my tiptoes.

Paige's expression changed. The pain was gone, her tears stopped streaming, and I could feel the waves of hatred rolling off her, face as hard as stone. Her focus shifted from Angela to me, and she lifted the bat and swung it like a striker right into the flat screen—the plasma cracking in circles from the center out. Delivering her final sentence.

Or so I thought.

She walked out swiping every surface on her way clean of photographs, papers, and books—her shoes breaking and cracking whatever she stepped over until she was out of the door. I didn't realize I was holding my breath until it came out of me in an audible gush.

Angela picked up her tee from the steps at the bottom of the stairs and put it on. I watched Paige march across the floor-to-ceiling window toward the garage. That was when we heard more smashing. She'd gotten to my car. My grandad's car. The vintage Mustang that had been his pride and joy, and that he had left to me.

I tried to run to the door, forgetting I was barefoot. A few steps in, I had to stop, a string of utter profanity pouring out of my mouth. Something had caught underneath my right foot. I made it out of the door cursing and limping.

"What the hell, Paige!?! Stop it! Get away from the damn car!" The noise changed, but it didn't stop. "Stop! That's my grandad's car!" I shouted trying to walk toward her, pain shooting up my leg, limping harder with every step. "You've smashed the fucking house already! I get it! I get it!" But the noise continued.

Only a few steps away from the house, I had to stop to yank away the offending piece of debris, blood gushing out, making me limp even more. "Stop! You stupid bitch!" Frustrated and at loss for what else to say, I screamed from the top of my lungs.

She hit something a couple of more times, then threw the bat at me wildly off target. Just to walk to the pedestrian gate and disappear. I stood there, hands in my hair—looking at the car, looking at the gate. Smashed lights, cracked windows, dented frame, the car alarm screaming at me without a hope in hell of being silenced if I couldn't find the keys. A timeless, classic Mustang turned into a battered old mule.

The house was a post-apocalyptic shitshow—broken glass and pieces of paper everywhere; books skewed under pieces of furniture and broken equipment; blood drops that had become red stains then bloody footprints that trailed all the way to me.

Time seemed to move in slow motion. I could hear things cracking under every single one of Angela's footsteps to the door. Halfway to the gate she smiled, flirting. "Once you get the psycho bitch sorted, call me."

And I saw it, clear as fucking day—the glint in her eye that told me she was happy about this. "Go to hell, Angela."

Her smile faded instantly. "Nice seeing you too, Celo." And she too disappeared out of the gate.

My foot was now gushing and throbbing, burning like it was on fire. Fists full of my hair, I took stock of the hell I'd created by my own doing, bewilderment and frustration turning me into a faulty pressure cooker. With nothing left to do, I blew my top and screamed.

CHAPTER 1
Marcelo

I WAS DOING THE STOCK TAKE BEHIND THE BAR WHEN MY PHONE buzzed. It rang twice before I could get it out of my pocket. One glance at the number and cold ran down my spine.

It had the international code for London.

"Hello?"

Nothing.

I said it again. "Hello?"

"Hi."

It was Paige.

I was so relieved to hear her voice that my legs felt like Jell-O. It had been nine months since she'd left Brazil without a trace and not a single one of us had heard from her; and over two months since she'd started talking to Lu again. I'd been watching my phone like a hawk after Lu told me she would call.

"Hi!" I sounded out of breath, but I wasn't. "Just... Just give me a minute. I'm at work. I just need to get myself into the office. Please don't hang up, ok?"

I waved at Leo, frantic, to tell him the bar was going to be unattended, but he didn't seem to see me. Ended up having to pull the phone away from my ear to shout at him. The door to my office shut, the quiet welcome, but unwelcoming.

"You still there?"

"Yes."

I'd wanted to speak to her for so long, but now that she was calling, I didn't know what to say. My mouth felt dry. I parked my ass on the desk, scrambled for a way to start the conversation.

"How are you?"

There was a long silence. "Fine." Her tone was flat, voice low. Unfriendly.

A thousand thoughts were going through my head. I needed something to occupy my mind and slow it down before the moronic side of my brain ruined any shot I had at redemption, so I reached into my pocket and started flipping the lighter on my fingers.

"I came looking for you. Turned up at Lu's door, but you had already gone."

The line went quiet.

"I've been trying to speak to you for months." It wasn't an accusation. I just didn't want her to think that I did what I did and then didn't care, didn't make an effort to try and fix things.

Silence. All I could hear was her breathing.

"I called, sent messages, emails, Insta. I tried everything." The memory put a knot in my throat. I swallowed it down.

"I heard."

I wanted to say it before she hung up on me. "Paige… I'm so sorry. I'm so… so sorry." The words came out rasping, catching on my teeth. "I know I fucked up something chronic. But please can we talk? Please can you give me a—"

"I need to tell you something." Her sharp, dry tone cut through my apology. "There is no nice way to say this, so I'm just going to come out with it."

My stomach turned. She was lining me up on the execution wall, and I was about to get gunned down. I'm sure she could hear my breathing and swallowing. I could.

But for what felt like a lifetime, she said nothing.

"You still there?"

"When I left Brazil, I was pregnant." The words came out in

a gush, as if she had to say it before she changed her mind. Her breathing grew faster on the other end of the line.

Out of all the scenarios I'd played in my head about this, that word didn't compute. "Pregnant? As in… with a baby?"

"Yes. Her name is Amber. She's just over a month old, and she's yours."

Pregnant. Baby. A month old. Yours.

I knew what the words meant, but they didn't make any sense. "Are you… are you telling me I have a kid?"

"Yes." Such a small word, said in a rush, but with such absoluteness that it weighed a ton.

I froze. My brain going to mush like I had wrapped it around a streetlamp at a hundred miles an hour. All thoughts obliterated from my head altogether. I literally had nothing, not a single word.

"Are you still there?"

"Why? Why didn't you tell me?" I gasped. As though someone else had said it, as if I wasn't in my body.

"I'm telling you now."

"Why didn't you tell me *before* you left?"

"I tried." She went quiet for a couple of seconds. "That's why I went to your house that day."

Realization hit me like a freight train. The day she caught me cheating, she had come to tell me she was pregnant with my baby. My fuck-up went from magnitude seven to off the fucking scale. Self-loathing and regret made me want to punch something. Out of options, I grabbed a handful of my hair until it hurt.

"You were pregnant for nine months after that and you didn't say anything. You didn't answer any of my calls, texts, nothing!" The math clicked into place. She left in June—now we were in March.

"Eight months. When I found out, I was already five weeks. And I didn't know what I was going to do." Her voice was strained, as if she was trying her hardest to keep an even tone.

"What do you mean 'you didn't know what you were going to do'?!" More words that also made no sense.

"I'm not expecting anything from you." That sharpened my senses like a slap across the face. My brain finally decided to join the conversation, homing in on every word with the precision of a laser beam. "I just… thought you had the right to know. I'm not calling for money and I don't—"

"*Stop.*" I cut her off. Anger, offense, and hurt turned my voice into an icy sharp sword. "I know you're upset with me, and you have all the right to be. But *do not* talk to me like I would abandon my kid."

She didn't respond. For a moment neither of us said anything.

"I'm flying to London. I will text this number once I have the flight booked. If you don't send me your address, I will knock on every fucking door until I find you and my kid." I cut the call.

To say I was pissed didn't cut it. Not just that she didn't tell me, but that when she did, she talked to me like I was a piece of shit. Like I wouldn't care about my own kid. Like I would do to my child what my parents did to me.

CHAPTER 2
Luciana

My door burst open. Marcelo had bypassed my assistant.

"I'm going to have to call you back." I put the phone down before he started screaming.

"You knew, didn't you? That's why you were so sure she was gonna call me. That's what you've been hiding." His voice didn't raise; it dropped lower. His finger pointed at me, the accusation coming out through his teeth in a low, angry tone, his voice smooth like silk.

"I'm kind of having a déjà vu moment. But last time this happened, it was Felipe bursting through my door." I waved at my assistant. "It's ok, Cecilia." She closed the door behind her. I stood up and walked around to the front of my desk. "I gather she finally told you."

"You knew."

"Of course, I knew. Who do you think took her to the doctors?"

His lips squeezed together, the muscles around his nose trembling, his head turning to the side, hands clenched into fists so tight, his knuckles went white. If I was a man, he would've punched me.

"And who do you think convinced her to tell you?"

His head returned to the center, the muscles stopped jumping, but his fists stayed balled up.

"Who else knows?"

"Nobody. Just me."

"All this time, you knew. Why didn't *you* tell me!?"

"Because if I had, I would have lost my best friend. We would both have lost her. Plus, when she left, I thought she'd gone back to England to have a termination. Terminations are easier if you do it in the first ten weeks. She was already five when she found out."

"She was going to have an abortion!?" His tone became high-pitched at the last word, his eyebrows screwed together in outrage. He gasped, pivoted on his foot. His fingers laced behind his head as he paced around the room like a crazy person.

"What did you expect, Celo? Put yourself in her shoes for a second. She was only twenty-four, pregnant from a guy she had dated for just over a month in another country—three weeks of which he spent depressed—and then she caught him cheating. What would *you* have done?"

He sat down on the chair. The same chair Felipe had sat on. This was a hundred per cent déjà vu. His hands rubbed over his face and down his neck, fingers like claws, as if he was trying to rip his own skin. Three thousand emotions passed over his face in one minute.

"She didn't though, Celo. She couldn't go through with it. Said the baby wasn't just yours, it was hers too."

He closed his eyes and sighed. Then leaned back on the chair and stared at nothing.

I waited a minute. "How are you feeling about it, now that you know?"

His head turned to me slowly, eyes angry. "I just found out Paige had my kid. And they are both across the fucking Atlantic. How do you think I feel?" He went back to staring at nothing.

"At least now you know where she is."

He scoffed.

"I just can't believe you're a dad. Fancy that!"

He frowned like the word didn't fit, didn't sit well with him.

"Did you ever think you'd have children?"

He shook his head, continued staring at nothing.

"Did she send you a picture?"

Another head shake.

"Do you want to see your baby girl?"

His head snapped in my direction, eyes focused on me sharper than an eagle. "You have a picture?" His voice was low, raspy, full of disbelief.

"I have better than that!"

Celo sat forward in his chair, and I leaned over my desk to grab my phone. By the time I had it opened, he was standing next to me.

"She told me she didn't know how to tell you. I told her to send you a picture. I knew that as soon as you saw the baby, you'd know she's yours. Believe me, there is no denying who's the daddy!"

I opened the video Paige had sent me the day after Amber was born. The chubby baby was in a hospital cot, name tag on her wrist, huge cheeks, dark unfocused eyes, frown on her little eyebrows, and masses of dark hair. Paige's voice boomed through the speakers. "Look who arrived last night, Auntie Lu! Two weeks late, like a proper queen, at a whopping eight and a half pounds. I have the stitches to prove it. Look at all this dark hair." Paige's hand rubbed the baby's head. "I think she'll have dark eyes too. And look at this cute grumpy face!" Her thumb rubbed the crease on Amber's forehead, the baby's head turning in response. "I guess your Brazilian saying was right."

He rewound the video, played it twice more. His eyebrows frowning, he looked tired. "What Brazilian saying is right?"

"That if the father makes the mother angry, the baby is born looking like him."

His sigh came out like a rushed puff. "She never had a chance. I messed it up pretty good on that front."

"There are more pictures and one more video."

He signaled with the phone, asking for permission.

I nodded. "There are a couple more before it to the left and some more to the right."

There was a photo of Paige pregnant, wearing a figure-hugging baby pink dress—hands cradling her bump, face turned downwards, looking at her stomach with a soft smile, belly huge. He stayed on this picture for a while, zoomed in on her face. His eyes softened and became sad, scanning every detail; his eyebrows arched upwards in the middle.

He missed her.

Then there was a video she'd recorded for me in the middle of the night. All you could see was her huge stomach and waves moving under her skin, turning her belly into a big lopsided shape. All of a sudden, a sharp bump poked out, as if an alien had invaded her body and was trying to break out. "Look at this, Lu. You think I'm joking? It's 3am and this little madam is playing football with my ribs. Oh! Right on cue, you even get to see the offending foot! Poppet, please let Mummy sleep. I'm so tired." And the video ended. He replayed this one too, frowning all the way.

There were also some hospital pictures—individual people holding the baby, Amber asleep, Paige holding Amber's little hand, miniature feet, their maternity bracelets next to each other.

"This is Paige's mum, Kate. And that's her dad, Ryan," I said as he swiped through the pictures.

"She looks like her father." His voice was a whisper.

"Just like your little girl looks like you. Maybe it's a family thing." It almost looked like Amber wasn't Paige's baby. Paige was caramel blonde, with light green eyes and very fair skin. Amber was a tiny dark bean next to her. "And these are her two half-sisters. They flew from the States when she had the baby."

He nodded, then whispered, "And we weren't there."

Had things worked out differently, our family would also have descended at the hospital in droves, like we did when Freddie, Felipe's little brother, was born.

"No. But at least she told you while Amber is still a newborn. Her mum didn't say anything till Paige was twenty-four. Count yourself lucky."

Paige and Marcelo's story was almost a replay of Kate and Ryan's, Paige's parents. Except, Ryan hadn't found out he had a daughter till much, much later. If it'd been up to Kate, he would never have known.

"At least she wasn't alone." He sighed, ran his hand down his face. "Can I send all these to myself?"

"Of course! She's *your* kid."

"Is the baby healthy? She was born ok, right?" His voice was low, anxious. "On the video Paige said she was two weeks late and she had stitches." His face was turned toward me, but he was staring at the floor.

"Are you kidding? That little dark bean weighs a fucking ton. Have you seen the size of her cheeks! I feel sorry for my friend, squeezing that watermelon through the space of a carrot!"

He looked at me with disapproval, as if I was being distasteful.

"True fact that!"

His phone vibrated; he checked it. "She sent me her address. I told her that if she didn't send it to me, I was going to knock on every damn door until I found her and my kid."

"May I?" I extended my hand out for his cell. He gave it to me. I wrote down the address on a Post-it. "When do you want to go?"

"Tomorrow. I need some time to organize things, so I can

go for a while." He had gone back to my phone. Rewatching one of the videos.

"For how long?"

A tap, and the device paused. His head lifted, hands asking for his cell back.

I handed it over. He studied his calendar for a moment. "I will have to come back before April twenty-seventh. I'll get the keys for the new bar then, and we'll need to start the building work to get it ready for opening. That's the only thing I can't shift." His voice was low, raspy, full of an exhaustion that I didn't think was physical.

"Of course." Celo was opening a second bar. Our firm was in charge of the refurbishments. I was project managing, and the turnaround was tight as he wanted it ready as soon as possible. The longer the venue stayed closed, the more money he lost.

He counted something down his screen. "That's five weeks. I need to be back on April twenty-sixth. If I hadn't signed the papers and paid the deposit already, I would pull out. But I can't now. The building team is booked; everything is in train. There's no turning back, and I have to be here."

I walked to the door and addressed my assistant. "Cecilia, please book business class tickets to London for tomorrow, coming back in five weeks, for Marcelo Costa. Also find a good hotel as close as possible to this address and book him in there. Send the confirmations to him. You'll have his details on the list of board members."

I walked back to him. "I've done as much as I can. Now you go, get our girls back and, please… don't fuck this up."

CHAPTER 3

Marcelo

I COULDN'T FIGURE OUT HOW TO SAY IT, HOW TO TELL PEOPLE I had a kid. It didn't feel real or sound right.

Told Leo that I was going to be away for five weeks, bribed him with a decent bonus so he wouldn't kick a sting. But when he asked me where I was going, I didn't know what to say. So I just showed him one of the photos. He looked at the picture, then at me, then back at the picture.

"When did you make that!?"

I shrugged.

"Bless her little soul. She inherited all your bad looks."

"How do you know it's a girl?"

He stared at me, both his eyebrows raising. "She's dressed in pink."

I looked at the picture. She was dressed in pink alright.

"Man, you need to do some reading. You don't have a clue, do you?" He laughed. Leo had two kids. "You're about to walk into a hurricane. Say goodbye to your life as you know it, dude."

"You make it sound like a bad thing, but all you do is talk about your kids."

"I love my kids. They're the best thing I've ever done. Man, when I get home and those two little faces scream with excitement just from seeing me, I'm on top of the world. They're more excited to see me than my Mrs.! And they think I'm a superhero. There is no bad day that won't fix. But if you're a good dad, it will change all your priorities, man. It'll shift everything."

Told Marisa I was going to be away and miss our holiday in Ilhabela this year. She'd started to protest until I showed her the picture.

"Holy shit!" She never swore. Her eyes were huge when she looked at me.

"Mom! You said a bad word!" Freddie was eavesdropping. "Let me see! I want to see!" I showed him the picture. He scrunched his nose. "Oh! It's just a baby!" He said it as if he was expecting something more exciting.

"It's Marcelo's baby, Freddie."

"Celo doesn't have a baby."

"He does now! I mean… I suppose I shouldn't be surprised, with all your antics. It was bound to happen sooner or later. Who is the mom?" Marisa's eyebrows were screwed together.

"Jesus, Risa, you make me sound like a…" I was going to say whore, but Freddie was listening like a radar. "… working girl."

She raised one eyebrow at me, puckered her lips, unimpressed. "Who is the mom?"

"Paige."

Risa's eyes grew even bigger and her jaw dropped; she sat down.

"I like Paige. You put a baby in Paige's tummy?" Freddie was now interested.

"It's not in her tummy anymore, bud."

"How did you put a baby there?" His face looked genuinely confused, eyebrows screwed together, nose wrinkled, mouth open.

My neck itched; I scratched it. At a loss for what to say, I looked at Risa. "Ah… I think your mom better explain that to you."

"Not now, Freddie. Go watch TV."

He shrugged and went back to watch his cartoons. Obviously, a baby just wasn't all that interesting.

"I'd say that's a hell of a plot twist. Wouldn't you? Jesus!"

"I didn't know until today. She didn't tell me."

"Sounds like you're lucky she told you at all."

"That's what Lu said." I stared at her for a moment; she still looked shocked. "I need to fix this, Risa. Now more than ever."

"By fixing it, do you mean getting back together with Paige?"

I nodded.

"Are you saying that just because of the baby? Because, you know, you're still her father, even if you're not with Paige."

I shook my head. "I want her back, Risa." Admitting it was like rubbing on a blister—uncomfortable, painful. It made me sound tired. "Sometimes I wish I didn't. It would be so much easier if I could just forget and move on, but I can't."

Risa's eyes softened; she reached for my arm and squeezed it.

"I considered it, you know. When the weeks turned into months, I thought that was it. Thought maybe I should let it go. Go out, have a drink, meet some women. But it just felt weird, wrong somehow." I rubbed a hand down my face. The whole thing honestly perplexed me. "I just didn't have it in me." My resignation came out as a sigh. "It has been months. *Months*, Risa! I keep on waiting to feel different, but I don't. I can't get her out of my head. Sometimes I feel like I'm going insane."

Risa's face twisted into something that looked like pity. And it was pitiful; there was no denying it. "You're not going insane. You just found your person, that's all." She paused for a beat. "You know getting her back won't be easy, right? I wish I could tell you everything is going to be ok, but you made some really poor choices."

I took a deep breath, stared at her hand squeezing my arm, and nodded.

"You betrayed her trust and broke her heart. If she's a smart woman, she'll make you work seriously hard to get those back, if she gives them back to you at all."

"I know. I have no doubt she'll make me pay. I would if I was her."

"One thing is to know someone is upset with you. But feeling their anger on your skin over and over again is quite another. Are you sure you're ready for that? Are you sure you can take it?"

"I want her back, Risa. And if I have to pay the price, so be it."

"It'll take a lot of patience. You're going to have to prove to her that you've learned your lesson and are serious about her and the baby. The only way you can do that is by being present, consistent, and quietly persistent. The proof will be in your actions, not in your words. If I know Paige, she won't settle for anything else. Are you sure you're ready for what this will cost you? Are you sure this is what you want?" Her voice sounded concerned.

"If I can get her back, I'll take whatever hell she brings down on me."

"What if you can't? Are you prepared for that?"

I had no answer. Something in me cracked just thinking about it. She squeezed my arm once more. The words that followed came out in a whisper. "I need her, Risa. Sometimes I miss her so bad, it feels like something in my body is missing. It's insane. It makes no sense. We didn't date for long. I can't explain it."

A frown revealed her worry, her hand rubbing my arm with such force it had stopped feeling like a caress. "You'll take your meds with you, right? Just in case?"

I hesitated but conceded and nodded. I'd take them, not

with any intention of taking any, but just to give her peace of mind.

Her expression cleared, and her chin dipped in one sharp move. "Well… if you can get through this as a couple, you can get through anything. And wouldn't *that* be something?" The squeeze she gave my arm matched the sharpness of her nod.

I mirrored her gesture, unlocked my phone, and the picture filled the screen. My kid was staring right at me. Lu was right—there was no denying she was mine. But it just felt bizarre, like I was daydreaming.

"You know Felipe will have something to say about this." The thought sneaked up on the hope I was feeling and tried to quash it.

"Yes, I should imagine so. He won't be happy, we know that. But unfortunately for him, babies are non-refundable."

I sighed. We would be back at ground zero. Felipe had just started attending family events again, after spending months behaving like I had some contagious disease.

"But you can only tackle one problem at a time, my son. And right now, Felipe should not be your priority." One last squeeze of my arm. "What are you doing standing here still? You have somewhere else to be. Pack a thick coat and gloves. It'll be cold in London this time of year. And please show some manners. Don't turn up there empty-handed." She stood up. Touched my face, placed her hands on my shoulders, straightened my shirt. "You're doing the right thing going over there." Then she looked at me for a second. "I can't believe you made me a grandma. I'm too young for that!" And slapped my arm.

♥♥♥

Me
Flight leaves 2nite. I'll be in London tomorrow 5pm. Will come over after I check in.

Paige
By the time you're done it will be too late to visit. Come the day after.

Me
10am then.

Paige
Fine.

Marisa wasn't kidding; it was freezing in London. Gray skies, wind hitting you like a thousand knives, and the air too cold to smell anything.

I felt like a caged animal—a build-up of nervous energy and tension that had twelve hours to marinate sitting in a flying can, then in a taxi for another hour before being unceremoniously spat out onto a sidewalk in Pimlico.

The hotel was in a residential area, facing a school: six floors of sheer brick wall covered in rows of white windows. Not the prettiest building I had ever seen. But once you got past reception, it was hallowed at its center, hiding a big garden with a water fountain at its heart, trees still looking like overgrown twigs, at odds with the emerald-green grass everywhere else. There was floor upon floor of orange brick surrounding the gardens—a fortress, clearly designed to keep the elite away from the masses. Ironic. In Brazil, buildings with exposed bricks were normally construction projects that had run out of money before they were finished.

My room turned out to actually be a one-bedroom serviced apartment. Modern, spacious, big windows. My home for the next five weeks. I knew something was seriously wrong with me when I caught myself giving too much thought to the fact I had a washing machine. How I was going to do my laundry was all of a sudden a big deal, as if I actually cared.

I hadn't paid much attention to anything in between the airport and the hotel. My mind was overthinking the scenarios, trying to prepare for what was to come without having a clue what it would be. Rehearsing what to say. Stomach turning at the thought of seeing Paige and the baby, at the same time as feeling like a kid the night before Christmas.

By the time I was all set, it was only 7.30pm. It wasn't too late to visit, but I wasn't gonna be difficult, start demanding things, making myself a nuisance. That wouldn't help my case. At least I knew where she was and when I was gonna see her. I had come this far; I could wait a little longer.

The hotel had a pool, so I did some laps, checked out their gym—the physical burn helped, but didn't quite manage to disperse the tension. Had some food. Had a drink at the bar, checked their cocktail menu. Read some more of the baby book I bought at the airport.

Apparently, one-month-old babies can't see much and have a very short memory. If I had been there during the pregnancy, the baby might've remembered my voice. But to my kid I was a complete stranger. If she didn't see me or hear me every day, she would forget me. I had to speak to her and hold her as much as possible so she would know who I am. Like a computer being programmed. Leo was right, reading about it was helpful. Would've never known that.

By 11pm I was restless. My body full of energy, still synced to the Brazilian time zone four hours behind; the hotel room feeling like the wing of a mental asylum. I had come all this way and was so close, but now I was just sitting here. Idling.

So I walked to Paige's address anyway. Told myself it was

only to know where I was going the next morning, but it wasn't. I just couldn't wait.

Her building was around the corner from a quaint row of shops. A residential street that, at this hour, was inhabited only by streetlamps and a cold wind that cut straight to my bones. It was exactly seven minutes' walk from my hotel. For all my complaining, Lu's assistant had done a great job booking me in somewhere real close.

Her apartment was in a townhouse. Three floors and very English. The street level was white, black railings around the ground floor with a mosaic path to the door, set not that far from the curb. A heavy, wide navy blue front door that told you the building was old. The two floors above were made of yellow brick and big windows, with white trims around them and on the edge of the roof.

I looked at the doorbell and Flat A wasn't on the list. That confused me and, for a minute, I thought she had sent me the wrong address. Then I spotted the small gate on the railings and steps going down. Flat A was the apartment in the basement.

The curtains were closed, but there was a gap in them where the fabric didn't quite meet, and the lights were still on. Through the opening I could just see the sliver of a living room and doors leading into what looked like a dining area.

I had been outside, leaning against a car for a few minutes —my ass, toes, and fingers going numb with the cold despite all my padding. I was about to leave when something moved.

And I saw her.

Paige walked into the room with a cup of something hot enough to steam and sat down on the armchair right in front of the gap. I'd be willing to bet it was English tea. Her hair was up in a messy bun. Her boobs were bigger, her face and figure a little rounder, but it was her.

After months of hanging suspended, seeing her was like

medicine. It relaxed my body and calmed my nerves. But it also made me ache. Ache for all the things I had missed—her smile, her skin, her freaky green eyes. The pregnancy, the birth. And the irony wasn't lost on me. Back then, I thought she was ruining my life. Now, it was clear I had done it all on my own.

I stood there watching her—feet tucked underneath her body on the seat, one hand propping the cup of tea on her knee, the other elbow leaning on the armrest; chin resting on her palm, fingers absentmindedly rubbing her lips, eyes staring at nothing. Deep in thought until something attracted her attention. Her head turned, she nodded, her expression serious, then said something and went back to staring at nothing while sipping her tea.

It was freezing, but I didn't care. I stayed until she left the room and switched the lights off.

The next morning, at 10am sharp, I knocked on the door. Her mom opened it.

"Hi. I'm Marcelo. I'm here to see—"

"Come on in." She interjected before I finished my sentence and moved out of the doorway so I could walk past her. "Paige is just feeding Amber. They will come through in a minute. I'm Kate, Paige's mum." She extended a hand to greet me. I moved the things I was holding to one arm and pulled off my glove to shake it. "Can I take your coat? Would you mind taking your shoes off?"

"These are for you." I handed her the flowers I had brought with me.

"Oh, thank you. Unnecessary, but very kind." Her voice was monotone, as though she'd said it out of politeness rather than anything else.

I continued juggling things from one arm to another to hand her my jacket and get out of my boots. "Where do you want them?" I signaled, boots in hand. She pointed to a mat in the hall; I put them on it.

"Come through. Would you like some tea?" She led me into the lounge I had seen the night before.

"I don't drink tea, sorry. But I'd love some water." Kate nodded and walked away.

My chest was constricting, turning itself inside out, stomach on fire. I hadn't been able to drink or eat anything before coming over, and I hadn't slept much. I'd waited for this for months and, now that I was here, I had no idea if I was going to sink or swim. Hanging on to the thin ledge of a precipice by a couple of fingertips, no matter how much I told myself to get a fucking grip.

I rolled my shoulders, moved my neck from side to side to try to get rid of some of the tension. To stop overthinking and pacing, I started looking at the pictures on the fireplace. Paige was white-blonde as a child, her eyes even bigger vivid pools of green, big round cheeky little face, dressed in a multitude of dancing outfits. By the time she was in her teens, she already looked like she did now. They were all only of Kate and Paige. No dad.

Looking around the room, I could see why Paige liked pastel colors. The walls were a pale green, the furniture cream, and all the other details in the room had these soft tones on them. She'd grown up with the same color palette. The sofa and chairs were covered in cushions; everything was pretty and had interesting textures or patterns to it. It was very calming, soothing. I needed that.

Kate came back with a tray—my water and two teas. It didn't look like she had any intention of leaving the room. She handed me my glass, pointed for me to sit on the sofa, and took a seat on the arm of a chair.

"So you're Amber's father." She took a sip of her tea, her eyes cutting into me like razors.

Lu had called Kate the 'Gates of Hades'. Apparently, she was a very difficult woman. And if Paige had told her anything about what had happened, I had no doubt she would hate my guts.

I nodded and drank some of my water.

"I'm under strict instructions from Paige's father not to give you a hard time."

"You can give me a hard time if you want, but what would that achieve? It won't really help anyone or make things any easier," I said, looking straight at her, keeping my voice calm and unthreatening. With difficult people, you are always better being a straight shooter and sticking to facts they can't refute.

She stared at me for a minute. Then smiled, raised her eyebrows, and sipped her tea. "Is Amber your first child?"

I nodded.

"How old are you?"

"Twenty-eight."

"What do you do for a living?" She took another sip of her tea.

"I own a couple of businesses."

"Like what?"

"One is a bar and restaurant—actually, two. I'm about to open a second venue. Two are a bar and restaurant, the other is an architecture and construction firm."

Her eyebrows raised; her chin tipped up and down. At least on that front, I knew she couldn't fault me. I wasn't some good-for-nothing that couldn't provide for her daughter.

"How long are you planning to stay?"

"Five weeks. But I will go, sort some things out, and come straight back."

"Why? Why come back at all?" she said, sitting there, an English lady drinking her tea, but snarling at me like a rottweiler.

"Because Paige and Amber are here."

"Paige doesn't want anything from you."

"Maybe. But I still want to give her, both of them, everything I can."

She nodded, drank more of her tea.

We sat in silence. Kate had a blank expression, but her eyes were throwing daggers at me.

Then Paige walked into the room.

She was wearing jeans and a V-neck loose tee, hair parted to the side, one half pushed behind her ear. At a distance, she was beautiful. But this close, she was eat-your-heart-out gorgeous. And God help me, I had missed her. Everything about her. Her laugh, her humor. The way she sassed me and put me in my place. The feeling was stuck in my throat, hard to swallow.

On one shoulder she had this little round bundle, a dark mass of hair above it. It was small, but solid. She stood by the door like she wasn't sure she wanted to come in.

We looked at each other for a long moment, her face unreadable.

CHAPTER 4

Paige

Marcelo stood up as soon as I walked into the sitting room. His lips pressed together, and he swallowed as though something had caught in his throat, his eyes wide and intent on me.

I didn't really want to look at him. But despite my best efforts, my eyes looked for him as soon as I walked into the room and refused to move elsewhere, rebelling against my will.

He looked taller, bigger somehow, like he'd been working out. All his tattoos were covered under a long-sleeved polo with no collar, buttoned up. His hair was down, parted to the side. And there was beard stubble I don't remember him having. He took up more space, appeared more imposing than he was when we first met.

I had dreaded this—seeing him. Had put it off yesterday and procrastinated feeding Amber to buy myself more time. If I could've walked back out of the door, I would've done. But Amber wiggled on my shoulder, and I remembered why he was here.

I moved her to face forward, facing him. "This is Amber." His gaze stayed on me a second longer, then turned to her. "She's milk drunk at the minute, so she's a little groggy."

For a moment, he didn't move—focus darting from me to Amber. Then his hands came together, and he squeezed one of them with so much force, I could see every single one of his knuckles from where I stood. His face had no expression, but his eyes looked… anxious, nervous. It made him look younger, childlike.

After a couple of minutes of uncomfortable silence and a hard swallow, he walked to me slowly, tentatively, coming to a stop so close, I could smell his aftershave. It was still the same.

This was going to be harder than I thought.

"Hi," he said, looking at my face, the word coming out in a gush of air as if he breathed it out rather than said it.

I averted my eyes to stare at the buttons on his shirt and didn't respond.

The silence dragged like he was waiting for an answer, but when he didn't get one, his attention turned to Amber. "Hey, baby girl." Fingers trailed the contour of her chubby cheek, his words still coming out in a breath rather than fully spoken. "Nice to meet you." His index finger rubbed over her hand, and her tiny fingers wrapped around it as if they were shaking hands.

I couldn't look at him when he was standing this close, smelling this good, eliciting a cold chill that told me my body would betray me if I let it; so I focused on the top of Amber's head instead.

"Can I…?" Palms facing upwards, he gestured toward Amber.

I felt like pulling her away from him and, if I'm honest, I didn't really want to hand her over.

But he was her father. This was why he was here.

I didn't want him this close to me either.

"You need to support her neck. She can't hold it by herself just yet."

He nodded.

I placed her in his hands, and he took a few steps back, rocking her up and down suspended in front of him, so he could look at her face. Her whole body fit inside his two palms; she looked incredibly small, tiny next to him. And they were two peas in a pod—same color skin, same hair, same eyes.

I took a seat next to my mother. Understanding how hard this was for me, she rubbed comforting circles on my back while we both watched Marcelo hold Amber.

For a while he didn't say or do anything, just looked at her. Holding her awkwardly away from his body like he was reading the label of a giant tin in the supermarket. His eyes scanned her face, throat working in compulsive swallows. The room felt weirdly still.

Then he inhaled one long breath and started talking to her in Portuguese.

For the first few sentences Amber stared at him, a frown on her little face like she was giving him a scolding. But then she gurgled, sticking her tongue out, making noises back at him as if she understood him. Her feet stuck out and touched his stomach, and her arms started waving.

Marcelo's expression softened; his shoulders relaxed. He smiled and continued talking to her in his language. She continued responding. And he brought her close to his face, kissed her chubby cheeks, talking to her, kissing her forehead. Soft eyes, small smile playing on his lips. He gave her the same look he used to give Freddie—the love look.

My chest tightened. When we were together, we had never spoken about children; I had no idea if he wanted any. And now, in hindsight, I could recognize that part of me worried he wouldn't want to know Amber. But I had quite literally just watched him fall in love with her right in front of me. I had to look away not to cry.

"What is he saying to her?" Mum whispered in my ear.

I shrugged. I didn't know. And it didn't matter. What mattered was that he was bonding with his daughter.

Marcelo walked to the window, turning his back to us, and

moved Amber so she was lying on one of his arms. He continued talking to her but every so often he would wipe at his face and sniffle, his arms raising up, his head dipping to kiss her head. And as angry, as upset as I was that he was here, I knew I had done the right thing. I couldn't take this away from my little girl. Or from him.

I was so focused on the scene in front of me that Mum's ringtone made me jump. She reached for her phone, showed me her screen—Ryan—and walked out of the room. He knew Marcelo was coming and probably wanted to know if Mum was behaving. They didn't use to speak, but since I'd announced I was pregnant and had a meltdown about it, they had taken to talking on the phone at night. First about me, then about other things. Slowly, the tone had changed from impassive news report to inside jokes and laughter. He asked her opinion on some of his projects—he was a property developer, she an interior designer. Now, they talked every day like they had never not spoken or weren't in a cold war with each other before I blew up my life.

The irony… Funny how one thing ends, and another begins.

Marcelo stayed at the window for a long time. Then rubbed the back of his hand on his face and turned around—eyes red, eyelashes wet.

"I need to take a photo for Marisa. She has messaged me non-stop wanting news."

"Who is Marisa?" Mum asked as she walked back into the room. She had become very protective of both Amber and me.

"My mom." I had never heard him call Marisa 'Mom'. That was new.

I nodded and stood up from my chair. "You're better taking a video. She pulls really weird faces in photos. It will take you ages to get a good one."

His head bounced up and down in agreement, a phone

coming out of his pocket. He unlocked it, found the camera, and handed it to me. I pointed it at him and nodded. He turned sideways, so Amber faced the front.

"Oi vovó, vovô, Freddie, Tia Lu." He picked up Amber's little arm and waved it at the camera. *"Meu pai veio me ver hoje. Eu bati uma real nele, sabe? Colocamos todos os pingos nos is."* Amber was staring at him and, on cue, as he started speaking, she started grunting. Marcelo looked at her, smiled, kissed her head. Then turned her in his arms so she was facing him once again. He nodded at her, talking in Portuguese like they were having a conversation, kissed her cheeks, touched his nose to hers.

And I couldn't watch it anymore. I stopped filming.

He moved Amber back to one arm; I handed the phone back to him. Four taps and it was shoved back in his pocket.

After all the changes in position, Amber started wiggling and whining in his arms. He tried to comfort her, but the whining soon became a full cry.

"I didn't pinch her, I promise." He looked at me not knowing what to do.

"You been holding her for over an hour. She probably just needs a nappy change." I extended my hands out to take her from him.

"I can do it."

I stared at him.

"I used to help Marisa with Freddie."

I continued staring.

"I'm not here just to see her and go home. I'm here to be her dad. A real dad."

The words caught me by surprise, and I hesitated. But after a couple of seconds my brain jump-started, and I nodded.

"Where is her nappy stuff?"

I signaled for him to follow me, and he walked behind me to the kitchen.

"You have to change her on smooth surfaces. Stay away from upholstery and carpets. She leaks."

"What do you mean 'she leaks'?"

I unrolled her changing mat on top of the dining table and got all the stuff out. Very gently, he placed her on the mat. Amber's crying increased in volume.

"She has a good set of lungs on her, doesn't she?"

I snorted. "They're particularly good at 3am."

"She wakes up at 3am every night?" He unbuttoned her onesie, getting her chubby legs out.

I nodded and heard him smile.

"I don't know why you think that's funny."

He pulled a couple of wipes from their packet. "3am is the time we met at the pool in Ilhabela." His eyes burned into the side of my face while he unwrapped Amber's nappy. "Remember?"

I didn't answer and didn't look at him.

With her skin exposed, Amber started peeing. "You might want to focus." I pointed at our baby.

"Oh shit!" He panicked, and rather than folding the nappy back over, he picked her up and held her suspended. Pee running down her legs and going everywhere, including all over his top.

After she was finished, he looked at the mess and nodded, lips pressing together. "She leaks."

"She does. It's the fresh air. Next time, just fold the nappy back over and wait."

"Copy that."

I cleaned the mat, took her clothes off, and wiped her legs while he held her suspended. As I went to get her clean clothes, he continued changing her nappy, but by the time I came back she was screaming twice as loud.

"Why is she still crying? She has a clean nappy." He was

frowning, a hand holding on to one of Amber's and rubbing her arm. His fingers looked huge next to hers.

"She doesn't like being naked. I think she feels exposed."

He gave me a distracted nod, his eyes on Amber. "Good. Let's hope she keeps that till she's thirty."

"Ironic, coming from the one that got a twenty-four-year-old pregnant and became a father at twenty-eight."

His head snapped toward me, stare digging into the side of my face for a moment, but he didn't bite into my goading. "Do you mind if I rinse my shirt in your sink? This stuff stinks." He was already unbuttoning his top.

"No, but it's not going to dry before you leave. This is not Brazil."

While I redressed Amber, he walked to the sink and pulled his polo off, opened the tap and started rinsing where the pee had hit. I had forgotten what he looked like undressed, with all his tattoos. And he was fitter, his muscles more defined.

I hated him even more. I looked like a postnatal plum, and he looked even better. Prick.

Mum walked into the kitchen. "What on earth are you two doing to that little girl? And why is *he* half naked?" She pointed at Marcelo but looked at me.

He looked at her, at his shirt under the tap, back at her. "Ah… Sorry, I don't normally strip the first time I meet people." Liar. He had shown unknown women a great deal more. "It was an accident."

"Amber peed on him. He's rinsing his top," I said, picking Amber up and raising her to my shoulder.

"I can see that." My mother's tone was flat. "But it's not going to dry before he leaves."

"I told him."

He twisted the wet part of the shirt in between his hands to get the water out and turned our way while pulling it over his head, the skin at his sides stretching over bone and muscle. My mother looked at me, one eyebrow raised.

And I hit my limit. "Well… I think that is enough for today."

He looked at me for a moment, then understanding what I meant, nodded. "Can I come back tomorrow? Same time?" He sounded disappointed.

I would have loved to say no. But this was why he was here, so I agreed.

We followed him to the hall. He put his boots back on; Mum handed him his coat. His top was wet, right down the middle, crinkles forming the shape of a rose where he had twisted it.

"It was nice meeting you, Kate." He nodded at my mother. She nodded back; her fingers crisscrossed in front of her lap like a school mistress. He stepped toward me, then to my side. "See you tomorrow, baby girl." His hand caressed Amber's head, and he leaned down to kiss her. His face coming incredibly close to mine.

It took everything in me not to recoil, stand still, and let him do it.

He shifted on his feet to stand in front of me. "Thanks for telling me and allowing me to visit. I know you could've chosen different." His voice was low, as if he only wanted me to hear it.

It wasn't what I thought he was going to say. Caught by surprise a second time, I looked at him. His eyes caught mine, and the muscles around his mouth raised a fraction, his eyes taking in my face. It was just a flash of something, and then it was gone, but I could feel the tingle from the base of my skull down to my shoulders. Not wanting to succumb to it, I averted my gaze and nodded. He stood there, looking at me for a moment longer, then made for the door.

"I almost forgot," he said, turning back to me, one hand on

the door handle. "The bags in the lounge are for you and the baby."

"Unnecessary." I adjusted Amber's clothes so I wouldn't have to engage in conversation.

"But yours anyway." The door opened and closed.

And as soon as he was gone, "Amber is his spitting image, isn't she? He couldn't deny it even if he wanted to." My mother was ready to give me her opinion. "I can see why you were attracted to him. He's kind of good-looking and has an imposing presence even when he doesn't say anything. Not sure about the long hair and tattoos, though."

"Mum..." I turned to her. "I don't really need a recap of why I found him interesting enough to let him impregnate me."

"He's here for five weeks, you know. I'm back to work tomorrow, so you will have to deal with him on your own. Are you sure you're ready for that?"

"No. But I have to get used to it. He *is* her father, and there is nothing I can do about that." I walked into the sitting room; she followed. The bags he mentioned glared at me from the sofa. "I need a minute."

Understanding what I meant, she nodded, and I let her take Amber from me.

I sat in my room, staring at the two bags for God knows how long, feeling utterly drained and hollow.

The first bag had a teddy bear in it. Caramel soft fur dressed in a Brazilian football shirt.

The second bag I recognized instantly. It was smaller, but similar to the one the bracelet he gave me had come in. The bracelet that was supposed to mean I was his and we were official. I hadn't worn it since the day I'd caught him with Angela.

I unwrapped the ribbon, opened the small box. A charm in the shape of a baby pram sat inside it.

I didn't want to. Tried my hardest not to think about it at all over the last few months. But flashbacks of the day he gave me the bracelet flooded my memory. *You know you're the only one, right?* he had said to me. Then he'd bent me over the arm of his sofa and given me the best orgasm I've ever had. My body exploding, air scaping my lungs like I couldn't breathe, the aftershock causing my muscles to tremble.

Just thinking about it made my body tingle.

But I wasn't the only one. He wasn't just mine, even though I had been completely and utterly his.

My eyes filled up and welled over without my permission. The hurt and disappointment I'd tried so hard to push down resurfacing and suffocating me. It made the bruise fresh, my ears ringing, uncomfortable like a dissonant song on repeat. Upset pulled me under water, making me feel like I was drowning, as if it was an anchor around my ankles.

For a while I could do nothing but cry. Lie with my face buried in the bed covers, wishing I could forget it all. Forget how small, stupid, and insignificant he made me feel— the dark grave he had put me in while I was still breathing.

When the tears finally dried, I walked to the chest of drawers and shoved the small box in with its mother, covering it in baby clothes to keep it from being seen and tormenting me. My anger and pride telling me I should throw them away. Better still, I should give them both back to him. But something else, something no doubt very stupid, refusing to let go. The fact I couldn't give it up making me even angrier. He had done it on purpose. Just to keep me in this hell.

I wouldn't give him the satisfaction. He wouldn't see me break. He didn't deserve it, and he wasn't worth it. I wasn't doing this for him. I was doing it for my baby.

♥♥♥

"How was it? Tell me everything." Lu video called me in the afternoon wanting the lowdown.

"Amber peed on him."

She laughed. "Good girl! Marisa sent me the video. He seems quite smitten with her."

I nodded. "I think he cried holding her but turned his back to us so we wouldn't see it."

"She's like his little Xerox."

"Is that another one of your Brazilian sayings?" Her weird, translated idioms always made me smile.

"I mean she's his carbon copy, his mini me."

"I know." My voice sounded melancholic.

Lu noticed. She noticed everything. Had the eyes of a bloody hawk that woman. "How was it? Having him there." Her voice was soft. She was approaching the subject with caution.

I didn't want to answer her question, had just managed to drag myself out of the dark hole it had put me in. Lu waited. I fiddled with the sleeve of my top. "Even harder than I thought." My eyes welled up. "If I had a choice, I would never see him again."

She nodded. Neither of us said anything.

"You didn't tell me he'd grown a beard, goatee, whatever that is."

"Five o'clock shadow. I didn't think you wanted to know. Every time I mentioned him you pretended you weren't listening. I didn't want to come across like I was lobbying. I mean… I was worried you would stop talking to me again if you felt I was pushing. I'm traumatized, after you were so mean to my lovely self and left me all alone in the world." Her lips pulled over her teeth into a mischievous smile.

At that, I had to laugh. "Alone with your thousand friends and busy social life? You're such a drama queen."

"Always."

We both went quiet.

"And are you? Lobbying?"

She sighed and grew serious for a moment. "I wish I could say no, because he was an asshole, and I know just how much he hurt you, but I am a little bit. It's hard not to be. You weren't here to see how upset he was when he found out you'd left. I think he thought he would have the chance to at least apologize and beg for forgiveness. I think he still very much wants that, and I see how hard he's trying. He's been keeping himself on the straight and narrow since you left, so you would give him a chance."

"What do you mean 'straight and narrow'?"

"He's doing therapy to sort out his family stuff. Has even accepted taking medication for his low moods, which he always said no to before. He doesn't go out partying, is not sleeping around, and these days he's all about work. He's opening a second bar, you know."

"Yeah, right… If you're telling me he has been celibate for almost a year, I'm sorry, but I don't believe you. You don't call him love rat for nothing." The last sentence was a replay of what she had said about him in Ilhabela, making me uneasy enough to fidget in my seat, and sad enough that my head went back under water.

"Did you notice how much bigger he is? He's been swimming and hitting the gym like a man possessed. I think he's been doing it to burn the tension. He doesn't do that when he's getting laid."

A memory flashed in my mind—Ilhabela, the pool, when he told me he swims to clear his head. When I had asked him from what, he had looked at me and not answered.

"Good for him."

"Plus, I'm pretty sure one of his arms is getting bigger than the other, if you get my drift."

"Lu!"

"He must be shooting blanks like crazy; it's been months! I'm just saying." She raised both her hands in the air.

Only Lu could make me laugh when everything else felt so grim. "You're impossible! There isn't a single conversation I have with you that doesn't end in some sort of sexual comment."

"He's got to be doing something! You said so yourself, it has been months." She hesitated for a moment, her eyes dropping—head tipping sideways, then refocusing on me. "Be honest now. Seeing him... Is there any part of you that missed him even a little bit?"

I didn't want to answer that question either. In all honesty, I didn't even want to entertain the thought.

"It doesn't matter, Lu. Because I look at him and all I see is him fucking someone else."

"I told you... You will continue to feel angry until you slap him. You should try it. Crack one right across his face. You will feel *way* better. He won't be happy about it, of course, but he'll let you do it. He knows he deserves the corporal punishment."

"Advocating for domestic violence much?"

"No. Just old-fashioned an eye for an eye."

"If that was the case, I should aim lower to a certain appendage."

"Would you really want to bruise the crown jewels? I hear that's his best asset."

"So not his personality then?"

Lu laughed.

"Would you have forgiven Alexandre?" My voice was sarcastic on purpose.

"Never. But Alex didn't spend months on his best behavior looking for me so I would give him a chance. He dumped me to go date Angela. Then within a month she dumped his sorry arse. Karma *is* a bitch. So... it's not the same." She wavered for a moment, as if she was deciding what to say. "I need to show you something. He posted this on Insta earlier. It's a trimmed version of the video Marisa sent me." I opened WhatsApp. The image showed him facing Amber. "The caption says 'met my baby girl for the first time today. Never thought I'd be a dad'. He's basically made her official to everyone who knows him. I think you lost your throne."

I laughed. "Good. She should be the only reason he's here."

"That's not all. Felipe saw the post and called me." She waited for a moment. When I said nothing, she continued. "He wanted to know who the Mum is."

"So he's speaking to you again?" My voice was heavy with sarcasm. I still found Felipe's grudge against Luciana ridiculous. If he wanted to be mad at anyone, it should be me. It had been my choice to date his brother. Lu had actually tried to persuade me otherwise.

"Just about." Her eyebrows raised and dropped, eyes widening and returning to normal size.

"Did you tell him?"

"Yeah. He laughed. Said 'for an unlucky bastard, Celo's luck never seems to run out'."

"Was that all?"

"No. But the rest isn't really worth repeating."

I rolled my eyes. "Out with it, Lu."

Her gaze dropped; she hesitated. Very unlike her. "He said he hoped you weren't stupid enough to forgive Celo."

The sentence hung between us. It wasn't just Felipe. There was a whole feminist school of thought dedicated to how a woman should never forgive a philanderer. If your man crossed that line, that was it: he was *persona non grata*. And staying with a cheater carried a whole level of shame. Women who did so were idiots. Deserved what they got, because leopards don't change their spots. Out of everything, that was the worst thing. The feeling you were being judged and taken for a fool if you chose to forgive.

"He's right. I'm not."

♥♥♥

At 10am on the dot Marcelo knocked on the door. That was odd. Brazilians were always late by at least fifteen minutes for everything. It was like a rule to them. Marcelo was normally late by a good half an hour for everything always.

He nodded at me, came in, and automatically hung his coat and took his gray Dr. Martens off, a little too familiar for my liking. His knitted gray jumper made his shoulders look broader, chest bigger. His black jeans were tighter from the knees down; the hems had been folded over to accommodate his boots. I pointed him toward the sitting room. Amber was lying on the floor in her play gym, kicking her legs, a couple of arches of soft toys dangling over her.

"Wow, that's one fancy toy right there," he said, kneeling down to kiss her head.

"Coffee?"

He looked at me and smiled. "Black, three sugars, please."

While I made my tea, and his coffee, I could hear him talking to her in Portuguese. I walked back into the room to find him lying on the floor next to the play gym, playing with the toys she had dangling. I placed his mug on the coffee table, and he sat up, perching on the floor with his back against the sofa; I sat on the chair opposite. His eyes trained on me; mine everywhere else—Amber, out of the window, the floor—but him.

"Your mom not here today?"

I shook my head.

"She working or something?"

I nodded.

"What does she do?"

"Interior designer."

He nodded, drank his coffee. "You look good."

I drank my tea. Cheap shot, liar. I hated him. But a small part of me, the one I wanted to throw in front of a train, was comforted that he was here and wanted to know Amber. "You grew…" I rotated my finger in front of my mouth without looking at him.

He shrugged. "You like it?"

We sat there, him staring at me, me trying not to look at him.

"Things with your mom look better. Last time I saw you, you two weren't really speaking."

"Life taught me a lesson."

From the corner of my eyes I saw him nod. His head turned, and he looked at Amber for a long while. He wasn't stupid. He knew things were better with my mother because now I kind of understood why she did what she did.

"The health visitor is coming at 2pm." I broke the awkward silence.

"Health visitor?"

"The nurse who looks after Amber. I struggled to breastfeed her after she was born, and she lost some weight. The health visitor is coming to do a check-up on her, make sure she's growing at the right rate. I thought you might want to hear what she has to say."

In my peripheral vision I saw his head bop up and down. His face turned to me, mine to Amber.

"I also have to register her birth the day after tomorrow. I need to know if you want to give her your surname."

"Definitely."

"You might need to come with me and bring your passport."

Another nod.

"I'll confirm and let you know."

"Whatever you need. I'm here for five weeks. Then I need

to go back to sort some things out, but I will come back to London after that."

I looked at him then.

"I'm not going to be the dad she only sees once a year and barely remembers," he said, staring right at me, almost like a challenge. "Would you really have registered her without my name?"

I raised my eyebrows at him, letting him know I would much prefer that he wasn't here. He snorted, shook his head, jaw muscles poking in and out under his skin. He drank his coffee.

"I was thinking her name could be Amber Lancaster-Costa then."

He nodded.

Brazilians always took both of their parents' surnames. I didn't see why I had to tell him that in the UK our tradition was to take just one—the dad's. Didn't see why he deserved the honor when I had carried and given birth to her on my own.

Another sip of coffee. "It should be Amber Costa, really. Your naming system is the same as the Americans, is it not?" He gave me a knowing smile. It hit the wrong cord. "But she is yours as well as mine, so Lancaster-Costa is fair."

Arsehole.

"Fair would be if she was called Amber Lancaster, bearing in mind I was the one who carried her for nine months and gave birth to her, and you did what exactly? Had fun for thirty seconds?"

He tsked, his eyes shifting to the side, and he half smiled, full of contempt. "I'm still her dad."

"Barely. Only by a cosmic joke at my expense. Not to mention that Costa is a chain of coffee shops in the UK."

He shrugged. "I like coffee. And she's like a little coffee bean next to you."

Double arsehole.

He put his drink down, lay on his stomach next to the play gym, and gave Amber one of his fingers; she grabbed hold of it. "I think that is how I'm going to call you," he told her, "my little Coffee Bean," and kissed her head.

Triple arsehole.

"Her name is *Amber*."

CHAPTER 5

Marcelo

Paige
I'm feeding Amber. Have left the door open, just come in.

TOOK THAT AS AN INVITATION TO BE FIFTEEN MINUTES EARLY FOR the nurse's appointment. Waiting at the hotel, without anything to do, just idling, was driving me insane.

"Paige?" I said as soon as I got through the door.

"In the sitting room."

She was sitting in her usual chair, a cushion on her lap, Coffee Bean sprawled on it. Her top was unbuttoned, exposing her cleavage, and one of her breasts was out—a tiny, tight chubby fist on top of it. I could hear Amber's breathing and sucking noises from the door.

I don't know why—she told me this is what she was doing—but I wasn't expecting that.

And I couldn't stop staring.

Lucky for me, she wasn't looking. One of Paige's hands was tapping Amber's nappy bottom; the other was covering her eyes. Her face twisting as if she was in pain.

"You ok?"

"You're early."

"I am. You didn't answer my question."

"Ouch! Amber, baby girl, please… Go easy on the nips! You're not a Dyson." She looked at me then. "No, I'm not ok. I think she's trying to suck my nipples off me. And I can't stop because if I stop, I stop producing milk, I'm in pain, or I drip and start leaking like a fucking tap. Do you want to let her latch on to you to see how you like it?" She was in pain and frustrated alright.

"We could try it, but I don't think she would find it very satisfying." I pointed at Amber.

Paige's cleavage was fuller, bigger. And, God help me, her breasts looked amazing! I actually felt envious I wasn't the one doing the sucking. As I thought that, I mentally noted that I should stop staring, but I couldn't.

"I'm going to… make some coffee." I took myself out of the room.

Fuck me! Literally, someone needed to put me out of my misery and fuck me, because I got a boner watching my daughter being breastfed while my girlfriend complained about being in pain. What the fuck was wrong with me!? Not getting any, that was what. This shit didn't agree with me.

I couldn't stop thinking about it. Fair, round, voluptuous skin that would feel awesome in my hands. A memory stuck to my mind like super glue—my nipples were dark; Paige's were this gorgeous sexy baby pink. Shit! I repositioned myself in my clothes, walked around the kitchen, jumped about a bit trying to disperse the energy. They used to raise like two little berries when she was turned on, when I kissed her neck. And I used to kiss right down the middle of her cleavage, then play with them. Fuck! Sometimes my mind was my worst enemy. The health visitor was going to be here in a minute. Worse, Paige's mother could walk in. Can you imagine? *Oh, hello to you, sir, and hello to your flagpole!* That's one quick way to make a bad impression.

I tried to think about something else. Politics, multiplication tables, the ugliest footballer I could remember. It wasn't working. So I decided to go outside and stand in the cold. Good fucking job the curtains were closed, and Paige wasn't paying attention.

As I started shivering, I felt like a pervert. Who the hell sexualizes breastfeeding! I'm sure if I said it out loud, someone would hunt me with pitchforks. So I did what everyone would do when they want to feel normal—googled it. Apparently, it is a thing for fathers not only to be turned on, but to also feel jealous of their babies when their partners are breastfeeding. Great. I had entered a new category of fucked up. Like I hadn't collected enough of them already.

"Hello there." I turned around; the nurse was standing on the sidewalk at the top of the steps. "Have you locked yourself out?"

"No. I just… needed some fresh air." Saved by frostbite and Google.

"It's too cold for fresh air without a coat and shoes, lovey."

I opened the door. "Come on in. They're in the lounge, first to the left."

"Are you Dad?"

"I am." Right now, that felt like a massive overstatement. So far, all I seemed to have done is gotten Paige pregnant and perved on her breastfeeding. "Can I get you anything?"

"Oooh! I would love a tea. Milk, two sugars please." English people and their damn tea.

I stood at the door, my eyes glued to the floor. "Paige? Do you still drink the same tea?"

"No, I can't. Can I have peppermint tea, please?"

I nodded and went to the kitchen. Had to look through every cupboard to find what I needed. But I was glad to come back and find that Paige had stopped feeding Coffee Bean. A blessing that.

The health visitor weighed and measured Amber, checking her eyes, her heart, her hips and reflexes, writing all the information in a red book. The nurse had to strip her out of her clothes to do all the checks, which she wasn't happy about, and she pretty much cried all the way like she was being tortured. Her chin quivered, little legs and arms outstretched as if she was crying for help, her yelling getting louder and louder and more desperate, tears running down her face despite both the nurse and Paige trying to settle her down. Her crying making Paige anxious, and ringing in my ears like a blackboard being scratched. I felt like a spare part and started pacing.

As soon as the nurse was done, and Paige had dressed Amber, I offered to take her. For some reason, it felt like my arms were the safest place for her. Once I had her, I talked to her in Portuguese, hugging and kissing her to calm her down. To calm both of us down.

"Ooh! That sounds lovely. What language is that?" the nurse asked.

"Portuguese," Paige answered. Amber had stopped crying. "She likes when he speaks to her in his language, seems to understand him."

"So you're Portuguese?"

"Brazilian," Paige answered for me. "He's Brazilian."

"Ooh! How exotic! I thought Brazilians spoke Spanish. You speak Portuguese as well?"

Paige shook her head. "I only understand bits."

"How often is she feeding now?"

"Every three hours, sometimes more often."

"The latching has improved? She certainly seems to be getting enough as she has gained some weight."

"I think so. But it's still hurting me."

"Has it not healed? Is it still cracked and sore?"

Great… They were going to talk about *them*, weren't they?

Paige looked over her shoulder for a second, then nodded.

"Can I have a look?"

Somebody fucking shoot me! I pretended to comfort Coffee

Bean so I could turn my back to them. Amber frowned at me like she knew what I was thinking.

"Don't look at me like that! In my defense, they were mine before they were yours," I told her in Portuguese.

Her frown got deeper.

"Stop judging me. I'm your dad. Show me some respect, little girl."

I could hear the sound of buttons being undone, so I started to mentally name all the Brazilian states and their capitals. I was always shit at Geography.

"Yeah, they are still very pink, aren't they?" *Shoot me! Minas Gerais – Belo Horizonte; DF – Brasília; Goiás – Goiânia…* "But it seems to be healing. There is no infection or anything; it's just that one of them was cracked a little deep." Fabric being ruffled, nails catching on buttons. "We don't recommend this as a first resort, breastfeeding helps with milk supply, skin-to-skin contact, bonding as well as other things, but if you need a break… you could look at expressing and giving her the bottle. Try to keep it to a minimum so it doesn't affect her latching and breastfeeding as a whole, especially after all the problems we had to get her to latch properly. But it might be good for Dad too…" I turned around when she said 'Dad', and she looked at me rocking Amber behind Paige. "He can do some of the feeding."

Paige nodded.

"Now, what about the stitches? They should all be gone now."

Paige fidgeted on her chair and looked over her shoulder as if she was uncomfortable answering the questions with me present.

The nurse picked up on it too. "Are you ok discussing this with him in the room? We can ask him to step out for a minute."

Now she asked the question!

Paige looked at me, looked at Amber. "It's fine." There was no chance she was going to let Coffee Bean out of her sight. "Stitches are fine. I think they are all gone now. I'm keeping the area clean, taking the arnica pills, taking short baths with tea-tree oil, and taking paracetamol when it's uncomfortable."

"Great stuff. And there is no redness, pus, pain or any signs of infection that you can see?"

"No."

"The bleeding still normal, no clots, and is it decreasing?"

More fidgeting. "No clots but still feels the same." Her voice was low.

"Ok. You're in week five of that. It should last between six to eight weeks. So we'll keep an eye on it. It should really be decreasing soon. And here, I'm obliged to give you a quick reminder that you can get pregnant again as early as three weeks after giving birth." The nurse looked from Paige to me.

I wish. I'd love to get my hands on her skin and get all this tension out of my body.

"We're not together, so that won't be a problem," Paige answered, her voice monotone.

It was a problem for me. I had a big problem with that whole sentence.

"And how are you feeling? Any low moods?"

Her head turned toward me. "Hmm… some. Especially the last few days."

"Do these include any self-harming thoughts or thoughts to harm the baby?"

Paige hesitated, then shook her head, but her gaze lowered. She didn't look at the nurse.

And it hit me like a kick in the balls.

Being pregnant and giving birth to our little girl had taken a lot out of her. I had come in, desperate to get what I wanted, only thinking about myself and what I'd missed. And I had completely ignored what toll the whole thing had taken on Paige.

I was such a selfish moron.

"How long do the low moods last?" The nurse's voice softened.

Paige cleared her throat. "At the minute… they're constant." I couldn't see her face, but her voice sounded strangled. Her tone, the unwilling admission of the truth she was trying to keep under wraps—probably many times worse than what she was actually saying.

"Do you need a minute, lovey?" The nurse reached for her, squeezed her hand.

Knowing she was upset made me want to bang my head on the wall. I knew she would be angry, but I never considered she would be feeling low.

Paige shook her head. "I think I'm a little hormonal, a little sleep deprived, and a little… rattled. It's a bit like the perfect storm." Her head dropped.

The nurse handed her a tissue, reached out and held on to her. And something in me tore in half. I wished I could do the same. Put my arms around her and comfort her like I had done to our baby, but I knew she wouldn't let me.

"It's ok and normal to feel a little blue after giving birth. Your body is still healing from labor…" She said the second sentence looking straight at me. She was saying it for my awareness. "Your hormones are still all over the place, and your body is still trying to level itself up after months of releasing them." Paige nodded. "But we need to keep an eye on it because, if the moods persist, you could have postnatal depression. Dad?" The nurse looked at me. "Maybe you could help by looking after the baby and allowing Mum to take a nap during the day while you're visiting? Sleep deprivation worsens and can cause low moods."

"Every day if she wants. I'll do anything she wants."

"Let's do some expressing so Dad can help with some of the feeding and give you a break too," the nurse said, then nodded at me, giving me my cue.

"I'll do whatever she wants me to do."

"There you go!" She turned to Paige. "Being a new mum is hard, lovey, and it takes some getting used to. You need to let your family and the baby's dad help you. You don't have to do it all on your own if you have people around you who want to help."

CHAPTER 6
Paige

He handed Amber back to me and took the health visitor to the door. I was hoping he would leave with her, but I wasn't that lucky. A few minutes later, he walked back into the room and sat on the sofa across from me—one arm on the arm rest, the other over the back of the sofa, stare a blow-torch heating my skin while I rocked Amber and rubbed my thumb from her tiny nose to her forehead until her eyes started to close. It had been an intense appointment for everyone.

He leaned forward on his elbows. "I didn't realize how heavy this was for you." His voice was husky.

I didn't answer. Just kept looking at Amber.

"I meant every word I said, Paige. I will do whatever you want me to do, whatever you need me to do."

I didn't answer or look at him.

Frustrated with my lack of response, he walked to me and crouched in front of my armchair—one hand on each armrest—his proximity making me uncomfortable. I readjusted myself in the seat to keep as far away from him as possible.

He sighed. "I'm here for the next five weeks whether you like it or not. I have no place to be but here, nothing to do but come here, and there is only so much swimming and going to the gym I can do. So you can sit there giving me the silent treatment and letting me make you feel uncomfortable, or you can listen to your nurse and use it to your advantage. Let me help, give me something to do that benefits you and our little girl. What is it going to be?" He was being direct, but his voice was tender, caring.

I looked at him then. "Anything I want, huh?"

His head dipped in one sharp and swift gesture, eyes watching me, face calm.

"I want you to let go of my chair and leave."

His chin rose up, the muscles on his jaw working, gaze disappointed. But he nodded, stood up, and stepped back from my chair.

"Fine. But I will be back tomorrow morning at ten."

He walked out of the room, and I could hear him putting his boots and coat on. The door opened and closed. Footsteps drummed on metal heading up the stairs, and then on the pavement.

And as soon as he was gone, I couldn't hold it in. I cried my eyes out.

I didn't know it was going to be this hard. I loved my baby. She was so small and defenseless, and it wasn't her fault. Having her had been my choice. But I had brought her into a mess. And this was brutal! I hadn't slept properly in months, my figure was destroyed, my nipples were dangling for dear life, breastfeeding was painful, I was bleeding like a massacre was happening inside my body, and I hated that he was here.

I wanted him to disappear and leave us alone, but he needed to be here for Amber. I didn't want her to grow up like I did. Always missing something. Always wondering why everyone had a dad and I didn't, why I didn't look like anyone in my family.

He wanted to come visit every fucking day. And I knew that was why he was here, but every time he turned up, the pieces of me that were left smashed a little smaller. I had loved him with everything I had. Had allowed him to do things to my body that I hadn't allowed anyone else. He had promised me things, then broke his word, and broke me. And now he was here, and I had to share the most precious thing I had with him.

Amber looked like a baby doll sleeping. Like she wasn't real. I hadn't told the health visitor, scared she would think I was an unfit mother after not being able to feed Amber properly for weeks, but I had considered it. I had considered how much easier it would be if both Amber and I didn't exist.

CHAPTER 7
Marcelo

KATE ANSWERED THE DOOR.

"Would you like some tea?"

"I don't drink tea, sorry. But I'd love a coffee if you have some." I took my coat and high tops off.

The lounge was empty; there was no Paige or Coffee Bean.

Kate walked into the kitchen and signaled for me to sit down at the table. While the kettle boiled, she turned to me. "They're both still asleep. It was a rough night."

I pulled a face so she would know I didn't quite get what she meant.

"Paige didn't sleep. And Amber seems to feed off her tension. The more stressed she is, the more Amber cries." She went quiet for a moment as if she was deciding what to tell me. "I came back from work, and she had been crying all afternoon. She was already struggling with certain things, but you being here has pushed her over the edge. She's only doing it for Amber, really." Kate looked at her own feet, hands behind her back on the counter, one of her ankles moving in and out. "Because she doesn't want to do to her daughter what I did to her."

"I know." I could have counted on my two hands the amount of times Paige had actually looked me in the eyes since I'd arrived. Whenever she had to face me, her eyes stayed on the middle of my chest; she refused to look at me. And her voice, her tone was always off. Cold, sharp, and distant. The spot at the back of my neck felt like it was on fire; I rubbed it.

Kate made the drinks and sat opposite me. "Why are you here? Are you doing this out of some sense of duty?"

I shook my head.

"Because if you are, nobody really needs you here. You can go back home, and we'll keep you posted." She took a sip of her tea. With Paige out of sight, all her knives were out, and she wasn't going to spare me a single blow.

"I'm not going anywhere. My daughter needs me. And she might not accept it, but Paige needs me too."

"My daughter doesn't need you. She was doing fine as a single mother before you came along." Another sip of tea. Her words were sharp, but she sat across from me like we were talking about the weather, and she was being pleasant.

"Paige is not a single mother. I'm right here." We stared at each other for a minute, but this standoff wasn't getting any of us closer to a solution. "The health visitor said Paige needs to rest, catch up on her sleep, and express milk so she can take a break from breastfeeding to heal quicker. I can help with that. I can look after Amber while she sleeps or just takes some time for herself. But she needs to let me."

"And in the meantime, she has to put up with your presence? The man who cheated on her, broke her heart, and sent her packing pregnant." The last words came out through her teeth.

"I didn't send her anywhere—she left. And I've been trying to find her and apologize ever since. I didn't know she was pregnant either."

"Oh yeah… because saying you're sorry will fix everything. Your apology will make her forget you're a two-timing bastard, will it?" Another sip of tea. Her voice dripped in politeness that had been weaponized, loaded, and able to pierce through bulletproof armor.

She was starting to piss me off. But I had no right to argue with her. She wasn't wrong.

"I made a *mistake* when I wasn't in a good place myself. And I know I was an asshole. But I love Paige, and I have been trekking through hell, hoping that she would give me a chance to make things right."

"You have a funny way to show you love her. I wonder what you do to the people you don't like."

Now I knew where Paige got her passive aggressiveness from, but I ignored her comment. "I will do *anything* she wants, anything she needs me to do."

"Just not leaving?"

"Just not leaving."

"Then I guess you won't do *anything*."

"I'm not walking away from my family." My statement seemed to ruffle her feathers even more.

"I knew that trip was a mistake; I could feel it in my bones. I begged her not to go. That's why she didn't come home after what happened. And why she didn't tell anyone she was pregnant until she had no choice. She went to Denver. Her father didn't really know her, not like I do. She knew he wouldn't know something was wrong. She has been a mess for months. *You* did that."

I didn't answer. Nothing I said would justify what I'd done. I'd fucked it up pretty good.

"She struggled her whole pregnancy. Torn between loving her baby and hating that she shared her with you. And now... she has to put up with you being here." A sarcastic laugh came out of her.

Kate was going for my jugular and, truth be told, there was next to nothing I could say in my defense. But in the last few months, therapy had told me that rather than getting defensive or feeling offended, I should take responsibility for what I'd done and genuinely apologize for the pain it had caused. That

I shouldn't drive myself insane dwelling on the mistakes and bad things I couldn't change or control. Instead, I should focus on what I could change and take positive steps to change my present and my future. Dr Fernandes had also drilled into me that I should express my feelings rather than bottling them up; let people see what was under my hood. Easier said than done when someone is throwing knives at you. I doubted anyone would want to look into my mess. But I guess it was time to find out if the good doctor was full of shit or not. So here went nothing…

"I never meant to hurt her, Kate. I wasn't thinking straight. I felt betrayed, was angry, self-sabotaging, and she got caught in my crossfire. It makes me want to crack my head open that she's still so upset with me. Every day I turn up and she doesn't look me in the face or recoils when I come near her… it *hurts* me." Admitting to it drained all my energy. It went deep against my grain to tear up and show anyone what was under my skin, especially when they were holding a guillotine over my neck. "I cannot change what I've done. Believe me, if I could, I would. I can only try to change what comes next. I'm not perfect, and I know I committed the greatest of sins, but I love Paige, and I love our baby. I want to be a good dad and give Paige everything I can, even if she doesn't take me back. And I will beg her for forgiveness on my knees if I have to. So no, I'm not leaving."

Kate was still staring at me, but at least it no longer looked like she wished I'd drop dead.

"Look… I spoke to the health visitor yesterday before she left. She couldn't tell me much about Paige without her consent, but she did tell me to try and support Paige as much as I could. I know you can't be here all the time, because if you could, you would be here every time I'm here. But I have all the time and flexibility you don't have. So you can hate me all you want, but since I'm here and not going anywhere, you need to let me help. Paige needs to let me help. I can do some of the work, give her some room to breathe."

Kate's eyes narrowed. She drank her tea. For a while she said nothing. Then she sighed. "Fine. I will speak to her. But you need to give her a break. She has not seen or spoken to you in months. Now you're here. Turning up every day like an eyesore, bringing all the bad memories to the surface. This is painful for her. At least give her today to get her head around things."

I wasn't happy about it, but I nodded. "Can you give her this?" I put the bags I'd brought on the table. "The nurse said she should try to express milk so she could have a break. I didn't know if she had them, so I got her a pump thing, bottles, and a sterilizer. The lady in the shop said this one is the best pump because she can wear it under her normal clothes. I got Amber some nappy stuff too. I know she goes through a lot of them."

Kate nodded.

I stood to leave. "There weren't just bad memories, you know. We also had some good ones." I could hear the sadness in my voice. The vulnerability giving me agony like a thousand bugs were crawling on my skin.

She didn't follow me to the hall as I got my stuff and let myself out.

♥♥♥

"Hello?" Luciana sounded sleepy. It was 10.30am in London, but 6.30am in São Paulo because of British Summer Time.

"I'm sorry to wake you up, Lu."

"Just a sec." I could hear Gabriel, her boyfriend, in the background. "Go back to sleep. I just need to take this call." He said something else. "It's Celo. I'll be back in a minute. Go back to sleep." A door opened and closed. "Celo?"

"Still here. Sorry to wake the whole house. I didn't know you were with Gabe."

"Is everything ok?"

"No. Paige is on the verge of postnatal depression, and she hates my guts."

On the other end of the line, Lu sighed. "Well… we knew this wasn't going to be a walk in the park."

"I know. I deserve all the shit she's giving me. I'm not calling for me. I'm calling for her. She needs someone she can talk to, Lu. Like, really talk to. I don't think she's giving her mom or her nurse the full picture, and right now my presence is doing more harm than good. She needs you, but I know she won't ask. So I'm asking for her. Can you come to London even if it's just for a short time?"

"You know…" She still sounded sleepy. "I think she told me that. When I spoke to her at Christmas, she said she was getting in touch with me because it was hard to go through everything without having a close friend."

"It's not looking good, Lu. And there is nothing I can do. She doesn't even look at me, so I'm not much help."

I could deal with Paige's anger. Anger, rage, were old acquaintances of mine. But the impotence, the feeling I could not do a damn thing, was driving me up the wall.

"How bad is it?"

"It's bad. She told the nurse her low moods are constant. And when the nurse asked her if she had any thoughts of harming herself or the baby, she said no but her body language was all wrong, Lu. That was yesterday. I went to see them today and she was still sleeping. Kate told me she didn't sleep all night and cried all afternoon yesterday."

"Jesus! Ok. I will check things and let you know when I'm coming."

"Please come as soon as you can? I know I'm imposing and it's just before you break for Easter, it's just that…"

"You're worried about her."

I didn't answer.

"You don't need to ask me twice. Paige is like a sister to me. I was going to come anyway; I just didn't think it was fair for me to meet your little girl before you. I will try to get there in the next couple of days. I just need to sort things in the office."

"Thanks, Lu."

"And how are you?"

I scrambled for an answer. "I'm better than she is. At least, I'm happy to see them, and I can hold my baby girl."

"How is fatherhood treating you?" Her voice had the upbeat of a smile.

"I was worried, I'm not gonna lie. I was worried I wouldn't…" It sounded so mean saying it out loud. Amber was so small and none of this was her fault, but I never thought I would have children.

"Love her? Bond with her?" Lu finished the thought for me.

"Yeah. And now I'm worried I won't be a good father to her."

"If you weren't, you wouldn't have rushed there. Taking all this heat to be near your family."

"She's so small, Lu. Like a big meatball. And she is my Xerox, like I'm looking in the mirror." Thinking of her little face and chubby cheeks made me smile. "And get this, when I speak to her in Portuguese, she makes noises at me like she's trying to talk to me. It's very sweet."

"I saw the video. You look very smitten."

"It's hard not to be. She's so small and innocent."

"Well, I don't think you could deny she's yours even if you wanted to." She laughed. "How are you getting on with the Gates of Hades?"

"She hates me. Today she told me to go back home and called me a cheating bastard." It was such a shitty situation, I could only laugh or cry, so I laughed.

"I can't say I'm surprised. She might not be happy to see me either. Not after her daughter came to visit me and came back pregnant." Lu let out a sarcastic laugh. "How is Paige with you?"

I had to take a deep breath before answering this one. "Doesn't look at me. Only speaks to me when she has to. And she uses this tone, you know… like I'm a stranger bothering her or something. Kate told me she is only putting up with me because of Coffee Bean." My own voice had a tiredness I didn't know I felt.

"Huh… I'm not so sure about that. You used to do the same thing to her when you were trying to stay away from her. But you still turned up everywhere we went. Remember?"

The memory made me smile. I did follow her around like a masochistic puppy dog. Not willing to give in, but unable to walk away. That felt like a lifetime ago. Things seemed so much simpler back then. Lucky as I am, things never seem to get easier, just harder.

We both went quiet for a moment.

"And how are you holding up? Sounds like you're under fire on all sides."

She'd already asked me this question, so I gave her a better answer. "It's shit. But I need to be here for them, even if nobody wants me to be. And I still want her back. Now, even more." My neck itched. "I was expecting her anger. Anger I can deal with. It's her pain and disappointment I can't stomach. Remorse doesn't quite cut it." It came out rasping. This business of being open didn't come naturally to me. Truth be told, I would've preferred not to say anything at all. But apparently, not verbalizing things wasn't good for me.

"Betrayal cuts as deep as the amount of love you have for someone. If she's still mad and upset, it's because her feelings run deep. Feelings like that don't disappear overnight. But loyalty is very important to Paige. Her head will be telling her she shouldn't forgive you, but her heart will be telling her something else. That's why she is so cut up. All you can do is be there and prove that you're sorry and mean business. It'll just take time to earn her trust back." She paused for a second. "She might have to slap you."

"What??" It was such a curveball, I could do little but laugh at the last thing she'd said.

"I'm serious. She went mad at your things, but she didn't go mad at you. She hasn't said a single word to you about it. She will have to get mad at you and blow out all that pent up anger before she can move past it. But she's English; they don't like confrontation like we do. So this could take a while."

I nodded as if she could see me. "If it gets me out of the doghouse, I will take it."

♥♥♥

Waiting feels like you're suspended, anxiety building, turning everything into the monster of your nightmares. Giving you the feeling you're about to get shot. And when you stop waiting… it feels like someone dropped you from a high, right into a cold lake—your mind struggling to make sense of what just happened. It takes you a minute to realize you're screwed no matter what.

Idling is no better. You know you're not staying where you are, you have somewhere else you want to be, but you sit there—motor running and ready, just waiting. Wasting fuel, the seconds ticking in slow motion, minutes stretching to infinity. The hope of an impending green light sitting on you like doomsday. And with too much time on its hands, your mind starts overthinking. Going over everything you said, everything you've done, fine-combing the details like you can change their outcome by thinking alone, driving yourself insane.

I had to move. Had to go outside, do something, anything, to avoid blowing a fuse. The day was gray and cold, but dry, so I went for a walk. On the way to the riverbank, I passed a gated garden. A path ran right across it straight to the other side. A round fountain in the middle worked as a rotatory, surrounded by trimmed rose bushes that had been pruned to a few centimeters off the floor. Garden arches stood at either side of the circle.

I tried the gate. The latch opened with a click and clank. Long, wide, flat lawns stretched to either side of me, surrounded by trees that were still bare but showing signs that spring was coming. The lawns were vivid green, bursting with purple, white, and yellow chunky flowers scattered around like someone had forgotten their picnic blankets. The air was cold, smelling of wet soil.

I picked a bench on the side. A couple of women were pushing prams and talking in a language that was all short and elongated vowels. Chinese maybe. An old lady seemed to be power walking on the path that followed the edges of the lawn in a big rectangle. The cold seeped through the seat of my jeans, reaching my bones. If I sat for too long, my toes and ass would start to freeze. The discomfort was a welcome distraction, making my mind focus elsewhere.

I watched as an array of people crossed the square—a gate clanking, shapes moving across the corner of my vision, another gate clanking. The old lady was on her third loop around the garden when she dropped something just as she walked past me.

"Excuse me, you dropped your purse."

She stopped in her tracks, twisted around, and walked a couple of steps back to me. "Ta, love." Her hand reached out to collect the purse from my hand, a smile gracing the face under her purplish-gray short curls. She was flirting.

I smiled back. "Are you playing the old 'drop the purse' trick on me?"

"Oh!" She smacked my arm with said purse. "Don't spoil an old bird's fun. Make me believe I still got it." She had a twang. Certain words were pronounced differently, the rhythm of her sentences melodic.

Her comment made me laugh. Something about her reminded me of my grandmother—her bubbliness, her energy maybe.

"You should smile more, love. You look even more handsome when you do, ya know."

"Now, now, take it easy on the flirting. You'll break my heart when I find out you have a husband at home."

"Oh no! He's long gone him. I'm all yours, my love."

I laughed harder. Don't think I had ever been called love so much in my life.

"You're not a serial killer after me money, are ya?"

"I think it's me who should be afraid of you."

She winked at me, turned, and started walking. "Come on then." With a lack of having anything better to do, I followed. "So why you sitting 'ere with a face like a smacked ass?"

"A what?"

"You know, sad like."

"I didn't realize I looked sad."

"Where're you from, lad? You have a bit of a mad accent."

"Brazil."

"You don't sound Brazilian. My cleaning lady is Brazilian; you don't sound like 'er."

"I lived in the US for a little while."

She nodded. The fast pace of her walk had started to warm me up.

"Are you from here?"

"Oh no! I'm a scouser, me."

"A scouser?"

"From Liverpool."

I nodded to show I understood.

"So what brings you 'ere then?"

"My daughter." I tried the words out. Somehow it no longer felt as strange telling people I had a kid.

"Ah! You have a daughter? How old is she?"

"Just over a month old."

"Ah! So she's just a baba. Why is your daughter 'ere then?"

"My girlfriend is English."

"And you live here now, do ya?"

I shook my head. We had gotten around half of the garden and were now back at the rotatory.

"I think this story needs a bevvy. This baltic weather is playing havoc on me rheumatics. Come on, love."

The gate clanked. We started to walk back in the same direction as I had come.

"So your baby and your bird are here, but you're not?"

I shook my head. "We're not together right now."

"So your ex-bird then." We turned the corner toward the hotel.

"I don't see it that way."

"Does *she* see it that way?"

I didn't answer, kept my eyes on the floor.

"Dear, dear. She's got a cob on then, has she?"

"She's got a what?"

"You know, like a face on. So you had murder?" I must have looked confused because she felt the need to clarify. "You've fallen out?"

"You could say that. How do you know I'm staying here?" I pointed at the entrance to the hotel.

"Because I've seen you knocking around in reception. I've got a little flat in the residential bit."

Realization made me smile. "So this was a premeditated hit. I knew I should be scared of you."

Her lips pulled over her teeth in a wide grin, shoulders shrugging, eyebrows raising. When she was younger, she must have been a hell-raiser.

We took a seat at the bar and ordered our drinks. I drank my coffee. She sipped her tea.

"You never told me your name."

"Siobhan Williams."

"Marcelo. Pleased to meet you, Siobhan." I extended my hand out to her.

She shook it. "The pleasure is all mine, my lovely. Now come on, tell me, what's with your bird? Why does she have a cob on?"

Before I replied, my phone buzzed. I excused the interference, explained I needed to respond. One hand waved her permission to me while she sipped her tea.

Paige
You need to come with me to the registry office tomorrow 11am. Bring your passport.

Me
Sure.

She wasn't being nice and was only talking to me about something we needed to do, but receiving a message from her still gave me some relief.

Me
Do I still come 10am? Can I help w/ anything?

She didn't reply for a while. By the time her answer came through, I had given Siobhan a shorter version of events. Talking to a stranger feeling like therapy and giving me an odd sense of relief.

Paige
Can you come at 9am? I'll use the pump. You can feed and look after Amber while I get ready?

Me
I meant what I said. I'll do whatever u want me 2 do, come whenever u need me there.

Paige
9am then.

"So, you've basically been a bit of a bellend and now you want a second chance. Do you reckon she will give it ya?" Another tea sip, her voice neutral, matter of fact.

My eyes stayed on the coffee mug I was rotating on the table.

"Do you regret it?"

"More than I'll ever be able to tell you. I don't know what the hell I was thinking."

She nodded. "I need a biccy with this tea. Ya know, I live 'ere years now and these tight bastards *still* only give me one." She waved at the waiter and asked for another biscuit. "So basically, you won't fuck it up again if she gives you another chance?"

I shook my head.

"Then I hope she does give ya the time of day, love."

CHAPTER 8
Paige

"DID YOU MESSAGE HIM?" MUM SAT DOWN AT THE TABLE WITH both our teas.

I nodded and wrapped my hands around the cup, the heat warming my fingers close to burning. The scent of peppermint swirling up my nostrils with the steam—a letdown. I'd kill for some caffeinated English tea right now; but it wouldn't do me any good, going into my breastmilk and leaving me with a hyper baby. I glanced at the tea police, swaying from one side to another in soothing figures of eight in her electric baby swing.

Mum took a sip of her tea. "Trust me, I don't like the idea any more than you do. But since he's here and not leaving anytime soon, he might as well make himself useful. At least you can get *something* out of it."

I took a sip of mine. "Now I kind of understand why you didn't tell Ryan." The words came out weak, like a whisper.

Mum reached out and held on to my hand. "I couldn't bring myself to do what you're doing. But you are better and stronger than I was. You're doing the right thing. And I'm very proud of you." Her fingers squeezed mine, eyes earnest, voice loaded with deep meaning.

We had never spoken about what happened. Both of us hopping around the subject like dog shit on a pavement, the stench hanging around us all the same. I stared at our hands when I whispered, "What happened, Mum? What did he do to you?"

Her hand retreated, another sip of her tea. "It was more what he didn't do." She smiled, but it didn't reach her eyes. Her cup went back on the table.

"How did you meet?" I back-pedaled, trying to ease us both into the conversation.

A smile. A real one this time. "At a bar in Denver. I had turned up with a girl I met on my travels; he was there with his friends. He kept looking at me. He was *so* handsome!" The word dragged. Another smile. Her fingers hugged her cup. "Americans look big, you know. Tall, bulky. I had dark hair, sun-kissed skin from traveling, and he was all light and air—blond, green eyes, freckles like you. Eventually he came over with one of his friends, to occupy my friend while he spoke to me."

The smile was permanent now. Her face taking a warmer tone, cheeks blushing a little, head tipping to the side.

"We ended up kissing, exchanged numbers, and kept on talking and meeting up. I ended up staying in Denver longer than I'd planned to. We both fell hard, you know? He told me he loved me in bed one night, in the middle of the dark." Her grin wrinkled the corner of her eyes, gaze dropping to her cup. And she got lost in thought. Her mind clearly remembering private moments she didn't want to share with me.

"Was he your first love?"

"My first and only." Both of her eyebrows raising and falling.

"Why did you break up?"

Her gaze snapped back to me. She drank her tea, paused, took a deep breath. "His mother. She had his whole life planned for him. For everyone really—his father, his sister. And Ryan was her pride and joy. She had chosen his university, his career, and… the good Christian girl he was going to marry. An English traveler wasn't quite what she had in mind for her precious son." A sarcastic laugh escaped from her. "The day he took me to meet them, she invited the girl she wanted him to date for dinner. Sat me across the table from them, giving me premier seats to watch Melody flirt with him as if I wasn't there."

"Melody?"

"The girl she wanted him to date." Her nail tapped the teacup on the table, reliving the annoyance in her memory. "He kept looking at me, uncomfortable, but didn't say a thing. Didn't correct his mother when she jabbered on about how they would make such a lovely couple, or how it would be great if they got together. When I stood up to go to the toilet, she caught me in the hallway. Told me Ryan was going places, and I should get out of his way. I told him on the way home; he promised me he would speak to her."

"Wow! She wasn't pulling any punches, was she?"

A headshake. "I didn't get it, you know? My parents were old hippies. All they wanted was for me to be happy." Her palms were up, hands moving animatedly, eyes scanning the room without looking at anything. "They never controlled me, always supported me. So I didn't understand why he couldn't just talk to his parents. I didn't have the wisdom to see that he had been brought up to please his mother from the cradle. He was under so much pressure from them. They had saved and paid so much for his education, he felt indebted to them. Trapped. They wanted him to be a doctor. She bragged about it nonstop."

"And I thought *you* were pushy!" We both laughed.

"Oh, your grandmother takes it to another level." The laughter continued, but it didn't last long. "I met them twice more, both times the same story. After the second time, I felt so humiliated that he didn't defend me, didn't stand up for us, that I decided he didn't deserve me. So I packed up and I left.

By the time I found out I was pregnant, I had been back in the UK for a couple of months. Before I called him, I called my friend—the one I was with when I met him. She told me he had started dating Melody. I was so *angry*!" Her whole demeanor changed—the smile gone, head bowed, shoulders hunched. "His mother would've never accepted us. She'd probably have accused me of doing it on purpose, and Ryan was too under the thumb to correct her. So I didn't see the point of putting both of us through the ordeal when I had left already. I mean, how was it going to work anyway? I was here; he was there." Her hands moved from one side of her body to the other.

"Is that why he doesn't really speak to her anymore?"

"No. He told me that, after doing exactly what she wanted, he found himself deeply unhappy in his career, in his marriage, with his whole life. Then he found out Melody was having an affair with another married man." Sarcasm made her laughter a little obnoxious. "Imagine that! The *perfect* Christian girl his mother had chosen for him not only had an affair but was also a homewrecker. Perfect, my arse!"

Her bitterness raised both my eyebrows.

"He told me that when he found out, he wasn't upset; he was actually relieved. After that, he changed career, divorced his wife, and faced up to his mother. She disapproved, of course, wanted him to fight for his marriage, even after he told her he was unhappy. That's why they're not really on good terms. I guess he fell off the pedestal she had put him on."

"Crazy that she would prefer him unhappy but doing what she wanted."

Mum nodded.

After a moment of quiet she reached out, her hands holding both of mine, thumb rubbing soothing circles. "I never meant to rob that life from you, Poppet. For what it's worth, I'm truly sorry. I was young, barely twenty, and I honestly thought I was protecting us. My mind didn't stretch as far as how you would feel growing up. It didn't even occur to me that you would miss something you never had." Her lips pressed together, eyebrows twisting into a frown, gaze seeking and holding mine to convey that she was truly apologizing.

It didn't fix it. It didn't give me back what I'd lost. But it explained it and, right now, I honestly understood.

"Why didn't you just tell me that, Mum?" My voice broke. This was a sore point for me. Something I still couldn't wrap my head around. Why she didn't just explain what had happened rather than being angry.

"The more years that passed, the harder it became. I got so used to telling you the same story, I ended up believing it myself."

"You got so angry with me," I whispered.

She nodded. "I was so embarrassed! You caught me in my biggest lie." The smile she gave was bitter. She didn't look at me. "Focusing on what you did was easier than facing up to what I'd done."

Her eyes traveled down to our hands. She was lost in thought again, darker ones this time, her face somber.

"It wasn't fair, Mum. All I wanted was the truth."

She looked at me then, hands squeezing mine, nose going red. "I know, Poppet. And I am sorry. I didn't really know how to handle it, but I wasn't mad at you. I was mad at myself." She squeezed me so tight, it was a little uncomfortable. "And before I could fix it, your father was here, and you were running."

"My middle name—Paige Pegging-It-Marie Lancaster."

We both laughed. The self-deprecating joke alleviating the mood dive the conversation had taken. "Only when you're heartbroken; otherwise, you're unfortunately quite feisty."

"I think it's the northerner in me."

"It is indeed." More giggling. She let go of my hands. We both drank our tea.

"So that's why you never dated?"

"Oh, I dated! You just never saw it."

"What?!" Now, that was a surprise.

"I never brought them home to you."

"Oh! So that's why you kept on palming me off to grandma's?"

She laughed. "Excuse me! I didn't palm you off!"

"Yeah, right!"

"I didn't! I needed to live my life too, you know. Being your mum isn't everything there is to me. I have needs too."

"Do I even want to know what your needs were?"

She raised her eyebrows at me. I laughed. Truly laughed. For the first time in a year since Mum and I had our bust up, we were talking like we used to. A ray of sunshine in the middle of the shit storm I seemed to be sailing through.

"Ok, maybe not."

"Are you sure? Because I could tell you about this Spanish guy I almost introduced to you. He was a firecracker!"

"Nope! Please don't. Stop it before I hear something I won't be able to forget."

CHAPTER 9

Marcelo

> **Paige**
> Left the door open. Just come in.

TOOK THAT AS MY INVITATION TO BE THIRTY-FIVE MINUTES EARLY. As soon as I opened the door, I could hear Coffee Bean screaming.

"Paige?"

"In the kitchen."

I removed my coat and boots as fast as I could. Paige was in her bathrobe; Amber in a type of half sleeping bag, half dungarees, bellowing her lungs out, her hair sticking up on the top of her head like she'd been dragged through a bush backward.

"Why is she crying?"

"She's hungry, and she's not a very patient customer."

Paige took a bottle from inside a container smoking with hot water and shook it. "She needs to be fed and changed. I set everything up for you." She nodded at the kitchen table and handed me the bottle. "Test it on the back of your hand to make sure it's not too hot before you give it to her." Then she handed me Coffee Bean. "I need to get ready. Are you sure you'll be ok with her?"

"We'll be fine." I tried to sound as reassuring as I could.

Paige hesitated, holding Amber's hand. She had never left me in charge of Coffee Bean before, and I could tell she was struggling with the idea, especially as Amber was screaming. Her crying had a way of getting into your bones.

As she leaned over to kiss Amber's head, she got real close to me. And I could feel the pull of her. It had always been like this. Whenever she was close, her body called to mine like a magnet, and I moved toward her without thinking. That was why I'd had to always keep a certain distance from her at the beginning. Then she was out of the door, leaving me with a sense of emptiness.

With Coffee Bean on one arm, I didn't have enough hands to try the milk on my hand before giving it to her, so I sucked on the bottle instead. It didn't taste like normal milk, but it wasn't hot. And as soon as I gave Amber the bottle, she stopped screaming—her miniature fists resting on her chest as if strapped by an invisible straitjacket, her eyes focused on me. I pulled a chair with my foot and sat down. Not long after, I heard the shower switching on down the corridor and a door closing. Paige had waited until Amber had stopped crying to get in the shower.

I was still feeding Coffee Bean when she reappeared—hair wet, barefoot, still in her bathrobe.

"You still ok with her?"

I nodded.

"Don't forget to burp her before you change her. And watch your clothes—"

"She leaks, I know."

Paige nodded but hovered in the doorway. She really didn't like leaving Amber.

"I got it. Don't worry."

She nodded and disappeared into the hall.

"Coffee Bean, you need to make me look good for your momma, ok?" I told the hungry meatball in Portuguese. "Otherwise, she won't let me do it again. I could really do with some brownie points. You need to help your daddy out."

Paige had picked this little dress, with tights and a top underneath, and she had laid everything out in the order they should go on. Like an idiot's guide to how to dress your baby. I did what I was told. Thanking Marisa for making me help her with Freddie when he was little, otherwise I would've been shitting my pants trying to dress Amber. Getting her legs into things was easy enough, getting her arms and big cheeks into things was another story. I don't know what moron decided that baby clothes should have small holes. Her tiny limp body got stuck each and every way, as if it didn't have any bones, which only added to my worry that I could pull and break something.

A hairdryer turned on somewhere deep inside the apartment.

Coffee Bean's chunky legs and arms looked like little lumps of bread dough, the fat on top of her feet making them look like small balls in her tiny baby shoes. But there was no amount of brushing that would make her hair go down. I tried to wet it and everything, nothing was taming her mop of hair. From the neck down she looked presentable, from the neck up she looked like a chubby punk rocker—big cheeks like a hamster and a disheveled cluster of dark hair pointing in all directions.

Paige reappeared—half her hair was pinned to the side, the green dress she was wearing giving her a killer figure—dark tights and boots that went all the way up to her knees. The black of her eyeliner made her eyes an even lighter shade of green, her lips an inviting glossy pink. She walked past me, leaving a trail of perfume I would recognize anyplace. And I couldn't stop looking at her. If we were in a different place, I would have kissed her, smelled her neck, told her she looked sexy as hell. But today, all I could do was drool over it from my doghouse. It was incredibly mean.

"You look beautiful."

"I don't feel it." She answered without looking at me, stashing Amber's bag with everything she thought she might need. Then she looked at Amber. "Oh gosh! What is going on with your hair, Poppet?"

"Yeah… I can't fix that. It's not coming down, I tried everything."

Paige's head bounced up and down, telling me she was used to this, and she vanished down the corridor, I assumed in search of some magical solution. When she came back, she had a thick headband with a big-ass bow on it. It subdued Amber's Mohican, but it made her look like a baby Carmen Miranda. By the time she was dressed in her polar bear ski suit and strapped to the car basket seat thing, she looked like a starfish, wrapped in layers of warm clothes with only her tiny face on show.

Paige reached for the handle and went to move the car seat from the table, but I put my hand on top of hers to stop her.

"It's heavy. I'll do it."

For a minute she didn't move, and we stood there—my hand on top of hers, me looking at her, her looking at our hands. Her hand was so warm. Paige was like a hot water bottle; her body always radiated heat. Now I knew why. In Brazil, we were built to lose heat and stay cool. In England, with the cold weather, they were built to keep it. I had missed the warmth of her skin.

Then she removed her hand from under mine, grabbed Amber's bag, and walked to the hall. As we got to street level, she got her keys out and opened a car. It was the same one I had leaned against while I'd watched her through the window on the first night I landed.

"You drive?" I didn't know she could drive or that she had a car.

"Of course I drive." She answered without looking at me.

"You never drove in Brazil."

"Nobody ever asked me to drive in Brazil. Doesn't mean I can't drive."

She opened one of the back doors and signaled for me to set Amber down on the seat. The car was low; she had to bend over to strap the car seat in—her dress riding up and sitting just under her ass. Memories of her bending over the sofa in my lounge at home filled my mind, and my eyes glued to her curves like a fly on a spider's web. I scratched my neck, ran a hand down my face to try and curb the memory. This shit was going to give me a heart attack, death by fucking boner. I'm sure this is a type of torture in some messed-up country. But this is what she had always done to me; she just didn't know it.

Paige closed the door and almost walked into me behind her. "You're on the wrong side. This is the driver's side."

Of course it was. Everything in this freezing country was on the wrong side. The measures were all different, their coffee was awful, they didn't have cheese dough balls, and now I was sat on the driver's side without a steering wheel, and Paige was on the passenger side driving. It just felt wrong. It wasn't that she was a bad driver, she wasn't. It was just that I always drove.

Paige connected her phone to the car, and the strong base music she liked started playing.

"So, this is your famous playlist?"

At first, she said nothing. "Can you keep an eye on Amber, please? I put her on the wrong side of the car, and I can't see her."

I nodded.

Whenever I tried to reach out to her and talk about memories of us, she shut me down. Like my mistake had erased everything good we ever did and there was nothing left, just Coffee Bean. If she wasn't going to accept the old ones, I would have to create new ones. I needed her to remember me when I made her smile, when my touch gave her goosebumps.

Everything had gone to shit, but before it did, we had three amazing weeks when we were both happy—going on dates, talking in bed, hugging, kissing, having sex so good it'd make your toes curl. And I missed it. I missed her smile, the way she looked at me like I was worth keeping. The way she held my hand and brought it to her face when I was driving. This purgatory I was in couldn't be farther away from that. I could actually feel her wall trying to push me out of the car.

We sat in the waiting room of the registry office—Paige, me, and the starfish in her starfish-mobile. Amber's stroller looked like a three-wheeler spaceship.

"Can you hold this for a minute, please?" Paige handed me a series of documents and started to unzip Amber's ski suit.

"Paige Marie?" Her driving license was on top of the pile of papers.

"It's my middle name. It was my grandmother's name."

I hadn't known she had another name apart from Lancaster.

The dots connected. "So you can give your child a middle name to honor somebody?"

She nodded but didn't look at me.

I looked at her driving license for a minute. She looked younger in the picture.

"Amber doesn't have a middle name."

"No."

"You chose her first name. Can I choose her middle one?"

She sighed, clearly unhappy with the idea. "Depends on what it is."

"Marisa." Her face turned to me then, but her eyes gazed at the floor. "She deserves all the credit I can give her. God knows I didn't make it easy on her."

Paige went quiet for a moment, then consented. "Amber Marisa Lancaster-Costa it is then."

One hour later, Coffee Bean was officially a person, and we

each had a piece of paper to prove we had made another human.

"Do you mind if I call Marisa before we get in the car?"

Paige shook her head.

I took Amber out of her stroller and had her face the phone as Marisa answered my video call. "Hello *vovó*."

"Oh, my goodness!" Marisa's voice took the squeaky tone women get when they see a baby. "She is *so* adorable! Look at those cheeks!"

Paige smiled. This was the first time I had seen her smile since I landed. She might not understand the words, but the squeaky tone was unmistakable.

"I want to see! I want to see!" The top of Freddie's head appeared on the screen. Risa lowered the phone to his eye level. "Oh, it's just a baby." And he still hadn't got the memo.

"It's Celo's baby, Freddie."

"What are you doing home, bud? Shouldn't you be at school?"

"I'm going to the dentist."

"I see. Freddie, your best friend is here." I flipped the conversation into English, turning the phone to Paige.

"Paige! Mom! It's Paige!" he shouted, all excited. His racket made everyone look at us; I turned the volume down.

"Hey Freddie. How are you?" Paige said, smiling and waving at the camera. The kid did have the moves. I couldn't make her smile for love nor money, but all he had to say was hi.

"When are you coming back? You missed my birthday." Freddie, as always, was as subtle as a bullet to the brain, but Paige laughed.

"I know! I'm sorry, bud. You've grown!"

"I'm in big school now."

"Lu told me. Well done! Do you like going to school?"

"No!" His face twisted as if his answer was obvious and she was being stupid, borderline patronizing.

Paige let out the most amazing laugh.

"We still have to watch Spider-Man. You promised." He was on a roll.

"I did. Next time I see you, we will watch it, ok?"

"Ok. When are you coming?"

I turned the phone back to me. "Hey bud, can I speak to your mom?" Before he landed me in trouble.

"Ok…" He sounded disappointed.

The screen turned back to Marisa. "Let me say hi to Paige." I handed the phone to Paige.

"Hi, Risa." She smiled and waved at the camera.

"Oh! You look so pretty. Motherhood is treating you well. How on Earth are you?!"

"I'm ok."

"Oh please! You're being polite; postnatal is brutal. I know, I had two." Paige smiled, embarrassed. "We have missed you on our beauty days. It's so nice to see you!"

"I know… I miss you guys too." She looked down, bit her lip. Then diverted the conversation. "Marcelo has something important to tell you. I'll hand it back to him." Apparently, not even Risa escaped Paige's ban on good memories from Brazil.

I took the phone back. "I know you're getting Freddie ready to go. I just wanted to tell you something real quick."

She sat down. "You're not having another baby, are you?" And laughed.

"At this rate… only if it's by immaculate conception." I looked at Paige. She looked at the floor, biting her lower lip. Man… she really had to stop doing that. It distracted me.

"I can't believe you made me a grandma! I'm only forgiving you because my grandbaby is so adorable."

"I'm actually calling you about her." Marisa's head tilted to the side, eyebrows frowning. "We have just done her birth certificate. They do this thing here in England where they give children a second name in honor of someone. It's called a middle name. Paige is Paige Marie because of her grandmother. So… I wanted to formally introduce you to Amber Marisa Lancaster-Costa." I turned the camera to Coffee Bean.

Risa went quiet for a long minute. "You gave her my name?" Her voice was choked.

"Paige let me pick the middle name. You're like… my mom. So… I thought if anyone deserved it, it was you."

She went silent. Then started fanning herself with her hand. "You are really going to make me cry at eight in the morning?"

"It wasn't the intention, no." I smiled at her.

"It only took you twenty years to call me that." Her face was going red.

"You know I'm complicated. But better late than never, no?"

She laughed. "At least you did it while I'm still alive to hear it. You're making me look a mess. Now I need to go fix my face." She sniffled.

"I know you need to go, so I'll catch up with you later. I just wanted to tell you."

She nodded. "I feel very honored. Thank you." A hand wiped her face. "Love you, son."

"Love you too, Mom." Her shoulders dropped, her head tilted to the side, and she smiled, a soft expression on her face. She liked it when I called her Mom. It felt good to me too, I had to admit. "Speak soon." And I cut the call.

Paige was looking at the floor, but she was smiling. "Did you ever tell Risa about the tattoo on your arm? The one you did for her."

"No. She hates my tattoos; she wouldn't see that as a compliment."

She shrugged. "I don't know… You mean something to

someone if they carry you on their skin for the rest of their lives. You should tell her." She started pushing the stroller to the door.

"We're in Chelsea, right?"

Paige nodded.

"Coffee Bean, what do you say we go celebrate you becoming an official person and making Risa happy?"

"Stop calling her that. Her name is *Amber*. You're holding the paper that proves it."

I turned my head like Coffee Bean was whispering in my ear. "What's that? You know a great restaurant in Chelsea. Excellent idea. I'm starving." Then I turned to Paige. "*Amber* and I want to go for lunch."

"Oh, really? Because her restaurant is standing right here." She was trying to keep a straight face, but her voice told me she found it funny.

"Then I guess you better come with."

She fidgeted on her feet, bit her lip, looked everywhere else but at me. "I don't think that's a good idea. Amber's about to get hungry and crabby soon."

"So? You're here, she has all the food she needs. We're already out, and you have packed everything but the kitchen basin in that bag for her."

"This is not Brazil. English people are not child-friendly. You walk into a restaurant with a baby, and everyone looks at you like you're carrying a bomb."

"Sounds like that's their problem to me. We're celebrating, and my money is as good as everyone else's."

Paige bit her lip, shook her head. "Amber will need a feed soon. I don't like breastfeeding in public."

Yes, there was that. It wouldn't do me any good staring at her breasts either.

I scrambled for a solution. "When Freddie was a baby, Risa used to put a blanket over her shoulder when she was feeding him. We have a blanket." I pointed at the pile of fabric on the stroller. "Or you can do it in the car before we walk into the restaurant. Come on, you must be hungry too. You didn't eat anything before we left."

"It's not a good idea." Her voice was dry, sharp.

"What is that, Coffee Bean?" Paige rolled her eyes at the name. But as I started talking to her, Amber started making noises back at me. "Hmm, I'll tell her. She says she wants to stay out of the house. That you spend too much time indoors like you're in prison."

"*Amber* said all that with one single gurgle, huh?" Paige's face turned to me, her eyes in the middle of my chest, but her eyebrows were raised, and she was smiling.

"She did. Behind these chubby cheeks there is a very powerful brain. Come on! Look at this cute face. How can you say no?" I turned sideways so Amber was facing Paige and tickled Amber's chin.

"Did you see that?" Paige pointed at Amber, her eyes wide.

"Did I see what?"

"She smiled!"

"She did??" Babies learned to smile after six weeks, according to my book. This was the first time Coffee Bean had done it.

"Did you smile at your dad being silly, Poppet?" Paige tickled her chin while smiling at her, and Coffee Bean opened the sweetest, toothless smile. It was all drool and gums, like she wasn't really in control of her face, but her little eyes were happy. "Oh my gosh! She did it again!" Paige looked me in the eyes then, all excited, big smile on her face—standing so close to me I could've kissed her. "She smiled!"

"She did." And I smiled with them.

"You're smiling, baby girl?" Paige cooed at her, holding Amber's hands and rubbing her cheeks with her fingers.

Coffee Bean not only giving her more smiles but also making noises back at her. "He is silly, isn't he?"

Things were still messed up, but for a couple of minutes, my two English girls were smiling, and Paige forgot she was angry with me. After three days feeling like I was banging my head against a solid concrete wall, this small break in the clouds gave me a high and a glimpse of why I was here. This is what I wanted, what I came here to win back—my own little family, my two girls and me. Happy. Together.

"I told you. She wants to go for lunch and is happy to be out of the house."

Paige was still smiling at Amber. "Fine. But only because *she* asked with a smile."

CHAPTER 10

Paige

I sat in the car feeding Amber under a blanket for forty minutes.

Told Marcelo he could stay in the car, but he insisted on standing outside, saying he was going to call the restaurant and book a table. None of the Brazilians I knew had any tolerance to the cold. The weather would be freezing to him; he paced up and down to keep himself warm—the hood of his hoodie pulled over his head, hands in the pockets of his parka. He was dressed like we were in the middle of winter, but it was early spring.

Winter clothes suited him, made him look even more imposing. Couple that with the warm tan no British person would naturally have after months of dark gray days, and a face that made you double-take him, and he stood out like a sore thumb. Passersby peeked at him while pretending not to look.

This is why I couldn't lock eyes with him. Looking at him too much had made me ignore the red flags and gotten me pregnant. Not at all dissimilar to an addiction that starts as something you do for fun, then you wake up and your life is ruined.

It was also hard to look at him and not think of what could have been. And as the minutes ticked by like sand piling up at the bottom of an hourglass, I started regretting my decision. I couldn't stand being close to him but now we were supposedly breaking bread. What on Earth possessed me to agree to this? Oh, I know, getting distracted by the smiling baby I gave birth to. I'm so goddamn gullible.

"Are you done, Poppet? Cause this is starting to feel like you're nibbling at me just for fun, like a vampire." Amber stared at me through hooded eyes. Double-chinned, little arms abandoned as though she was now too heavy to move them. A droplet of milk still sitting on her chin. I put myself away, sorted my dress, and started burping her. "Any chance you can puke all over me? You do it all the time, but now would actually be a great time."

Nothing. She just stared into the ether, milk drunk, belching to her heart's content. Where is baby puke when you need some?

Marcelo carried the car seat to the restaurant, the motion of walking and a full stomach sending Amber to sleep. So much for her wanting to go for lunch! She brought him here, distracted me, got me to agree my life away, and then she deserted me and left me to deal with lunch all by myself. She was definitely her father's daughter.

"How do you know about this place?" I asked as we both removed our coats to sit at the table.

He shrugged. "You only let me visit for two hours. I can't really work from here and can only swim and gym so many hours a day. So I spend a lot of time googling stuff and wandering around. By this time next week, I will know London better than you."

We sat across the table from each other. I didn't want to think about it, but this very much felt like the first time he took me out for food—sans Harley Davidson, avec a sleeping baby as an icebreaker. Talk about an alternate reality!

His eyes were on me as they had been back then. It was like he was daring me to look at him, but I busied myself looking around the restaurant. The waiter brought our drinks.

"Can you fill some gaps for me?"

"Fill some gaps?"

"Yeah. I know you were pregnant, and we had a baby, but I don't know anything else."

"Like what?"

"When did you find out you were pregnant?" He leaned on his elbows, hands busy playing with the lighter between his fingers. Not to look at him, I stared at the silver box going back and forth in his hands.

A sigh escaped without my permission. "The same day I went to your house."

"How did you know you were…?"

"I didn't. I wasn't late or anything."

"So how did you find out?"

"I fainted in the kitchen. Lu got worried and took me to the doctors."

"You fainted?"

I nodded. There was a pattern to the way he flipped the lighter, like a choreography his fingers had learned and danced on repeat. His hands were what I remembered: gorilla hands, big palms, meaty fingers, and short nails.

"When Risa was pregnant with Freddie, she wanted to eat all sorts of weird stuff. Did you get that?"

"No. But I was obsessed with chicken noodles, and those little eggs you guys serve with the pink sauce."

"Quail eggs?" He sounded surprised.

I nodded.

"I can't imagine they were easy to find over here."

"They weren't. I never ate any."

He grunted, and in my peripheral vision I saw him smile. "Risa also got funny about smells. She hated everyone's perfume. Did you have that?"

"No. But I loved the smell of concrete when it rained after a hot day. I only smelled it in Denver, though. It wasn't the same in London."

"Did you have any like… issues when you were pregnant?"

I had plenty of issues, the biggest one being him. "I got a lot of morning sickness around four months. And I was the size of a house toward the end, so I had a lot of back pain and shortness of breath, but nothing serious. She was just a big baby."

"You had a natural birth, and she was two weeks overdue."

"Yes. She was due on the fourth of February, but she wasn't born until the seventeenth."

Like magic, the lighter disappeared from his hands, Celo opening his palms to show me he no longer had it. My eyes instantly refocused on his face. While he'd asked me the questions, he'd slowly raised his arms up to rest on his elbows. I was so busy focusing on it—on his hands and the questions he was asking—I hadn't noticed. He had done it on purpose, so I would look him in the eye.

And once our eyes locked, I couldn't look away. Sitting across a table from me, he still had the same gravitational pull. His chocolate orbs reaching out like hands that could touch me. It made him a little hypnotic. It was painful.

"Hi." The corners of his lips lifted into a small smile; his expression softened as though this was the first time he was seeing me today. As if he hadn't spent the whole morning with me already.

I didn't respond.

The fight with Felipe had left a scar on his lip and a mark on his cheek. I remembered kissing those. His blood had smeared all over my mouth.

"I have a hard question."

I shrugged.

"Lu said you considered an abortion." When I didn't

volunteer any information, he asked an actual question. "What made you change your mind?"

For a moment, I debated if I should tell him the truth.

"They didn't know how far I was exactly, so I had to do an ultrasound. I was nine weeks. She already looked like a little person and had a heartbeat." I shifted in my seat, uncomfortable. "And I couldn't do it. She is my daughter too, not just yours. If my mother had taken the easy way out, I wouldn't be here either." I remembered his post on Instagram. He'd said he never thought he'd be a dad. "Why? Would you have told me to do it?" The question came out of my mouth before I could edit. I don't know why it mattered. It shouldn't matter. I had decided to have Amber without him.

He shook his head, puckering his lips together like that would've never been an option. "Did you want kids?"

"Not at twenty-five, no. Did *you*?" I sounded sarcastic on purpose.

Another head shake. "I didn't think I'd date anyone either. And yet… here we are." He gazed at me as if he meant we were still dating. "For what's worth, I'm glad you didn't. Have an abortion, I mean."

Our food arrived. He rearranged how he was sitting to eat his meal, and his eyes moved from me, setting me free. That was a relief. I had been unable to stop looking at him out of my own volition.

"Why did you choose Amber for her name? Did you already have it, or did you choose it after she was born?" he asked after we had both fallen silent, halfway through eating his food.

"It was the first name I saw after I found out she was a girl. It's the name of a gemstone. She is precious to me, so it seemed fitting." I could feel his gaze burning on me while I looked at Amber fast asleep in her car seat.

"It's also what remains after a fire. You can set it alight

again if you give it some oxygen." He followed my gaze; his voice sounded pensive.

"That's ember, not Amber."

His eyes didn't move from our baby. "She doesn't look real when she sleeps. Like a little doll." It dawned on me that he had never seen her asleep. Whenever he visited, she was always awake. "Will she sleep for long?"

"She moves when she is dreaming. And no. She'll wake up in an hour or two." He nodded, but looked relieved. "Are you missing your playmate or something?" I said, finishing my plate.

He shrugged. "You'll make me leave soon. I was just wondering if I'd get to speak to her before I left."

"You speak like you can actually talk to her. You know she doesn't understand you, right?"

Marcelo nodded. He had also finished his plate. "Babies don't remember people unless they hear their voice a lot."

The penny dropped. "You're trying to make her remember you?"

He shrugged. "She's my kid. But I don't have the privilege of doing anything a dad would do. All I can do is talk to her and hold her for two hours a day." His voice was low, eyes on Amber, and he looked genuinely sad. Like he longed not to be a visiting stranger, but someone who had a bigger part in her life.

Ryan had told me about this. His sadness that he had never seen me say my first words, take my first steps. That he would never get to read me a bedtime story. He told me he felt robbed of something he would never be able to replace or get back. That he was my father, but he hadn't been allowed to be my dad like he had been to his other daughters. If my mother had married, I might have felt different, but I felt it too. I had missed out on something important, on memories I would never get to have. Being a mum was hard, but I couldn't imagine how I would feel if the roles were reversed and someone had taken Amber away from me.

We drove back to the flat in silence, exhaustion starting to take its toll. I had barely slept, and this was the longest Amber and I had ever stayed out of the house since she was born. But by the time I parked up, she had woken up and was screaming. We walked in, me holding her, Celo carrying everything else.

"Is she hungry again?" he asked walking behind me.

"No. She needs a nappy change."

"How do you know?"

"She has different types of cries."

His head turned. "It sounds the same to me."

"You'll hear the difference eventually. I didn't hear it in the beginning either."

"I can change her, if you want."

I didn't answer.

"Look… I can see you're tired. I'm not. I can change her, and I can stay with her for a while so you can rest."

He had already stayed longer than he would have done on a normal day. I had only asked him to come earlier because I genuinely couldn't sort Amber and myself out in time.

When I didn't answer, he said, "That's what the nurse said I needed to do. That I should help take care of Coffee Bean while you caught up on some sleep."

No way in hell would I leave her with him. I wanted him to leave. "Her name is *Amber*."

"Paige, you look exhausted. Let me do what the nurse told me to do. I promise as soon as you wake up, I'll leave."

No answer.

"Ok, then I'll change her, and I'll leave. Why don't you go sit down for a minute?"

I didn't like his suggestion one bit, but since he was here, he might as well make himself useful. I wasn't happy about it, but I nodded.

"I'll change her. You go sit down."

He took his coat and shoes off, picked up the bag, and took Amber from me. I sat down on the sofa, my body thanking me for sitting somewhere comfortable and plush. I leaned sideways to rest my head for a minute, and the last thing I remember was hearing him talk to Amber while he changed her, but she wasn't crying.

♥♥♥

I was dimly aware of something touching my hair, resting on my neck, gently stroking my cheek back and forth. But I was so comfortable and relaxed, I didn't want to move. Then Amber's crying cut through the warm and fuzzy, awareness returning to me slowly as if it was a car's headlights in the distance, getting bigger and bigger as it got closer.

"Paige?" The voice was smooth, gentle. "Paige?"

I opened my eyes. Marcelo was crouched on the floor next to the sofa, face at eye level with mine, his hand on my face, a blanket draped over me.

"Hey…" He smiled, retrieving his hand. "You fell asleep, but I think Amber's hungry now, and I can't find a bottle." His voice was still smooth, low, apologetic for waking me up.

My eyes adjusted. He was holding Amber, and she had started to whine. The type of crying she did before going into a full meltdown. I sat up.

"You let me sleep!" It was a full accusation.

"You were tired." He stood up.

"You were just supposed to change her and give her back to me." My senses were still slow, surfacing from sleep.

"No, I'm supposed to look after her so you can catch up on your sleep. You didn't want to listen to your nurse, but you were so tired, you were out cold in seconds. I just did what I was told and let you sleep."

I scowled at him, hands automatically unbuttoning my dress so I could feed Amber.

"Don't worry, I'm going now." He handed me the breastfeeding cushion, kissed Amber's head and handed her back to me. "I'll see you tomorrow, Lewis." A smile creeped on his face, satisfied that I had been too tired to stand strong and he had gotten what he wanted.

I pulled one of my breasts out while glaring at him even harder.

His gaze dropped to my cleavage as my nipple hit the side of Amber's face and she desperately searched for it open-mouthed, crying, then latched on and went silent.

"This is not Broadway. And I'm not some freak show for you to watch," I said when I felt he had been staring for too long.

He blinked twice, eyebrows screwing together as though I had slapped him and he was confused as to why. His eyes returned to my face for a second. And without another word, he went to the hall, put his stuff back on, and let himself out.

CHAPTER 11
Paige

"PAIGE?"

"Sitting room."

I had messaged him to tell him the door was open, and he was thirty minutes early. Without even thinking, I adjusted my clothes and instantly wanted someone to slap me. It annoyed me to no end that the concern to look attractive whenever he was around still got the best of me. What he thought of me didn't matter. It shouldn't matter when I hated his guts.

I straightened the small bow clip in Amber's hair. She was only little, but she had masses of dark hair like her father.

He smiled as soon as he spotted us on the floor. "What are you doing?" He took a seat next to me.

"Development exercises. We're almost finished," I said, halfway through making Amber's hand reach for the opposite knee. "Eight… nine… ten." She smiled at me. "Well done, Poppet. Should we do your legs? Yes, we should. Yes, we should." I cooed at her encouragingly, letting her look at my face.

He watched me. "Babies have to gym?"

"They don't *have* to. But it's good for their coordination and brain development. And we want you to be a clever girl, don't we, Poppet? Let's do the bicycle," I cooed at her, as I moved her tiny legs like she was on a bike, then stretched and pushed them back into her tummy. Ten repetitions. "And rotisserie chicken." She smiled at me, as I gathered her little limbs and rocked her barrow-shaped body from side to side. "Almost done. Just one minute of tummy time and you're done."

As I placed her face down on the mat, she started complaining.

"I know, Poppet, I know you don't like this one. Nobody likes going to the gym. No pain, no gain."

Marcelo smiled, but his face quickly turned to a frown.

"Is that not dangerous?" He pointed at Amber. Granted, it looked precarious—the top of her small body lifted while she wiggled her head around like she didn't have enough control of it to keep herself from suffocating against the mat. "She looks like she's struggling."

"It's supposed to help strengthen their neck and shoulders. She's only meant to do it for a minute. But yes… I don't like it either. It doesn't look very comfortable. I guess that's why you're not supposed to leave her unattended." I placed a baby mirror in front of Amber to distract her from whining. "Look! Who is this? I know, Poppet. These are harder than when you had the cushion, I know. But you're a big girl now. You need to start doing the floor ones."

"How often does she need to do these?"

"Every day. We do it in the mornings before your dad comes, don't we, Poppet? But he decided to turn up early." I *was* goading. He was meant to be here at ten, not nine thirty.

He ignored my jab. "Can I pick her up? This is giving me agony. She looks like she'll suffocate in a minute."

Amber had done her minute anyway, so I waved a hand from him to her, and he didn't hesitate before picking her up.

"Oi, princesinha. Mas que linda! De laço no cabelo. Você sentiu saudade do papai?" Something about her looking pretty, something about her hair, I assumed the bow. And *saudade* meant missing something. He kissed her cheeks. She instantly smiled and gave him long loving blinks. Apparently, not even female infants escaped his charm.

I got up. "I'm in the kitchen if she needs anything."

But I heard him follow and turned around to find Amber facing me from his arms, sitting as if she was on a throne, her back resting against the front of him, chubby cheeks piling on top of one of his hands like a deflated round balloon.

"Can I help you?" I made sure my tone was annoyed as I turned around to face him.

"Coffee."

"You know where the kettle is." He had turned up every day for the last six days. He was out of his bloody mind if he thought I would wait on him with pots of coffee at the ready.

Celo walked to the worktop, and I turned around and started folding the baby clothes I had taken out of the dryer earlier. The tap turned on; water filled a container to the top. The kettle clicked; the hissing of it filling the silence. I could feel the heat of his stare at the back of my head.

A thud sounded through the hallway just as the kettle started to whistle. Someone was at the door. But Marcelo was already here, and I wasn't expecting any more visitors. I looked at him confused; he smiled. It made me nervous. That was the cocky smirk he wore when he thought he was being clever. Another knock.

"Are you going to get that?" His smugness made me even more suspicious.

I marched through the hallway and threw the door open.

"Lu??"

"Surprise!!"

"On my God! Lu!" And I threw my arms around her. I was so happy to see her, I had no words. Then I noticed the smiling figure behind her. "Gabe??"

"Hey, beautiful." Gabriel smiled at me, holding a bouquet of flowers and a teddy bear.

"Gosh! Come in, come in, it's cold!" I barely let them inside before I threw my arms around Lu again.

"Ok… can't… breathe." My arms eased. "I missed you too, flower," she told me with a big smile, squeezing me tighter. "Now… where is the little Coffee Bean? Cause you know, sorry, but we didn't come to see you."

"Don't *you* start calling her that as well." I pointed an accusatory finger at her.

Just as I said it, Marcelo emerged from the kitchen, big smile on his face. He'd known they were coming.

"Oh my gosh! She is even cuter in person!" Lu shrugged her coat off and handed it to Gabe. "Come to your favorite auntie *ever*!"

"You have to support her neck, Lu," Marcelo said as he handed Amber over, then went to greet Gabriel.

"Goodness me! I could dip you in chocolate and eat you! How cute are you!? And look at all that hair!" Lu turned to Marcelo. "How did a monkey-looking thing like you make something as cute as this?"

Marcelo snorted, but his lips parted into a smile. The self-righteous smile he wore when he was satisfied with his own performance. Like he was proud of producing a child. Ironically, he had done fuck-all but orgasm without a condom.

"I knew she looked like you, man, but gee! Father yes; mother maybe. Sorry, Paige." One of Gabriel's fingers tickled Amber's cheek. "You're a cutie, aren't you?"

Amber smiled at him.

"On my gosh!" Lu's voice went an octave higher in girlie squeakiness. "Look at that smile!" Then she turned to Gabe. "She is definitely Paige's baby. Celo's a grumpy sod."

"I'm standing right here, Lu." He laughed. But he was happy. Proud even.

"Come through, guys! Do you want something hot to warm up?" I offered.

"God yeah! It's only a short walk, but I think my nuts have shrunk to peanuts." Gabe was rubbing his arms.

"It's not that cold."

"You're forgetting where we came from, flower. It's the end of summer back home."

Lu and Gabriel looked so cute holding Amber. She was clearly not their child, but I could see it. The way Gabe looked at Lu, I could definitely see a family on the cards for them. He hovered, always aware of where she was, his hands never far away, always on her or around her like he didn't want her to go far. And Lu, for all her 'I don't need a man', never went far either. Her body was always angled toward him, eyes glancing at him every so often. She looked… happy.

Marcelo was sitting on the corner of the sofa—one arm over the back of it, the other over its arm, watching them like I was.

Until his eyes met mine, a sad expression like a stamp over them. He was thinking the same as me. Regret and longing all there, bare for anyone to see. What we could have been, what we lost.

Lu and Gabe noticed. The two of them were as bad as each other at noticing everything and reading people like books.

"So how is motherhood treating you, flower?"

I took a deep breath, trying to figure out how to word my response. "Do you want the truth? Or do you want me to be polite?"

Celo's eyes narrowed, the muscles on his jaw working.

"Ok… I guess, the truth." The words dragged, loaded with caution and suspicion, her eyebrows raised.

"I love that little bundle you're holding. Absolutely adore her. Would kill and die for her in a blink of an eye. But I haven't slept a full night in months, my social life is pretty much nonexistent, and I feel like I'm a milking cow. So… I would say motherhood is bittersweet."

"Right… Celo, I think this is our cue to take pocket-size mini you here for a walk and let the girls talk through their girl stuff." Gabe stood up. "Do you have a baby-mobile we could carry her majesty in, Paige?"

"Gabe, I don't think—"

"Don't worry." He interrupted my protest, both his hands up in the air. "I give you my word we'll bring her back in one piece. Is one hour ok, pocket rocket?"

Lu nodded. Gabe leaned down to kiss her.

Marcelo didn't move. He knew damn well I had never let him out of earshot with our baby, let alone out of the house. "We're not taking her anywhere unless Paige is ok with it." His eyes stayed on me, his voice flat, factual.

"It'll be fine, flower. Gabe knows I'd kill him if anything happens to her, and Celo has a vested interest in keeping her alive, bearing in mind she's his offspring and all."

The three of them looked at me, waiting for a response.

"Paige, come on. They can take her for an hour and come back. I haven't seen you in ages! I want to talk to you without these two bulls jamming the line."

That made me look at Lu. Her weird sayings never ceased to amaze me. "These two what?"

"You know what I mean. Without these two gossiping old ladies eavesdropping on our every word."

"Hey! I resent that!" Gabriel protested, but he was smiling.

Three sets of eyes came back to me.

I didn't really like the idea, but I suppose I needed to get used to Marcelo taking her places. I could do an hour. Sixty minutes sounded like a manageable first step. At least with Lu here, I wouldn't be going out of my mind worrying.

"I'll get her coat," I said standing up. "The pram is in the boot of the car right outside."

CHAPTER 12

Luciana

Paige watched as Gabe and Celo walked up the stairs with the baby, her eyes anxious, one of her hands squeezing the flesh on her arm.

"They will be fine, don't worry. Celo used to babysit Freddie for Marisa." I rubbed her back in a big circle. "He's surprisingly good with children."

"He told me. But she's only tiny, Lu."

"Hey…" I turned her around, so she was looking at me. "Celo adores that little girl. He'll take good care of her."

She nodded, but her eyes were still anxious.

"Plus, Gabe hates the cold. They won't go very far, trust me. Probably only make it as far as those cute cafés you have at the end of your road, so don't worry. Now, come on…" I held her by the arm and guided her to the sofa so we could sit down. "Now you can tell me what that 'motherhood is bittersweet' business was all about."

"Did he ask you to come?" Her tone was unimpressed, one of her eyebrows raised.

"I was coming anyway. But yes, he did." I drank my coffee. "He's worried about you. Celo has been through some pretty low points himself, you know, so he can spot the signs. And I'm not going to lie; I was worried about him too."

"Worried about *him*?" Another raised eyebrow.

"This is not easy for either of you, flower. It's not easy for you to have him here, but it's also not easy for him to be here when everyone dislikes him and wants him gone."

She scoffed, sipped her tea.

"I'm worried about *both* of you. That's why I brought Gabe." I smiled and nudged her with my shoulder. "So I can give you my full attention while Celo also has someone to talk to. A little bit of home, if you like."

"So you two are tag teaming us?" Disconcerted, she laughed.

"No!" I drank my coffee. She raised both of her eyebrows at me. "Ok, maybe a little. You're both our friends. Well… to me, more like family. Anyway, we just wanted to make sure you're both ok with everything that's going on."

Paige nodded, but her eyes were on the floor.

"Although, I will be honest, I just wanted to meet my goddaughter. She's way cuter than both of you. We're no longer friends if you don't make me her godmother."

That earned me a headshake and an amused smile. Both of us sipped our drinks.

"You look so happy, Lu. I'm really happy for you." Her face opened in a genuine, heartfelt smile. "You two make such a cute couple."

"Yeah… Gabe is great. He's so level-headed, it's actually annoying. Nothing seems to faze him. But anyway… I'm not here to talk about me. How are you, flower? What is really going on?"

Paige took a deep breath, the sigh that followed equally as long. She placed her tea mug on the side table, eyes dropping to the sleeves of her jumper, and she picked at the hems, biting her lip. I had asked her this on the phone several times, but she was very good at sidestepping my question when I wasn't sitting in front of her.

I reached out and squeezed her hand. "You know you can tell me, flower. It won't get out of this room, I promise you."

She looked at me for a moment, then nodded. But it still took her a couple of minutes to figure out how to say it.

"You know… You have this baby, and you're supposed to plug it into your boob, then off you go being an amazing mum. But that has not happened to me. This is just so hard, Lu." Her voice caught. "I absolutely love her. She's my world. But she doesn't let me sleep. I can't even go to the toilet or take a shower without having to put her in her car seat and take her to the bathroom with me, because if she doesn't hear my voice, she screams the house down. I'm twenty-five and my body is destroyed. Breastfeeding is killing me. It's like I have stopped existing and now I live just for her. And even complaining about it makes me feel like a shit mum."

Paige looked up at me, her eyes tearing up, her nose going red.

"I feel like my life is over. And then *he* turns up every fucking day. Looking hotter than he did when we dated. Completely unaffected by anything, expecting me to be nice when all I want to do is gouge his eyes out and scream in his face. It makes me want to disappear."

"So you still think he's hot? Is he giving you funny flutters?"

"Lu! Out of everything I said this is what you focus on!? You're impossible!"

"I know. That's why you love me." I nudged my shoulder into hers.

Paige's smile didn't reach her eyes or stay on her face. Her tears started overspilling.

"Flower… your life isn't over. You had a baby, you're not dead. I spoke to Mum and Risa about this—"

"Lu! Really? You've all been talking about me?" Her face was going pink, distorted into embarrassment. "Great! Now everyone over two fucking countries knows how much of a shit mum I am!" Both of her hands covered her face.

"Unless you count my angelic imaginary children, I don't have kids, flower. I'm not going to sit here pretending I know what it's like, because I don't. It's hardly like I could talk from experience. So, before I came, I spoke to the two women I knew could." I reached out and lowered her hands from her face, giving both of them a gentle squeeze. "Nobody thinks you're a bad mum. Celo just said you were having a hard time, and he was worried about you. You don't need to be upset or embarrassed about it. Unfortunately for you, that little cute baby has granted you a one-way ticket to the mad house of Brazilian families. And once you're part of one, a good one, your pain is our pain. We're family now. We're all here for you, and we'll stick together through thick and thin. Now, do you want to know what Mum and Risa said?"

She shrugged, defeated. Cheeks going deeper red, eyes focused on our hands.

"That motherhood is like swimming the sea just to die on the beach."

"This is not a good time for one of your crazy sayings that don't quite translate, Lu." And she laughed a self-deprecating laugh. "What the hell is that even supposed to mean anyway?" She wiped her face.

"That it's fucking hard work! Come on, it has the word die in it! Stay with me!" I laughed and she followed. "They said it changes everything, and that it takes some getting used to. Risa actually said it's a new phase of life, a curve on the road so to speak. But that it's more like a rollercoaster curve, you know what I mean? One of those that throws you to the other side of the car even when you're strapped with a cage of a seatbelt. Nobody goes through that curve without feeling like their lungs are about to burst. So, it's normal to feel what you're feeling. That doesn't make you a bad mum. It just makes you a woman that is going through a life-changing event."

Paige looked at me, big eyes like a kitten, guilt and relief all wrapped in one.

"Risa and Mum have also told me that it gets easier, once she gets a little older."

Paige nodded. "Everyone says that."

"Yeah… but you're also doing it wrong, flower."

Her eyebrows pushed together, eyes surprised as if I had kissed then slapped her.

"I know you're still mad at Celo, but here you are—going through all this shit without having a second to yourself, while he whizzes in and out and only sees his daughter when she's in a good mood and looking like a little angel. Fuck that shit! How good is anger when you are the only one suffering?

"*Make. Him. Pay.* Don't sit suffering in silence, get fucking even! If I were you, he would be changing every pooey nappy and babysitting while I take long baths, go to the gym and get my nails done. I would be sending him to the supermarket to get me tampons like my little bitch. So you're hurt and upset, but he gets the best deal? Fuck that! Put him to work!

"He wants to fill his mouth to say he's a dad? Call him at 3am and make him come over here, when Amber is crying the house down and driving you insane, so you can get some sleep. No… Take none of this shit! He wants to be a dad, let him. Give him all the shitty jobs. This business of 'I'm upset, so I don't want his help'… This is where you're going wrong. Be upset, and if you're suffering, make him suffer with you. He was happy to have a good time when it was pleasure, right? Well… sometimes pleasure comes hand-in-hand with pain."

Paige burst out laughing. "I don't think Gabe knows what is waiting for him around the rollercoaster bend."

"Oh! He knows! Serves him right for breaking through my wall. He did it of his own accord, so I have no sympathy."

Paige laughed, a genuine, loud belly laugh.

"Seriously, though, let Celo pull his weight. Amber's his

daughter too. Why are you trying to do all the work on your own?"

She took a deep breath, staring at my hand holding hers.

"It's really hard to have him here, Lu. I can't stand it." Her voice was low, just above a whisper.

"Is that cause you're mad at him still? Or because you want to be mad at him, but you know you still have feelings for him?"

She didn't look at me, but her nose started going red and more tears spilled over.

"Because he's not good for me, Lu. He has never been really." Her hands tried to wipe the tears away, but they just got replaced by new ones. "I gave him everything I could give him, and what did he do? Threw it all back in my face in a matter of weeks. Now, he turns up here like nothing happened."

"What if your assessment of him is wrong?"

She looked at me, shoulders raising, eyebrows coming together, head shaking as if to tell me that what I was saying didn't make any sense.

"It's not true that he's unaffected. I don't bring this up because I know you don't want to hear it, but I know for a fact he feels incredibly guilty, misses you, and wants you back. His words to me on the phone were 'remorse doesn't quite cut it'."

"Don't Lu…"

"Flower, I'm not trying to defend what he did. It was beyond shitty, and I know you're still really upset. You have all the right to be. But I also happen to know how you feel about each other. I saw the way you two were looking at each other before. This is why it's so hard to have him here, isn't it?" I lowered my head to try and make her look me in the eyes. "You're struggling to let him help you because, if he's nice and it stops stinging, you might actually remember you like him."

Paige stood up and moved away from me. "If you're not

trying to defend him, then why are we talking about this?" Anger tinged her words.

"Because I know you still have feelings for him, and him for you. It's at least worth a conversation, is it not?"

"A conversation about what, Lu? About how he has all these feelings for me but fucked someone else?"

"What he did was stupid, but I know for a fact it was one single time when he wasn't in his right mind. I'm just saying this would be a really good way to see if he is genuinely sorry. If he's serious about fixing things with you, he'll step up and do anything you want just to be in your good graces and stay close to you. If it was me, I would use it to my advantage. At the very least, it's a way to have the help you need—and a little revenge; and at its best, it's a way to see if he deserves a second chance."

"A second chance!?" she scoffed, sarcastic, borderline offended. "It's so easy for him, isn't it? To want a second chance. He wasn't the one betrayed, pregnant, and heartbroken. I can't believe you are trying to convince me to take him back. Really, Lu? After everything that happened?"

I tried to give her my softest voice. I knew I was pushing it talking about it so soon, but with the two of them, everything was intertwined. It was almost impossible to separate one thing from the other.

"Flower, I'm your friend. And because I'm your friend, I will always tell you the truth. You know this. We agreed back in uni that we would be each other's conscience, and call a spoon, a spoon. I never said you should forgive him. You made a statement about him, and I told you what I know about it. What I'm saying is that he's here, practically begging you for a second chance or, at the very least, the opportunity to be a dad to his little girl. You have the option to make him prove to you that he means business and he's serious about you and Amber. At its worst, you will have help when you need it; and at its best, you will know if he deserves a second chance or not. If after that, you still feel there is no future, and nothing has changed… by all means, set the house on fire and burn it to the ground. He'll still be in Amber's life, but at least you'll know for sure, and you can both move on. Now, if after everything, you genuinely think he has proven to you that he's worthy of forgiveness, and you're still feel something for him… what would you rather be: bitter or happy?"

Paige stared at me, frustrated and indignant. But I don't even think she was mad at me. She was angry because her proud brain was telling her that she shouldn't forgive him, but her heart was telling her that maybe, just maybe, she could. She knew I was right.

"Hey"—I raised both my hands up in the air—"I'm not saying forgive him for free. I'm saying forgive him if he proves to you that he's worth it. And don't worry… If you decide to forgive him and he fucks this up a second time, you and I will fight for the knife to kill him." I stood up and walked to where she stood. "Flower, I'm not saying this because he's like a brother to me. I'm saying this because *you* are like a sister to me, and I know that underneath all this fucked-up mess, you two really care for one another. If you think he's worth the forgiveness and what you had is worth saving, you need to allow yourself to be happy. Don't let pride make you blind and bitter."

Her expression mellowed, her eyebrows met in the middle, and she avoided my eyes.

"Wait… I just thought about what I said then… That sounded really wrong. If he's my brother and you're my sister, that would be incest, wouldn't it? That didn't quite come out the way I thought it would."

Paige looked at me blankly for a moment. Then started laughing. "You are impossible!"

"If you remove the incest part, it was a good speech, though."

We both laughed for a moment.

"Look at me, Lu." She opened her arms then let them slap against her thighs. "I look like a postnatal zombie. I would kill for a decent night asleep."

"Like I said, put daddy boy to work. Plus, your baby is under two months old, give yourself a break. When you feel like it, start going to the gym and you'll be in shape in no time. You're young, your body will bounce back."

"You know I hate the gym."

"Then go back to dancing." Her eyes came back to me. "You love dancing. Go back to your old studio and start dancing again. You won't even know you're exercising. And while you're at it, put Celo to work looking after Amber for you. Make him sweat for those brownie points."

"I'm giving him no damn brownie points," she mumbled.

"Are you sure? Cause last I heard you still thought he was hot."

She shot me a disapproving look, her eyebrows raising, lips pressing together.

CHAPTER 13
Marcelo

We sat at the café—me, Gabriel, and the spaceship cocoon that was Amber's stroller.

I'd known Gabe for years, but over the months he had played at Eight and dated Lu, he and I had become close friends. In fact, it was through me that he had met Lu, and they started going out around the same time I started going out with Paige.

"Don't you think it's crazy that Lu and I, and you and Paige started going out around the same time, and here you are with a kid? I've only just managed to get Lu to date me, but you managed to make an entire human being."

"Make an entire human being *and* set my world on fire, get my face smashed, lose a brother, lose my girlfriend, get my house and car trashed, get stitches on my foot, and fall right into Angela's trap like a sitting duck. Do you wanna swap?" I crossed my arms and leaned back into my chair.

"Yeah… That's a tough gig, dude."

"And you haven't even met Paige's mother. Now I know why Lu calls her the Gates of Hades. Kate sits in front of you like she is this prim and proper English lady, but she spits venom three meters high like a cobra. I'd only been here three days before she called me a two-timing bastard and told me Paige doesn't need me, and I should fuck off back home."

"Did she say it like that?"

"No. She said it dripping in British politeness, which is worse."

"You know it's gonna take time, and you're gonna have to pay your penance. You did commit the ultimate cardinal sin."

I didn't need to be reminded. The guilt weighed on me like concrete tied to my ankles. With nothing I could say in my defense, I sighed and nodded. The sigh came out of me in a long puff, heavy and loaded like my conscience.

"And how are things with you and Paige?"

"Purgatory. All I want is for her to speak to me normally, you know? Look at me the way she used to. I waited months just to see her, but she hates my guts and won't let me anywhere near her. She refuses to look me in the face, like I'm not standing right there; talks to me like I'm some dog shit she stepped on." I drank some of my coffee. Dark roast—bitter and far too strong, but I carried on drinking it. Just like my situation. "Worse still, everything about her turns me on, dude. And because I'm on a sex ban, I'm going up the wall. The other day, I caught myself feeling jealous of her breastfeeding. Perving on it even. I'll have a damn stroke at this rate."

Gabe choked and almost spat out his drink. My admission had caught him mid-gulp, and he seemed to find what I'd said funny.

"Don't laugh, man. It's not funny. Fucking weird kink, completely out of line. I need an exorcist or something."

Gabe tried and failed to stop laughing.

"Yeah… You laugh. You laugh cause you're getting everything I'm not. It's almost ten months for me, man; but, hey! Who's counting?" The tension sat in my body like nervous energy. Zapping me and making itself known at the most inopportune moments. Frustrated, I took a deep breath and rubbed a hand down my face.

"How the hell are you dealing with that? You used to have what? A date a week?"

I scoffed. "Try multiple dates a week. It fries my brain how far my life is from what it was this time last year. Might as well be in prison."

His laugh got louder; my purgatory was apparently amusing for some. "True. And if Paige heard you were still playing around, there wouldn't be a chance in hell you would ever earn her forgiveness. Lu would one hundred per cent tell her. Kid or no kid."

"It's not just about Paige either. Dr. Fernandes was another one that told me I should consider staying off it for a while, until my head was in the right place, and I was doing it for the right reasons. Apparently, and I quote, 'I should stop using sex as an emotional Band-Aid'." I raised my eyebrows and nodded at him, so he would understand just how screwed I was on all fronts. No pun intended.

"Makes sense. I wouldn't like to be in your shoes but makes sense."

"No joke. I don't wanna be in my shoes either."

"I have to ask, though. Why her? I know you're not short for choice, so why this obsession with getting back with Paige? You guys didn't even date that long. Is it because of the baby?"

I gave him a head shake. "I've asked myself that question many times. Some days I honestly wish it wasn't her. But it's like asking why I like coffee and not tea. Or why I like black coffee, not latte. I don't have a damn clue. I just do. It's just her."

"Do you think all this madness and angst made things more intense? You know… Made you zoom in on her. Want what you can't have, sort of thing. Things with you guys have always been a little extreme."

I shrugged, shook my head. If he knew the answer, he was one step ahead of me. "You're starting to sound like my therapist."

"You still doing therapy?"

"Every week."

He thought about it for a beat. "Do you think you'll feel the same way if things calm down? A few years down the line when you've been together for a while."

Another shrug, another head shake. "I don't know. But I know this—I have never met someone I actually wanted to date. Sure, I met a lot of nice women. Some of whom were amazing in bed. But I never saw myself with them on the daily, wishing I woke up with them every day, came home to them every night. I have that with her." I glanced at Coffee Bean. "She reads my thoughts, dude. Sometimes I don't need to say anything, and she knows exactly what I'm thinking. Only Risa and Lu can do that. You know, translate my face. It's like she's known me my whole life."

His question made me think, so I started rotating my coffee cup on the counter. Keeping my hands busy always helped me think better.

"At first, I just wanted what I always want, you know?" The handle of my cup moved ninety degrees. "But when I started spending time with her, it wasn't enough. I wanted more. More time to get… to *be* closer to her. Looked forward even to her texting me. It's almost pathetic really."

"No, it's not pathetic. Lu is always up before me. She always texts me before I text her in the mornings. If I wake up and I don't have a text, I think something is wrong. And if nothing is wrong, I find myself complaining that she forgot to text me."

"Sounds like we caught the same virus," I said, head bouncing in agreement, my cup turning another ninety degrees. "I know I said she turns me into a horny teenager, but that's not why. If it was, I would get it, you know? I can't even explain it. She gets things out of me that I don't tell anyone. She changes the way I see things. The way I see the future, the way I see myself. When she's around, I'm…" I struggled to find the right word. "I'm… hopeful, I guess. I can see a life where we can build something. A life where I'm happy, have two children and a dog. Where I am a better person than I actually am. It's hard to explain."

"No, I get it. You're always thinking about them, miss their voice, their smell, right? Something happens and the first thing you want to do is share it with them."

I nodded. Stabbed the air with an open palm so he would see just how strongly I agreed with what he said.

"I never asked, cause it's none of my business, but if you feel that way about her, why did you sleep with Angela?"

I took a deep breath. That was the million-dollar question everyone wanted an answer to, including me. It took me a moment to answer.

"It's all so fucking moronic. If I wasn't paying for it, I'd find it funny. But it was all because of a misunderstanding." I laughed, but it had no humor. "I thought Paige was leaving me and coming back to England. Saw this message on her phone from the airline, and I was so cut up about it that I didn't dare ask her the question. It was straight after the fight with Felipe. I was physically and mentally mangled, man, and she and I had argued. Things were all messed up and we weren't the same. I thought she'd changed her mind and decided to go back home." The coffee cup turned a full three-sixty. "I guess I figured it wouldn't make any difference. She would leave, and I would go back to my old life. And Angie… Angie was just there, biding her time. Now that I think back to our conversations… Man, she turned up every day, always when I was alone, and she would drop these hints in conversation, you know. Making me feel everything got harder after I started dating Paige. Pointing out how much fun we had, how things were uncomplicated before Paige turned up. You know… even if Paige hadn't caught us, I think she'd have created a way for her to find out. She left marks all over my body, man. Scratches, love bites. She has never done that. And I was such a blind fool, I didn't clock what she was doing. It was all very convenient for her. It was like she knew it was coming." Another hundred-and-eighty turn for my cup. "Maybe she did know. She was the one who set Felipe on me."

Gabe nodded. He stared at the floor as though he was trying to piece the puzzle together.

"I know it sounds like I'm blaming Angela, but I'm not. It was my mistake. I shouldn't have done it. It just annoys the fuck out of me that I didn't see her angling."

Another nod. "Your kid is cute, though. And she looks just like you, it's scary."

That made me smile, my hand automatically going to the stroller and bringing it closer to us. Coffee Bean was still in her ski suit; her legs had kicked the blanket off her as she stared at the mobiles strapped to the handle of her car seat.

"What is that smell?" Gabe's nose had the creases of disgust.

"What smell?"

"A little like dog shit."

We both looked under the soles of our shoes. Then at each other, Gabe's eyes going wide as realization set in.

"No… No way!" I leaned into the stroller, the stench going straight up my nostrils and hitting the back of my throat. "Yep. That's the source." I pointed at Coffee Bean.

Carefully, I rolled her over. The squashy mustard-yellow stain had spread all the way up to her hoodie.

"Are you kidding me?" As I laid Amber back over, she stretched and kicked her legs. "Stop moving Coffee Bean, you're making it worse! Drink up Gabe, we're gonna have to head back before she stinks the whole place out. That's just my damn luck. The first time Paige actually lets me take her out, I bring the kid back with shit all the way up to her hair."

At the flat, Gabe put the stroller back in the trunk of the car, and I carried Coffee Bean's basket down the stairs.

"Paige!" My voice sounded urgent. That was a mistake.

She ran into the hallway, eyes wide, expecting some sort of baby-killing disaster. It was just shit. A lot of it.

"What? What!? What is wrong? What happened?" Panic imprinted on her face.

I lifted Coffee Bean from the car seat, the stain of yellow now spread across the whole of her back, the car seat also stained in patches, stench filling the room like something was rotten.

"Is that what I think it is?" Lu started to gag.

"I don't know what happened. She was fine one minute, the next she was covered in shit, stinking out the whole café. It's all the way up to her hair, Paige! What the fuck!?"

For a minute Paige stared at me, no expression on her face. This is when mothers either go nuts or take it with some humor. Then she burst out laughing. Humor it was.

"Why are you laughing? I'm honestly scared to open this jumpsuit!" A trace of the smell hit the back of my throat and made me retch. "Jesus, Coffee Bean!" I kissed her cheek. "I love you, but you reek."

"I think you just learned the meaning of poonami." Paige was still laughing.

"Oh my God, that's disgusting." Lu was still dry heaving.

"A what now??" I honestly didn't know what that meant. Had a feeling I didn't want to know either.

Gabe patted me on the shoulder. "A tsunami of shit, bro."

"Ok…" Another gag. "I love you both, but unless you want to clean her poo and my vomit, Gabe and I are leaving. We'll see you later, ok?" Lu grabbed their coats and started pushing Gabe out of the door, the lock hitting home before either of us could plea for help.

"Why are you laughing, Paige? This is not funny!"

"Your face is priceless. Wait, let me take a picture." She pulled her phone out and snapped a shot.

She was literally howling, bending over, laughing at my face. For *minutes*!

"Are you done laughing? Cause you know, not urgent or anything, but our daughter is covered in her own shit."

"Welcome to my world. Enjoying fatherhood yet?"

"Paige!! Not funny!"

"Ok, ok… Come on, she needs a shower."

She walked ahead of me to the bathroom, while I held Amber suspended in front of me.

"Hold her over the bath. I will take her clothes off and bin them; we can then wash her. She won't be happy to be naked and suspended, so brace your ears."

I nodded.

"You might be better kneeling down. If I rinse it and you're holding her too high up, it will go everywhere."

I got down on my knees. The bathroom stank. Amber's clothes were all stained in puke-colored yellow, and I'm pretty sure my fingers were touching some of the shit.

"Wait, can you take my sweater off for me? It's cashmere. If this mustard thing goes on it, I won't be able to get it off."

She looked at me and raised one of her eyebrows, unimpressed.

"Fine. Then you take Coffee Bean, and I'll take it off myself. But I'm telling you, I can feel shit on my fingers."

"Her name is *Amber*. Put her down in the bath. You can take it off yourself."

I did as I was told. Had to wash my hands before I could take my top off. I held Coffee Bean suspended, while Paige stripped her off. Amber's crying echoed in the small bathroom and pierced my eardrums.

"Oh Lord, have mercy!" I gagged once Paige got to her nappy. It looked like a nuclear explosion had gone off in there.

"Why are you laughing? This is fucking disturbing. How can someone so small create this much carnage?"

"Yes, but I'm not the one with my fingers in poop."

Talking about our baby like that made me feel instantly guilty. "I'm sorry." I kissed her cheek. "Not you, Coffee Bean. You're not disturbing. I'm talking about the Chernobyl in your pants."

Children have a way to kick you off your pedestal like nothing can. Amber had me on my knees, reduced to shoveling dung with my own bare hands. The whole thing was so stomach-turning that I had to laugh not to spew. But Paige's mood had shifted from thunderstorms to sunshine. She was talking and laughing like everything was fine.

After rinsing away the thick of it, she cleaned the bath and filled it with some water. Then produced a giant egg-like thing.

"Sit her on this. Since you're here, you might as well learn how to bathe her."

"Is this thing just to give her a bath?"

"Yeah. Means your hands are free to wash her. Otherwise, you'd have to hold her the whole time."

"This kid has more gadgets than I have."

"No kidding."

Paige sat on the toilet and guided me through how to wash Amber.

"You know I'm gonna have to give her a soapy Mohican and take a picture, right?" I said as I was soaping Amber's hair.

"You didn't have to ask Lu to come, you know. I'm fine."

"Yeah… I say I'm fine too. Then I go and do something dumb." I said it without thinking, while trying to take a picture of Coffee Bean with her soapy hairdo. When my brain caught up to my words, I lowered the phone and looked at her. "Paige, I'm—"

"Right! I think we're done here." She cut me off. "Can you

go get her towel from my room while I rinse the shampoo off her hair?"

I continued looking at her. Every time I had tried to apologize, she hadn't let me even finish a sentence. "Can I just speak to you for a second?"

"You can go get the towel or I will. Which one is it?" She avoided looking at me, turned the little shower head on, and tested the temperature.

Defeated, I nodded. "Which door is it?" Trying to apologize over a screaming baby maybe wasn't such a good idea anyway.

"Next one on the left. Her towel is behind the door."

Paige's room had the light colors of the lounge. A cot with one of the sides missing sat adjoining the bed. The teddy bear I had given Amber at one end. The whole room smelled like Paige. I found the towel behind the door, then noticed the notice board above the chest of drawers. There were several pictures of Paige dancing, her friends, her and Lu, her mom and dad, Amber. Mementos of events and trips. Nothing from Brazil.

"Hey! Where is that towel?" I heard her shouting from down the hall. "My ears are bleeding here!"

Coffee Bean got wrapped like a chunky burrito. The hood of her towel covering her wet head, the teddy ears on it sticking up. I followed Paige back to her room.

The front door opened and closed. "Paige?" Kate was back.

"In my room."

Seconds later, Kate appeared at the door, her eyes coming straight to me. Shirtless. Again.

"Seriously? Why is it that every time I see you, you end up topless?"

I pointed at Amber. "Poonami."

"I can see that's under control now. So why are you still here, half naked?"

"I was teaching him how to bathe Amber," Paige responded without looking at either of us, putting a clean nappy on the screaming, now naked, burrito.

"Excellent. But I'm sure you arrived here dressed. Don't you have a shirt or something you can go put back on?"

It was a good time to make a swift exit. "I'm leaving now anyway." Instinctively, my hand went to Paige's back, and I leaned in to whisper in her ear, "See you tomorrow, Lewis." With her attention focused on Amber, she didn't have time to pull away from me. Her hands stopped moving. I leaned down and kissed our baby's head. "Be good for your momma, Coffee Bean."

I walked past Kate scowling at me. And as I picked up my sweater from the bathroom and got ready to leave, she stood in the corridor, arms crossed, eyes narrowed as if she was trying to laser beam my ass into non-existence.

She had clocked it as well. I hadn't meant to touch Paige or whisper in her ear. With so much going on, it had happened out of habit. But I was smiling, because she had gasped, her arms had gotten covered in goosebumps, and her hands had stopped moving. She was mad at me, but she wasn't immune to me. I still had the same effect on her. It didn't fix anything, but it was something. And I was going to hold on to it like I had just seen the faint memory of light at the end of a very long, very dark tunnel.

As though she could hear my thoughts, Kate marched down the corridor. "Wipe that smug look off your face. I need to talk to you," she whispered, as if Paige could hear us over Coffee Bean's crying.

I straightened up, any happiness I was feeling going straight out of the window. Last time she spoke to me, she told me to get lost.

"I'm going on a business trip soon, and I'll be gone for three days. You need to keep an eye on them. Paige won't ask for your help, but she'll call me. And if she calls me, I'll call you. Give me your number." She pushed a phone into my chest. "I don't like you. But I know how bad things get when both of them don't sleep. So if I call you, you better get your ass here pronto and make yourself useful."

I nodded, put my number in her phone as she told me to, and handed it back to her—politely. I wouldn't call it an improvement, but at least she was trying to work with me, not against me. Didn't change her face, though. She was still scowling at me, arms crossed, when I closed the front door.

CHAPTER 14
Paige

"WHY NOT?" LU WAS HELLBENT ON CONVINCING ME.

"Because driving to central London is a pain. You have to pay the congestion charge, traffic is awful, and parking is ridiculously expensive."

"You know we are good for the parking."

"We wouldn't all fit in the car anyway, not with the baby seat."

Celo and Gabe were sitting on the floor, watching Amber in her play gym and pretending not to care about what we were discussing, but very much eavesdropping.

"We can take the tube then."

"Do you know how much of a nightmare it is to take a pram to central London on the tube? Most of the stations are super old and don't have lifts. It's a pain to get up the steps even when you have help," I answered, without looking at her.

Lu waved at Celo to give her the bag he had brought in. He stood up to bring it to her, handed it over, then walked back, but didn't sit down.

"Then we'll use this." She pulled a baby sling out of the bag. "We can all take turns carrying her so it's not too heavy for anyone."

"It's cold, Lu."

"And I'm sure everyone here has a coat. Flower, you can't hide in here forever. I know you haven't really been out of the house since she was born."

I shot Celo an accusatory look. He pretended not to notice.

"Come on! Gabe has never been to London. This is the perfect opportunity to kill two birds with one stone."

I scowled at her.

"There are four of us. We can all take turns. It doesn't get any better than this for you going out."

Celo crossed his arms, watching us from the corner of his eye.

I grabbed hold of her wrist and pulled her into the kitchen. "Lu, if we go out, I will have to breastfeed her in public. I don't wanna do that," I whispered, not intending for my words to be heard by anyone else.

"You're expressing, right? You must have a couple of bottles ready? We can work out a route with plenty of stops. Gabe can't take the cold for long anyway. He'll be worse than Amber, trust me."

"I heard that!" Gabe shouted from the sitting room.

She stepped closer to me. "Flower, you need to get out of this flat before you go stir-crazy. And there is no better or more comfortable way to do it than when there are three of us to help you. Don't you wanna get some of your life back? Go back to doing normal things? Wasn't that what you were complaining about yesterday?"

I didn't respond, went over to the kitchen, and started putting some of the bottles in the sterilizer while considering my options. I didn't want to play happy families; there was nothing happy about this. But Lu wasn't wrong; I had to start venturing out sooner or later and doing it with help was indeed easier.

She walked over to me. "Come on! You know I'm doing this to get you out of the house and back in the land of the living."

I sighed and conceded. "Fine."

♥♥♥

The first person to wear the baby carrier was Celo. It was obviously his baby, but I had my suspicions he was just trying to keep me close. He knew damn well I wouldn't be far from Amber. The problem was that Amber attracted more than just me. The baby strapped to his chest and dressed like a teddy bear seemed to work as some weird aphrodisiac. Whenever a woman saw he was carrying a baby, her face softened. Some even flirted. He pretended not to notice, but he a hundred per cent did. Naivety wasn't one of his endearing qualities.

"I thought it'd be bigger." Gabe cocked his head looking at Big Ben.

"Is that what Lu says to you?" Celo had inuendo written all over his face.

"No. She just screams my name." Gabe winked at Lu.

"You wish. And how original and grown-up of both of you."

"Sorry, Lu. Couldn't resist." Celo's words were an apology, but his face showed no regret.

"Seriously, what is the point of calling it Big Ben when it's not big?"

"I think it refers to the bell inside the tower, not the tower itself, Gabe. But I get you. Fun fact, apparently, the clock at the Liver Building in Liverpool is bigger than this one. The north does it better." I laughed at my own private joke. Lu laughed with me. She was the only one who knew I was a northerner. "But I guess Big Ben is just an affectionate nickname that stuck."

"Why did you both laugh?" Marcelo, unfortunately, was paying attention.

"She always says the north is better cause she's from the north. Manchester, isn't it?"

I nodded.

"So you're not from London?" Ever since we walked out of the flat, almost every sentence that came out of Gabe's mouth had been a question.

"No. I came here for uni and ended up staying. Unfortunately, there are more opportunities down here for dancers."

Celo frowned, his hands holding on to Amber's, the baby carrier matching the color of his jumper perfectly and looking like an extension of his belly—a kangaroo pouch with the little joey's head popping out.

"So you're a foreigner here, like we are?" Gabe's gaze moved from the Houses of Parliament to me.

I laughed. "I guess you could say that."

We had a quick look at Westminster Abby, then walked up Whitehall, passing Downing Street, and the Household Calvary with their Royal House Guards—taking all the obligatory pictures, so Gabe could live the tourist experience, including being bitten by one of the guard horses.

We walked through Trafalgar Square and into the National Gallery. I sat on one of the wooden benches overlooking some of the art. Amber was in my arms, my feet and back aching from all the walking. A flurry of people moved through the room around us, the sound of shoes tapping on a wooden floor and rushed whispers the only things you could hear. I always found it curious how people in museums behaved like they were in a library without anyone telling them to be quiet.

The walls were a deep gray, spotted with evenly spaced heavy gilded frames. Paintings with pops of bright orange, red, and blue in a decadent traditional style. Voluptuous women covered in layers of fabric that seemed to defy gravity. Immortalized in time and space. The arrangement so aesthetically pleasing you couldn't stop staring.

Marcelo came to sit next to me. Lu and Gabe noticed us following behind but kept moving.

"I think I need to find the baby changing room."

We both looked around for signs of where it could possibly be. "I can change her, if you want."

"Are you sure?"

His nod came paired with a lazy single blink.

I handed Amber over, and Marcelo held her suspended in front of him—her arms at a ninety-degree angle, double-chin sitting deep in her shoulders. He lowered her back and forth, bringing her nose close to his in some sort of game.

It was too much moving. I had given her one of the two bottles I had not long ago. "I wouldn't do that if—" Before I could finish the thought, she had regurgitated milk all over the front of him.

He looked down at his top. "Why do I get the feeling Coffee Bean has a vendetta against me?"

"Because I've trained her to attack you with bodily fluids as soon as she sees a certain hand gesture, like a circus monkey. You're lucky she missed your mouth."

His head turned toward me, eyebrows raised.

"Don't be ridiculous. She is a month and a half old. It's not her fault you decided to shake her like a champagne bottle when you know she was just fed." I shrugged.

The baby changing room was miles away through a selection of other equally stunning gallery rooms. I locked the door; set up the changing table, and he placed Amber on the changing mat.

"Why is she going red?"

I peered over his shoulder to look at her. "Have a wild guess."

"You really gonna give me the triple whammy, huh, Coffee Bean?"

Just then, a noise that sounded like bubbling farting trumpets filled the room. I wish I could say they were cute little baby puffs. They weren't.

Marcelo's head snapped toward me, eyes wide open. Poonami trauma resurfacing faster than a squash ball that has just hit the wall.

Silence.

More trumpets. Amber's eyelids turned ruby red. Her hands balled into tight fists close to her body.

For a moment we just looked at each other.

And we both burst out laughing. Heartfelt, belly-aching laughs, while Amber looked confused, then disapproving of our giggling fit. Babies have a way to make you stare at the most primal behaviors right in the face. No filter, no shame.

By the time we rejoined Lu and Gabe, the laughter had subdued, but we were still giggling. Celo was now sporting just the tee he had on underneath, his jumper bundled into the baby bag.

"What's so funny?" Gabe asked as we got closer.

"Parental trauma bonding," Celo replied, smiling.

Gabe looked at Lu, shrugged—hands turning upwards, head tipping sideways, the corner of his lips dropping.

She shrugged back. "I'm kinda hungry. Should we check out one of their restaurants?"

After Buckingham Palace and a wander around St. James's and Green Park, Celo suggested we should call it a day, not to push our luck with the baby—or Gabe's tolerance of the cold.

By the time we got on the tube, it was rush hour, and I was wearing the baby carrier. The train carriages filled to the brim like potato sacks. We let three trains go past before finding one that had enough space for the five of us. There were only two stops to go, but one of them was Victoria—one of the busier stations.

As the train stopped on the platform, an avalanche of people tried to walk past us. My hands protectively wrapped around Amber, the flux of people pushing and squeezing me into a corner, but it didn't last long. As quickly as I got cornered, Marcelo appeared in front of me, arms braced on the walls behind my head, body shielding us from the flux of people getting off and getting on. A glance sideways told me Lu was in a similar situation, being smaller than most. Gabe had both his arms around her, holding on to one of the stanchion poles, keeping her safe from strangers inside the circle of his embrace like a smooth box crab. She smiled at me, holding on to him, not the pole.

She and I had been on the underground plenty of times, squeezed like sardines just like we were. Lu had been perfectly capable of holding her own space. Yet it was nice that now she didn't have to, and she was more than happy to step into her female energy and let Gabe guard her surroundings. It was actually quite heartwarming to watch, especially because Lu was so short in stature.

"Are you ok?" Marcelo asked, head tipped down toward me, forehead almost touching mine. The wall of him far too close.

I nodded. Uncomfortable with his presence, but grateful not to be squeezed by strangers. He was doing for me and Amber the same thing Gabe was doing for Lu.

The train stopped at Pimlico, and the platform was on the opposite side of the carriage from where we stood. We would have to squeeze through the wall of bodies to get out. Before I could think too much about how we would do that, Marcelo took hold of my hand and turned, going first, clearing the way like a snowplow, so Amber and I had clear passage. I instinctively held on to the back of his coat, his hold on my hand keeping us close.

"Jesus! That was a squeeze." Gabe pointed from the platform. "I don't know how you guys do it on these slim trains. In *Sampa* the wagons are twice the width. That's crazy! The amount of people squeezed on these things."

"Our trains are bigger, but we have a third more people, so

at rush hour it actually makes no difference. You still get squeezed into a shoe that is far too small," Marcelo commented, watching the train leave the platform. "From now on, we should plan to miss rush hour."

Lu and Gabe agreed as they walked to the exit, still holding hands. Marcelo turned to move, still holding mine as if he had forgotten he was doing it. I pulled it out of his grip, and he stopped, turned back to look at me.

Understanding my gesture, he waved one arm, indicating that I should walk ahead of him. I stomped past him, both my arms wrapped around Amber in her baby carrier, and he walked behind me. Everywhere I went, he had been just behind me. Like a German-bloody-shepherd keeping watch.

"What do you think? Should we take them to our old uni tomorrow, flower? Show them where we met? We could take the river bus; that will give them a good view of some of the other sights in one hit," Lu suggested as we walked back to the flat.

I nodded. We were all talking and laughing like the old days, when the four of us went out together. Largely thanks to Gabe and Lu who were hilarious individually and as a pair. As much as I would never admit it, I was actually enjoying myself. For the first time in months, the fact I was a mother didn't mean the world underneath my feet had shifted. The baby strapped to me wasn't a bomb. I was just me, going out with my friends, having fun, despite the undercurrent of drama.

We walked through the door of the flat, talking, joking, in a flurry of coats and shoes being taken off, Amber hanging precariously from underneath me in the baby sling as I struggled to unzip my boots.

"Let me do it for you."

I had all the intentions of saying no, but Marcelo crouched down and his fingers pushed mine aside, my back thanking me for not dangling the extra weight strapped to me at its expense.

Gabe stood up straight and grew serious, each one of us looking in the same direction and going quiet in turn, until there was just my voice echoing through the hall. I looked behind me.

"Oh, hi Mum." She was standing just outside the door to the sitting room. Hands crisscrossed in front of her lap. Eyes trained on Celo, on his knees at my feet.

"I was wondering where you'd gone." I hadn't thought to message her and let her know we were going out.

I removed one foot from inside a boot. "We went sightseeing. Gabe has never been to London." Marcelo unzipped the other boot.

"I assume you're Gabe." My mother's serious face turned to Gabriel.

I removed my other foot and turned to face her. Marcelo got to his feet.

"Pleasure to make your acquaintance, ma'am."

"Where did that cowboy English come from?" Lu turned in his arms to frown at him.

We all started making fun of him in the spirit of the conversation we were having just before.

"It's called manners. Maybe you three should learn it." Gabe was having none of our jokes.

"You can be polite without sounding like you're in a Western!" Lu wouldn't drop it.

In the commotion, none of us had paid attention to the fact Mum had walked closer. She hugged Lu, who seemed utterly confused by the gesture.

"Thanks for coming, Lu. Really." She whispered something else I couldn't hear.

Lu's arms wrapped around her. "No problem. She's my

girl." When my mum retreated, they both smiled. The effect was contagious, going from Gabe to Celo and eventually me.

"Would you guys like a drink and nibbles to warm up?" Mum's voice was upbeat, her expression open—genuinely happy, welcoming.

"Yes, please! I could murder a cup of tea." I was the first one to break formation and head to the kitchen.

CHAPTER 15

Luciana

When we turned up to pick up Paige the next day, both she and Amber were dressed and ready to go. The next one to carry Coffee Bean was Gabe. And Paige wasn't wrong, the little cutie worked as a babe magnet, even though it was clear she wasn't his baby.

Although it wasn't the closest pier stop from where we were, we headed back to Westminster to get the river bus. Paige insisted we see something first.

"Right, this is a bit of a joke, but it's just after midday now, the weather is sunny, *and* it's the right time of the year, so the perfect time for it." We stood on the bridge looking back at Big Ben. "Ready?"

Three heads bopped up and down.

"Look at the floor."

The parapet of the bridge was decorated with trefoil carvings, repeated over and over for the whole length of the bridge. With the sun hitting it at an angle, it created elongated shadows on the pavement that all looked like a line of giant—

"Behold, the Westminster Bridge penises!" Paige announced, arms stretched wide to either side of her, almost hitting passersby.

The three of us burst out laughing.

"Are you serious?" Gabe couldn't get over it. "The bridge of parliament is covered in dicks at lunchtime?" He couldn't stop laughing.

"Yes. But only in late winter and early spring. And the real question is: design flaw or genius joke? Nobody really knows."

"Whatever it is, it's awesome!"

"I knew you would appreciate the perverse sense of humor, Gabe."

Everyone dug for their phones to try and get snaps of the phalluses with Big Ben as the backdrop. People around us started paying attention, laughing, and taking pictures too.

"I get the feeling you know some interesting spots. What is your favorite part of London, Paige? Where would you go if it was up to you?" As much as Gabe liked doing the tourist thing, he was always more interested in walking off the beaten track.

She thought for a moment. "The Sky Gardens in the Walkie-Talkie building, or the Barbican Conservatory, a way to be outdoors but indoors for the nine months of the year when the weather is miserable. North Dock at Canary Wharf when the weather's nice, to have a drink and people-watch. Greenwich Market, or what we're doing now actually—taking the river bus to North Greenwich, but when the sun is setting. You get to see some of the major sights from the river when the streetlights are coming on. It's my favorite view of London. When you get to East London you can also see the green laser for the Greenwich Meridian. It cuts through the skyline."

"Can we do that then?"

Celo's posture changed, his head tipping slightly as if to warn Gabe that wasn't the plan. Asking Paige to come sightseeing had been Celo's idea, but he knew that if he asked, the no would have been automatic. So I was sent as a double agent. Keen to keep her out of the house, he had carefully planned a route that included several baby-changing facilities along the way, and Gabe had just come out with a curveball and thrown it into the wind.

Paige nodded. "Some of it. I don't see why not. The gardens

are in the opposite direction we're going, but we could have lunch at the O2 Arena, then head to Canary Wharf. They have a Brazilian restaurant in the O2, and everything is mostly indoors, so you won't feel the cold."

"Thank God for that! I was going to say I'm not giving her little majesty back to you. She's a heat pump. I'm pretty sure she's the only thing keeping me warm right now."

"We can head back on the river bus around 6pm when the streetlights are turning on and you get the best views. If nobody objects, that is."

"No, nobody objects," Gabe responded, but Celo looked like he was about to have an aneurysm.

We boarded the boat, Celo and Gabe standing outside to take pictures, Paige, Amber and I staying inside where it was warmer.

"Are you ok, flower? Is being back out in the wild as traumatic as you thought it would be?"

She laughed. "No. I have to admit I'm enjoying it. It's nice to be out of the house doing something. Trust you to dig me out of my hut." She squeezed my hand.

"I'd love to take all the credit, but unfortunately I can't."

"Why not?"

"It was Celo's idea. He wanted you to get some fresh air. Said you had locked yourself inside the flat like you were in prison. He thought you'd say no if he asked, so I did. He organized the whole thing. And I'm pretty sure he planned the whole route based on you having enough changing rooms for Amber. I thought he was going to deck Gabe when he suggested we deviate from the plan. You should've seen his face." I couldn't resist giggling.

Paige's head turned, and she looked at our boys standing on the outside of the boat. "He planned it all?"

"Uh-huh"

Like he sensed she was looking at him, Celo's head lifted.

They looked at each other for a moment until he nodded, and she nodded back. He asking the question, she confirming everything was ok.

Coming off the river bus always made me think of being swallowed whole—the bridge connecting the shore to the pier covered by a tunnel that looked like the inside of a giant worm as you walked through it.

"You weren't kidding when you said the building was one of a kind. It's like perforated paper," Gabe remarked as we stood outside our old university.

It wasn't a bad assessment. Covered in mosaics, with a facia littered with round windows, it indeed looked like perforated paper. Although, I preferred thinking of it as being more like lace.

"So, *this* is where the magic happened." Celo was staring up at the building.

Paige and I exchanged a look. We'd had an amazing time studying here. It was hard work, don't get me wrong, but some of the best days of our lives.

As we entered the main doors, the boys admired the modern interior, Paige and I reminisced about our student days, and we decided to go for a coffee at the café. The building was buzzing with activity. In two months, all years would be due their final projects, and students moved around like busy little ants as we finally found a table where the five of us could sit down.

"Paige? Is that you?" Someone shouted as she was just about to finish telling Gabe and Celo a funny mishap from our student days.

Paige's head turned to place the call.

"Elliot??" Her forehead creased into a frown—a guess, not a certainty. "Elliot!" She was genuinely happy and surprised to see him.

"Fancy finding you here, stranger!" The man came our way.

Paige stood up to greet him, and he enveloped her in a hug she was more than happy to reciprocate.

"How on Earth have you been?" He touched the side of her face, stayed close—too close, too comfortable—his whole expression excited, eyes vivid.

Celo's head tilted to the side. He crossed his arms, leaned back in his chair.

"I'm good! How have you been? Didn't you go to the States in some internship or something? I thought that'd be you gone to Hollywood."

"I did. But it was only for a year. Had to come back. Best year ever, though. Learned so much. It was quite unreal." He stared at her, then placed both of his hands on her shoulders. "Sorry, I can't believe I bumped into you! I'm lost for words. This is crazy!"

"Do you remember Lu?" Paige swiped a hand toward me. I waved. Then I recognized him—one of Paige's old *ficantes*, a TV and Media student. He'd changed his appearance, but it was him.

"Wildcat Lu. But of course!" His tone was heavy with meaning. He waved back.

"Wildcat, huh?" Gabe whispered, for my ears only.

"This is Gabriel, my boyfriend."

"Boyfriend now?" Elliot's eyebrows raised to match his high-pitched tone, as if he was surprised. He walked closer to the table and extended a hand to Gabe. "I have to shake your hand, man. You have managed to tame the untamable. I take my hat off to you."

Gabe leaned in to accept the greeting, his other arm making sure Amber's back didn't hit the table. "Why? You tried?" He said it as a joke, with a smile, but I knew he was trying to figure out who Elliot was and if we had any history.

"Oh no! Don't worry. I was always into *this* one." His arm wrapped around Paige's waist. Celo gave me a look. "But I watched many try and fail. And you have a baby?!"

He had always been into Paige. If my memory served me right, she had snogged him at a party in our first year, hooked up with him a few times after, then lost interest. And he'd chased after her for the two years that followed, posing as a close friend.

"Funny story, actually." Paige scratched the side of her forehead, uncomfortable. "The baby is mine."

"*You* had a baby?" He leaned sideways to look at her, but his arm stayed put at her waist.

Paige's eyebrows rose, lips stretched into a smile that didn't show any teeth, and she nodded.

"What happened to your dancing career? Weren't you dancing for—"

"I took a break." She interrupted him. "Went traveling—"

"Had a baby!" he repeated, as if she had broken the laws of physics. Celo kicked my foot under the table.

"Do you work here now, Elliot?" I asked, motioned into action by Celo's literal kickstart.

"No, I came back to do my Master's. I work in TV production now." He looked at me momentarily but went back to Paige just as quickly. "I still can't believe you're here and you had a baby! That's wild! We should have coffee sometime. Let me get your number." He reached for his back pocket, one arm still holding on to Paige.

Celo stood up, the legs of his chair scratching the floor. "We weren't introduced." He edged closer to them, hand shooting out for a handshake. "I'm Marcelo. The father of her baby."

Elliot's face twisted in surprise. He shook Celo's hand, but when he tried to let go, Celo held on—smiled, unblinking, his fingers tightening, squeezing. Elliot's gaze dropped to their hands; he swayed slightly on his feet, let go of Paige's waist, and stepped away from her a smidge. Celo let go.

"I can't believe we've bumped into you! What are the chances?!" Paige touched his shoulder—either ignoring the awkward exchange or trying to smooth it over.

"So… the two of you…?" Elliot's index pointed from Paige to Celo on repeat.

Paige smiled as if she didn't understand the question. Celo raised his eyebrows, a smirk plastered on his face as though the answer was obvious. Neither of them verbally confirming or denying it.

"You're a lucky man." Elliot's voice took a disappointed tone.

Celo smiled, but it wasn't friendly.

"Well… It was great seeing you both." He nodded at Paige and me. "I'm pretty sure I still have you on Insta," he said to Paige. "I'll DM you. Hopefully, we'll catch up some time soon." A hand stroked out and gave her arm a squeeze that was just meant for emphasis. He smiled.

Out of politeness, three of us agreed. Celo didn't. Everyone sat back down, and Elliot disappeared through the main doors.

For a moment we all sipped our drinks.

"Well, that was awkward." Gabe broke the weary quiet. "Interesting fashion sense, though."

I laughed. "You just can't help it, can you?"

"Another old boyfriend of yours, is he?" Celo had no expression, his voice flat in a monotone, eyes on Paige, coffee cup being rotated on its saucer.

"He was into her alright." I responded before she did, trying to defuse the escalating weirdness. "*He* wanted to date her. *She* friend-zoned him, and he tottered after her for two years." I drank some of my coffee.

Celo's eyebrows raised to acknowledge the information

was received, his head nodding, coffee cup still rotating in place, and he glanced sideways at Paige—expression serious.

Paige smiled into her tea. The fact she said nothing, actually said a lot. If she didn't like Celo's behavior she wouldn't stand for any of it. As it was, she seemed to find it endearing that he marked his territory like a dog peeing on a lamppost. Or… maybe… she was enjoying that he was the one feeling uncomfortable for a change.

We wandered into the O2, whizzed around the shops, and headed for the Brazilian restaurant.

"Hmm…" Paige's appreciation almost sounded like an orgasm. "I actually missed this food."

"You're more than welcome to come back to Brazil! You know, taste the real thing," I told her. Celo and Gabe hummed in agreement.

She smiled, head tilting to the side, eyebrows raising, but didn't respond.

"You know that has caffeine, right?" Celo pointed at her *Guaraná* can.

"Now you tell me!"

"You can't have caffeine?" Gabe made it sound like it was sacrilege.

Celo pointed at the baby in Paige's arm.

Gabe's chin lifted, his eyebrows raising, mouth open. "Breastfeeding. Got it."

"Let me cut that for you."

"No nee—" Paige started replying, but Celo was already cutting her steak into bitesize pieces she could fork and eat while holding the baby, her refusal falling flat.

"Yes! *Pão de queijo* and good coffee! Do you know how much I missed this?" Celo shook a cheese dough ball up in the air.

"Do you have access to a kitchen where you're staying?" Paige asked while he stuffed his mouth with dough balls.

A nod.

"Ask them if they will sell you some frozen ones. When Lu was here, they used to smuggle her some."

His eyes brightened.

"They'll defrost before we get back, though," I pointed out.

Paige's head bopped—half sideways nod, half shrug.

"I'm going to hunt down a Brazilian *mercearia*. There's gotta be one somewhere in London."

After wandering around Canary Wharf and sharing nibbles inside an igloo by the north docks—Gabe refusing to sit outside in the cold, even though the weather was nice and they had patio heaters—we got back on the river bus. With the sun setting, the air definitely felt cooler. The river worked like a channel for the cold breeze, but we all stayed outside to look at the lights coming on. Paige wasn't wrong, the view was indeed gorgeous.

Like most big cities, London seemed more glamorous after dark, pools of warm yellow lights emanating from the buildings, making even ordinary homes look like they had dressed up and put on a cocktail dress. Landmarks and bridges were lit up in mood lighting that made you see details you'd never noticed during the day. It nodded at its history, but it also gave it an air of romance.

As the boat glided through the river and around a bend, we lost sight of Canary Wharf's skyscrapers with the Greenwich Meridian laser crossing its skyline, and Central London started to reveal itself in the distance.

"See this small white house here on the right?" Paige pointed at something on the shore. "The one that looks way smaller than the two buildings to either side of it? That's a very old pub. When the tide is low, it has a bit of a beach in front of it. That beach is one of London's old execution sites. They still have on it old gallows to mark where they used to hang people, mostly pirates." She pointed it out then checked Coffee

Bean's head was still covered from the wind. The precious bundle was attached to her, shrouded in a blanket as well as her coat to keep her warm.

"How does she know all this?" Gabe asked me.

"Because she's a pain," I answered, then bumped into her with my shoulder and we both smiled. She knew exactly what I was going to say. "Whenever we went anywhere and she found anything interesting, she would get straight on Google Maps trying to figure out what it was."

"See this blue thing floating up ahead? Looks like a pier but it's not. That's actually the River Thames Police Station. The Thames has its own police unit."

"See what I mean."

On the other side of her, Celo grinned, glanced at Paige, then back at the river shore. He clearly found it endearing that she was full of random knowledge. Because he was the damn same. Full of obscure information, always reading some book about something random. It was one of the things they had in common.

Ahead of us the Shard stood miles above everything else, all lit up with its crystal top. Tower Bridge at its feet, looking majestic. Modern and traditional coexisting side by side.

"The tall building to the left is the Shard," Paige continued, our tour guide by default.

"There is a restaurant in there that has amazing views. We'll go there before you guys head back home." Celo pitched in, removing one of his gloves, and reaching for one of Paige's hands holding the blanket in place over Coffee Bean. "Your hands are freezing. Here, take my gloves and I'll use my pockets."

Her fingers must have been about to drop off, because she didn't put up a fight. Instead, she held alternating hands out so he could get the gloves on to them. "Fun fact, the famous bridge coming up now is Tower Bridge, *not* London Bridge.

London *does* have a bridge called London Bridge, but it's not this one, even though that's what everyone calls it. Tower Bridge is also the only bascule bridge in central London. The only one that lifts and opens up at the middle for tall ships."

"I think you missed your calling in life; you should've been a tour guide," Celo told her, smiling, while he fastened the second glove at the wrist.

She shrugged. "Gabe has never been to London. I'm just giving him some context."

Going under Tower Bridge was fascinating. It looked regal anyway, but when it was lit up and looming over you, it looked magical as though it was the portal to some fairytale kingdom. Everyone stopped to take pictures.

Paige continued pointing out the sights to Gabe, naming buildings, relaying bits of history. "Now *this* is the actual London Bridge. It's almost dull by comparison, isn't it?" The minimalist bridge in question had no frills or detailing. Indeed a letdown after admiring Tower Bridge. We sailed past Southbank, Shakespeare's Theatre, the London Eye, Westminster, and several other sights and bridges, before disembarking by the Tate Britain.

"I'm glad to be going home, but I have to admit I missed London," I confessed as we walked back to Paige's via the riverbank. "It's a beautiful city."

"São Paulo is the same, but in a modernist, organic kind of way. Some cities make you feel at home, don't they?" Paige's step faltered, as if she'd just realized she'd said it out loud.

"Would you ever come back to visit?" Gabe was holding on to Amber. As soon as we got off the boat, he had asked to carry her, refusing to let anyone else benefit from her hot water bottle services.

Paige shrugged but didn't answer.

♥♥♥

The next day, we went back to exploring Paige's off-the-beaten-track favorite spots. Greenwich Market was actually a collection of alleyways that took you to a covered square, full of market stalls, surrounded by quaint little shops. It was enclosed by buildings shielding us from the cold wind, for Gabe's happiness; a Brazilian stall sold more *pão de queijos*, for Celo's utter bliss; and another sold Brazilian churros filled with toffee—the latter for *my* indulgence. Colorful heart-shaped bunting hung from the skylighted ceiling. The alleyways leading to it made you feel like you were stepping back in history that had been reimagined with a heavy dose of hippie chic.

"I don't remember it having this many Brazilian stalls when we were here."

"It's gorgeous, isn't it? Still my favorite market, even though it's not the biggest or the most famous in London," Paige explained.

"Which one is the most famous?" Gabe, as always, another sponge in search of random knowledge.

"Probably Borough Market. Also, one of the oldest and largest markets in the city."

"But you prefer this one?" Celo sipped his coffee.

"It's just small and cute, you know." Paige shrugged. "Also more artisanal, I guess. Borough is more about food and produce."

After stuffing our faces and warming up at the market—Celo making sure to bring some *pão de queijos* back with him—we headed to the *Cutty Sark*, a ship turned museum. Its hull was surrounded by a glass dome as if it was sailing on frozen waters, the three sail masts above it making it quite regal and imposing. Across the river from it, the cluster of skyscrapers from Canary Wharf that we had visited the day before.

"It used to ship tea leaves from Asia to thirsty Victorian Britain." Paige was in full tour guide mode now. "This whole area we are in was very heavily into the shipping industry. That's why you have the Old Royal Naval College and the Maritime Museum all around the corner from here."

"You seem to know a lot about this place." Celo was never far away from her.

"This is where Lu and I rented a flat. Our old uni isn't far from here. So this was where we spent a lot of our free time."

"When we weren't burning a dance floor somewhere on a student night," I added.

"Very true." Paige smiled, reminiscing.

We wandered around the Maritime Museum for a little while, Gabe reading every note stuck to a placard or wall, while Celo gave Amber a bottle. Afterwards we went to pay the Prime Meridian our respects—the walk up the hill keeping us warm, despite the cold breeze. At the top by the observatory, a stripe on the floor indicated where the Greenwich line cut through London. Either side of it was decorated with the latitude of big cities around the world. Brasília at forty-seven degrees west, Rio de Janeiro at forty-three degrees west. São Paulo wasn't marked on the line, despite being the Brazilian New York.

"That's so crazy! Only four degrees difference. They look so close together here, but they're almost two hours' flight from each other." Gabe tried to do the math.

"Crazy is that if you stand with one foot to either side of this line, you're officially standing in two hemispheres—one foot in the west and one foot in the east," Paige was quick to point out.

Of course, we all had to take a picture striding the meridian. Gabe and I decided to take one with our toes touching, fingers intertwined together, and each one of us leaning in one of the directions, like an inverted pyramid pointing at the line.

"Now you two," I said to Celo and Paige. "Give Coffee Bean and the baby bag to Gabe."

Celo must have thought that Paige was going to put up some resistance, because he looked genuinely surprised when she didn't. They positioned themselves on the line, toe to toe. I positioned my camera ready for the shot. Her head tipped slightly up to look at him. His down to look at her.

And someone pressed pause.

For a long moment they stared at each other, not pulling the pose. Tourists galore moved around them, taking pictures of the meridian—but they didn't move. It made me think of one of those timelapses when you see someone standing still while a flux of people flows around them.

Not wanting to spoil the moment, I held the camera in place and took pictures, but said nothing. Gabe and I exchanged a look. He was thinking exactly the same as me—the chemistry between them was as heavy now as it had been back then.

Slowly, without taking his eyes off her, Celo's hands touched Paige's arms, just above the elbow, and ran down to her hands. He intertwined his fingers with hers and gave her a short nod. She nodded back. And they both leaned in opposite directions. He smiled at her—soft, loving, no teeth. She smiled back just the same. I took the picture, but they didn't look at the camera.

On the way back from leaning, he held on to her waist to steady them both. And she broke away, leaving him standing on the line.

"Did you get it?" she asked me, a little out of breath, walking in my direction.

"I did. I think it's my best yet from this holiday."

She came over to look. Celo went over to Gabe to retrieve Amber.

"It's lovely," she agreed without really looking at it.

"Can I hold on to her majesty the Coffee Bean?" Gabe was again trying to hog the mobile source of heat. "This breeze is going straight through me."

On our way out, Celo spotted something on the wall. "So these are your weird measurements." He pointed at a plaque showing the length of a British yard, two feet, one foot, six inches, and one inch. "Confuses the hell out of me. I don't know why you haven't moved into metrics like the rest of the world."

"We shall never surrender." Paige shook her head and smiled.

"Are you quoting Winston Churchill at me?"

"Never give in—in nothing, great or small, large or petty—never give in except to convictions of honor and good sense."

Celo seemed to think for a second. Then he smiled, accepting the challenge. "I have nothing to offer but blood, toil, tears, and sweat. Victory in spite of all fear, victory however long and hard the road may be." He raised his two eyebrows at her, the back and forth somehow not feeling like it was just an exchange of Churchill quotes.

"That's a heck of a paraphrase."

"You and your quotes, Lewis." He smiled.

She smiled back. Both beaming with teeth. An inside joke underpinning the conversation in a way that only the two of them knew how.

CHAPTER 16

Paige

"DO YOU THINK YOUR MUM WOULD MIND BABYSITTING COFFEE Bean for us later today?" Lu asked, as she, Amber, and I sat on the tube on our way home, Gabe and Celo standing in front of us.

The damn name had stuck. Now everyone was calling her Coffee Bean. "I don't think so, why?"

"It's our last night in London. Celo managed to book at table at the Shard, and I was thinking… maybe we could go for drinks as well as food?"

"And you don't want a baby spoiling your night out?" I teased. I must have sounded more convincing than I thought, because for a moment she wasn't sure what to say. "I'm pulling your leg, Lu."

"Gosh! Don't do that! I genuinely thought you'd taken offense!"

"I would love a night sans baby. Alcohol, spicy food, caffeine…" I grabbed her hand as I dreamed about all the things the pint-size food police didn't allow me to have.

"A good snog and hot sex," Lu whispered back.

"What?" I stared at her blankly.

"Just saying! I happen to know someone who would be more than happy to oblige if you're interested."

"Pity that someone would be happy to oblige to half the world as well. Now *I am* offended." I retrieved my hand.

"Don't be mad at me." She linked her arm with mine. "It was just an innocent suggestion."

"Nothing innocent about it," I mumbled, and without thinking I scanned the potential service provider, towering over us, one hand holding on to a hanging strap. High tops, straight-cut jeans snug at the thighs, high-neck jumper, scarf, open parka, beanie covering his head. He was deep in conversation with Gabe, but the bastard seemed to have spider senses every time I looked at him, because he always caught me staring.

His head turned, gaze meeting mine, and he half smiled—smug, satisfied I was checking him out. He swapped hands on the hanging strap and rubbed Amber's head, eyes coming back to me before he changed his hands back over and returned to his conversation with Gabe. His body turned my way, pose and demeanor almost saying: 'I'm enjoying that you're looking. Look all you want.'

So bloody vexing.

I gave Lu a look that said, 'See what you made me do?'

She smiled. "Moving on… So, you could have a drink with us?"

"I will if I have enough bottles in the fridge. I'll have to pump and dump the whole day after if I drink."

"Maybe we could go dancing?" Her voice was tentative, but her eyes widened, smile broadened, and a hand squeezed my arm, as if she had just realized all her possibilities.

"Maybe we could."

Lu clapped, short fast little claps, lips over her teeth in a smile full of glee. "I can't wait!"

"The socializing withdrawal symptoms kicked in, have they?" I laughed, shaking my head.

♥♥♥

Paige
This is a nightmare. I've been pumping breast milk like a cow since I got home and none of my clothes fit!

Lu
You have nothing to go out in? xx

Paige
I haven't bought anything to go out since I got pregnant and none of my old stuff fits! 😢

Lu
I'm coming over. xx

By the time she arrived, my room was a mess, and I was ready to throw in the towel and say I wasn't coming.

She reviewed the clothes I had strewn over the bed and made a few suggestions, all of which I had already tried or turned down as not dressy enough. "What about the red dress?"

"What red dress?"

"The one you wore in Ilhabela. The bandage one."

"I don't know if I have the confidence to wear that."

"I don't know why you say that. You're curvier, but that's all. You still look delicious. And it's elastic, right? Thick elastic. So hopefully that will do the trick. But if not, maybe your mum has some Spanx?"

I dug through my drawers to find it. And I hated to admit it, but she was right. The horizontal and vertical lines were incredibly flattering, the industrial strength Spanx seeming to control all the extra flesh I had on me. It was tighter and a little boobier than last time I wore it, and I looked more voluptuous, but it wasn't bad. Lu grinned at me, pleased her suggestion had worked.

We stood in the bathroom, slamming on the paint, giggling over how this reminded us of our uni days getting ready to go out. With the minor exception that I still had a milk pump latched to my person, and we were going somewhere way fancier than the type of venues I had been able to afford on my student budget.

"It's so nice to see you girls excited and laughing." Mum peeked her head around the bathroom door with Amber. "You both look stunning." She looked genuinely happy and relieved the mood in our house had shifted.

"Even with my bionic cleavage?" I teased, hands waving at the breast pump.

"You never know! You might set a trend." Mum winked at me.

"Talking about that, it's time to get rid of it, flower. The boys are going to be here in a minute."

Gabriel knocked on the door, while Marcelo waited with the taxi. Lu and I wrapped in our coats, and our heels chimed and clanked against the metal stairs as we climbed to street level.

The restaurant's interior was elegant and classy with a big flower arrangement hanging from the ceiling. Our table was at the window, overlooking the skyline of the city as far as your eyes could see from the thirty-fifth floor.

Marcelo took off his coat, pushed his scarf down one of the sleeves and placed it on the back of a chair. Black polo neck—snuggly fitted—showing toned arms, shoulders, and chest. Gray tailored trousers, all-black smart high tops, hair parted to the side. I scratched my forehead. *Good snog and hot sex*—Lu's comment played on my mind like it was engraved in my memory with hot iron, coming back to haunt me.

"Let me help you with that," he offered as I started to shrug off my coat, and I turned around to let him do it.

"You can see all the way to Canary Wharf from here." I

focused on the view, not wanting to dwell too much on my memory.

He didn't answer. When I turned around, he went into a coughing fit.

"Are you ok?" I asked after a minute.

He nodded—closed fist hitting the middle of his chest, cough still going.

A member of staff came to take our coats, and he rushed to hand over his and mine. His eyes coming straight back to me, the cough subduing. He pulled at his collar.

"Are you ok there, Celo?" Lu had a wicked smile. "You look a bit… on edge," she said as Gabriel pulled a chair out for her.

He scoffed, his eyebrows lifting and dropping.

Gabriel patted his shoulder, but he too had a glint in his eye. "Try not to choke on your own spit."

"Funny." Marcelo's response was sarcastic.

"Ok… Why do I feel I'm the only one that doesn't get the joke?" I said, suspicious, while Marcelo pulled a chair out for me.

Three sets of shoulders shrugged.

"I don't know what you mean." Lu's voice was high-pitched, pretending an innocence not reflected in her face.

The rest of the meal went without mention of whatever it was. The food was Asian, delicious, with a hint of spice. The cocktails… divine; their consumption made only too easy by Marcelo, who encouraged us all to try different ones in his attempt to taste his way through the menu. Apparently, 'seeking inspiration for his new bar'. The three of them talked animatedly about the new project, designed to be a live music venue.

We reminisced about the best of our three days' sightseeing, the moments that were funny when they happened and funny in hindsight; Gabe's experience visiting

London for the first time versus mine visiting São Paulo; the differences we liked and disliked between our two countries. And all of a sudden, the memories I'd tried so hard to avoid reliving for months no longer seemed to hurt. The conversation flowing with so much ease, that I actually forgot I was angry. I had not felt this good, this normal, this myself, in a long time.

"So when did this happen?" I asked Gabe, pointing at him and Lu. "When did you guys go from hooking up to officially dating? How did you manage to get past Lu's commitment phobia?"

"When she came to stay at my place without me asking. She never stayed. She always left after she used and abused me." The last sentence laden with mock disapproval and outrage.

Lu scoffed. "I think you mean after *you enjoyed* me using and abusing you."

"Very much so, yes."

We all laughed.

"Actually, it was something Celo said the day after you left that made me change my mind," Lu admitted, mid-laughter.

"What did he say?" I asked, still smiling.

"That we were the same. Using sex for comfort and sabotaging good people out of our lives for fear of getting hurt. I realized there and then that I didn't want to be in the position he was in—losing someone he loves and regretting it dearly."

She had said it without thinking, as a reflex, probably springboarded by all the cocktails we had tasted. But as soon as she realized what she'd admitted to, her eyes went straight to Celo, her smile fading.

Someone he loves? Without meaning to, my head snapped in his direction.

He returned my stare. His expression was blank, but his eyebrows arched toward each other ever so slightly, his eyes heavy with meaning, sad even, searching my face for a reaction it didn't give because I was still processing.

The table nosedived from laughter to awkward silence.

Someone he loves. He had never actually said that to me. There were feelings there, sure. But neither of us had come out with the three big words.

"So I have you to blame for being under the thumb of a pocket-sized dictator? Thanks a lot." Gabe broke the awkwardness.

Celo's head turned toward him. "Glad I could be of assistance." He smiled, but it didn't reach his eyes.

Lu hit Gabe with a backhanded slap. "Don't talk about the love of your life like that."

Celo's gaze dropped to his hands, and his aura shifted to something darker. So did mine.

"I didn't say I don't enjoy being under *your* thumb." Gabe grabbed her face, tender, endearing, and planted a kiss on her lips. "You can boss me around all you want, pocket rocket. Especially if you're wearing a sexy outfit."

She hit him again.

The contrast between their relationship and ours left an imprint on Celo's face and mine. Regret on his, disappointment on mine. We were sitting so close, literally next to each other, but the distance felt like a cliff neither of us could jump.

When the meal was done, we made our way to the Sky Bar, Lu and I sitting on bar stools, the boys standing. The plan was to go dancing, but after so much food, none of us felt like making the effort to move far. Everyone, even Celo, was a little too merry from the cocktail tasting bonanza.

I didn't know if it was the copious amounts of alcohol or how busy the place was, but he got closer and closer—his hand resting at the bar behind me, then the back of my chair, and eventually my back. A finger rubbing back and forth where it found bare skin just above the zipper between my shoulder blades.

I shouldn't have let it happen, but he behaved like he didn't know what his hand was doing—talking and laughing with Lu and Gabe, discussing the merit of each new cocktail as though it was fine food, talking to me like nothing was happening. And if I was honest, I was secretly enjoying it.

At some point in the night Lu and Gabe became self-absorbed—whispering to each other, kissing. And I seized the moment.

"Hey!"

Celo lowered his head so he could hear me, his hand moving away from my back.

"What was the joke earlier?" It had bothered me, made me feel something was off.

His eyes raked my face, hungry, heavy. "There was no joke."

"You were all talking in code about something. Come on, you can tell me. What was it?"

He inhaled, sighed. "You really don't know?"

I shook my head.

For a moment he just looked at me. "They were making fun of my face, my coughing fit, when I saw what you're wearing."

It made sense. He hadn't seen what I had on until we got to the restaurant. And I hadn't seen his face because I had my back turned to him. For a second I checked myself, dreading something was out of place. Had I leaked? Did I have milk stains on my boobs? Could he see my Spanx peeping through the edge of the dress? But everything seemed kosher.

"Why?"

His other hand moved, up and down twice toward me.

"The dress?"

He nodded. Lazy blink.

"Is something wrong? Does it look bad?"

He smiled. Another headshake, another lazy blink. "It looks too good." He leaned in closer, so he could whisper it in my ear. "Good enough to eat." And he planted a kiss—quick, short, and stolen—just below my ear at the corner of my jaw, before straightening up back to standing.

It happened so quickly that if my whole skin hadn't erupted in goosebumps and my breath faltered, I would've questioned if it really happened. The chill stayed in my spine for minutes after.

He smacked Gabe's shoulder. "Stop it you two, there are children present."

Gabriel moved his face away from Lu's neck to look at him. "What children? You left yours at home."

"Yeah, but show some mercy to the guy that can't get any. We should go before the two of you stop being PG."

I was the first one to get dropped off, Marcelo sending Lu and Gabe away in the taxi to walk me to the door.

"You didn't need to do that, you know. You could have gone back with them."

"No, I couldn't. Their PDA was getting a little intense." His voice sounded moody and tired.

"Right?!" I turned to him, laughing in agreement, pulling the scarf off my neck, keys in my hand.

His eyes dropped to the gap in my coat. "That's the same one from Ilhabela, right?" His index pointed at my dress, voice low, rasping.

"You remember?" I matched his tone.

"Do I remember?" His smile was self-deprecating, head turning to the side then back to me. "I don't think I've ever felt so jealous in my life. You kissed Felipe, then you came down the stairs wearing it."

"I wasn't the only one that kissed somebody." I fiddled with my keys.

"I didn't kiss that chick. She kissed me."

"I don't remember you complaining." I jabbed and put the keys in the lock but didn't open the door.

"Because I needed the distraction. Felipe was all over you. It was hard to watch. I wanted to punch him hard enough to knock his lights out," he admitted without reservation. Dutch courage making us both honest.

We stared at each other for a beat. *Someone he loves.* Lu's words played in my mind. We'd had such a good night; it'd felt so good. I wanted to press pause for a minute, forget that we were on opposite sides of the battlefield just for the night.

"You coming in for a drink?" I will blame the booze here.

He blinked twice before shaking his head. "We've both had too much to drink. I'm not sure I can keep pretending I'm a gentleman. I've been thinking about it the whole night."

The chill was back in my spine, running down my legs. He smelled and looked so good. "Thinking about what?" I will blame the alcohol for this too.

He got closer, sighed, gaze locked on my mouth, expression sleepy, lazy. A thumb rubbed across my lips. "Kissing you..." Fingers caressed the side of my face. "Your neck..." His full palm ran down my breastbone. "Down your cleavage." Digits and eyes trailed my skin following every single one of his words, his touch light and heavy at the same time, burning with electricity, leaving a wake on my skin until his index inserted itself in between my boobs—once, twice, rubbing, squeezing its way through. "Those two birth marks you like to torture me with." He touched his forehead to mine, eyes closed. "I've missed you so much." His words spilled out in a whisper. "I'm trying to do the right thing here, cause we're both drunk, and I don't want you to regret this, but you're making it really difficult. Please go inside." His index was still hooked on my dress, our breaths mixing together in smoky puffs in the cold air.

I gasped and felt lightheaded before I vaguely remembered

I was supposed to be mad at him. And I nodded. He took a step back to give me space. I unlocked the door; he placed his forehead on the doorframe.

"See you tomorrow then."

He blinked once, deliberate.

I closed the door.

CHAPTER 17
Luciana

Gabe and I had decided to have a drink before heading to our room. But as we climbed the stairs to the bar, we came across Siobhan sitting by the window, engrossed in a book, glass of wine in hand.

Celo had introduced us the night we landed, and she had joined us for dinner on a couple of occasions. Neither her nor him had family nearby, and they seemed to have found each other as surrogate grandmother and grandson.

"Siobhan?" I called for her, surprised she was up so late.

Her head lifted and she found us, lips parting into a welcoming smile. A bookmark was placed between the pages of her novel, and she put it down on the table.

"Do you mind if we join you?"

"Of course not, my lovely. Sit down, sit down." She patted the seat next to her.

"Should I get you a top up?" Gabe pointed at her glass.

"Oh yeah, go on, love!"

"Rioja?"

"You know me well." She winked at him.

He nodded, his hand snaking its way under my hair and caressing my neck. "You want your usual?"

I smiled at him. He always knew what to get me.

"I like your fella. He's a good egg like," she commented as Gabe headed to the bar.

"He is. Is everything ok? Why are you up so late?"

"Everything is fine, girl. The older I get, the less I seem to need sleep. But, come on, tell us! How was your night in town? Did our boy get his bird?"

I smiled, I couldn't help it. "They looked very cozy by the end of dinner. And we left both of them at Paige's flat just now."

"Oooohhh…" Her eyes widened, lips rounded. "Do you think they will finally crack on with it?"

"I hope so. There is so much chemistry between them, you could cut it with a knife. I hope they at least stop beating around the bush and talk about things."

"Marcelo said he tried to talk to her a couple of times, like, but she wasn't having any of it."

"Yeah, unfortunately, for her it has become a bit of a badge of honor not to forgive him."

"Don't blame her, girl! It's a hard pill to swallow, even if he had his reasons."

"I get her, I honestly do. It's what everyone expects, right? Your man cheats, you scrap him. But there is nothing about their story that is box standard. How it happened, why it happened, the baby, how cut up he is about it, how much they love each other—and I honestly do believe they love each other, none of it is your cut and dry cheating tale."

Gabe came back to the table. "They're bringing our drinks over." He took a seat next to me, his arm going over my head, resting on my shoulder and pulling me closer to him.

"I was just saying to Siobhan that nothing about Paige and Marcelo's story is box standard."

"True." His head bopped in agreement with his word. "It's anything but straight forward."

We had only been talking for a few minutes when Siobhan looked out of the window and squinted. "Is that our Marcelo walking down to us?"

We all looked in the direction of the walking figure.

"I think it is," Gabe confirmed.

"Oh, God." Siobhan's lips pressed together, corners dropping, chin crinkling. "She still has a cob on then."

"Go get him." I tapped Gabe's leg as Celo got closer to the building.

"What happened? Why are you back here already?" I asked him as soon as he got up the stairs, but he ignored me.

"Do you want a drink?" Gabe asked him before sitting down.

"No. Thanks, man."

They both took a seat at our table. Gabe next to me, Celo next to Siobhan.

"Are you alright, love?" Siobhan asked the same question I had, but in a nicer tone.

He smiled at her, but it was more of an endearing smile than an answer to her question.

"You don't look it." I stated the obvious. "I thought you were going to stay at Paige's for a little while."

He shook his head, eyes dropping to his hands, his demeanor that of a defeated man. He pulled the lighter out of his pocket and started flipping it in his fingers, his mood definitely in a lower tone.

"Was she having none of it, love?" Siobhan tried to coerce the information out of him gently.

"No, she was friendly. Invited me in for a drink and everything."

The three of us looked at each other confused. The words sounded good, like progress had been made, but his tone and body language were the opposite.

"And?" I broke the silence. Patience had never been my strong suit, and he was testing it.

His eyes focused on me then. "I can't do it, Lu."

"So, she asked you in and you refused?" Gabe double-checked.

Celo nodded, gaze back on the lighter.

"I don't get it, man. I thought this was what you wanted?"

"We drank too much."

More confused looks. He might have been a little merry, but he clearly wasn't drunk.

"I get it. Rule number two, right? No drunk women." Celo wasn't one for rules, but he had two he didn't compromise on. Number one: no fooling around while he was working. Work first, play later. Number two: he didn't engage with women he thought were under the influence of anything. He considered them not sober enough to consent.

"That too." He took a deep breath, hand dragging down his face. "I wanted it so bad, it's almost a joke. But I only have one shot at it. One." His index raised to emphasize his point. "I can't mess this up. Can't fuck it up because I want to short-cut it or rush it."

"You're stressing she would wake up tomorrow and regret?" Siobhan got to the heart of the matter.

He looked at her, nodded.

"It's complicated. We have Amber, we're in different countries. If I lose Paige for good, I can lose my daughter. So I need to do this right. She can't be drunk or upset. We have to clear the air and sort things out before I go falling on her mouth first. Because if the timing and the reasons are wrong, she will bounce back like an elastic band and..." He trailed off, head shaking, eyes dropping to his hands.

"Right now, your relationship can't take it." I completed the thought for him.

He nodded. "The last thing I need is for her to wake up and feel like I've taken advantage of her not being on the ball. I also need to know she's..." He stopped mid-sentence, as if he'd thought better and decided not to say it.

"She's what, love?" Siobhan gave his arm a gentle squeeze, encouraging him to finish.

He took a deep breath, sighed. "That she's doing it because she wants it, wants us… wants me. Not because of the baby or for comfort." His voice was riddled with insecurity, despite his best effort to keep it hidden.

I had never seen Celo like this—hesitating. He'd always been so confident, so sure of himself. Almost cocky. But right now, he really was uncertain of Paige's feelings. And this wasn't about her. This was about self-preservation.

"The right reasons." Gabe's nod hinted at something that had been discussed when I wasn't there.

Celo's head bopped up and down.

"So what's your game plan?" Gabe was being his normal level-headed self.

"I need to wait until she's ready to talk to me about everything."

"What do you want to happen? Ideally."

"I want to take her back home with me. I want my family."

"Do you think she would come?"

He shrugged. "Until we talk, I don't know. She has family here. It's complicated."

"And if she says no?" Siobhan's voice was gentle.

"Maybe we can do fifty-fifty. Half a year here, half there. Or maybe I'll have to move here. Either way, my daughter is not growing up without me. Even if Paige doesn't want me back."

I reached over and squeezed his hand. "I don't think it'll come to that. Last I heard, she invited you in for a drink. What happened last time she did that?"

For a moment, his face told me nothing. Then he smiled.

CHAPTER 18
Paige

"Hi." He was the last of the three to cross the threshold, gaze trying to read me.

"Morning." I smiled at him, a little embarrassed. Yesterday's moment just outside the same door hung suspended between us.

Lu and Gabe were absorbed in conversation, coats and shoes being taken off, while we stood awkwardly next to each other exchanging furtive side looks. Well… mine were furtive, his were staring. His aftershave assaulted me in the closeness, wooden and some sort of citrus—he smelled so bloody masculine and good.

"We can't go far today as we're on the clock." Lu brought me back into the room. As she moved out of the way, he stepped forward to remove his coat and boots. "We need to be on our way to the airport at 6pm."

Sunday, and their last day in London, had come around too quickly. The reminder that she was leaving shifted my focus. She'd only managed to get a few days off work at short notice, and the twelve-hour flight with a long check-in meant she lost almost two days traveling. All I got was four days. Four days where I felt normal. Four days where the drama seemed to pack up and go on a city break too.

It made me think of the power of true friendships. A little like your health, you don't notice how it makes a difference until you don't have it with you. Lu was the sister I chose. My confidant, the one I could have whole conversations with without saying a word, the one that always told me the truth without it hurting. Saying goodbye to her always brought me to tears.

I felt sad but incredibly blessed. Blessed to have a friend like her, who spared no expense and subjected herself to grueling flight schedules to come to my rescue in my hour of need. Worth her weight in gold three times over.

"Think about what I said, ok flower? Don't be stubborn. Use it to your advantage," she whispered in my ear as she hugged me goodbye. "Don't be too sad for me. I'm off to Ilhabela for Easter." She winked, trying to lift the mood. But my tears started spilling anyway. "There is no need to cry either. We have phones and video call. We'll talk in twelve hours," she reassured me, but she was also crying.

All goodbyes said, hugs distributed as though we would see each other soon, Gabe and Lu got into the taxi and disappeared out of view after it turned the corner.

"Let me walk you back to your place." Marcelo's voice was tentative, but he wasn't asking a question. "If your mom doesn't mind, we could stop at that little deli on the corner and have a bite."

"I'm not going to be good company. Maybe it's better we don't."

He nodded.

I set off walking. He didn't say a thing, but he walked alongside me. When we got to the deli, my feet halted. He took a couple of steps before looking back at me. I really wanted to stick to my guns, tell him I wasn't going to sit with him for food or anything else. But I was dreading going back to the way I was feeling before Lu arrived. The incredible sense of being overwhelmed and unprepared, sinking more than swimming. I couldn't quite face going back into mum mode just yet.

Without a word, I went into the deli. He followed. I ordered English tea and a slice of Victoria sponge; he, toast with cured meats and some juice. We sat in silence, basking in the early spring sun coming through the window. Lu had brought the sunshine with her too; I was willing to bet it would rain now that she'd left. And we people-watched in possibly the quietest corner of Pimlico, full of shops that were named after people, making it hard to know what they actually sold.

"I love and hate this street."

Celo's hands paused halfway through slicing some Parma ham and he smiled at me—only a small, fast one, letting me know he was relieved I had chosen not to stay silent.

"Why?"

"Because the shops are named after people. How are you supposed to know what they do? And because even the dry cleaner at the end looks like a designer shop. It's all very oblique and pretty, like everyone receives guidelines on how to do their shop fronts. An unattainable and obnoxious level of perfection."

"Maybe they do. Maybe they want it to look exclusive. It's working, though. It's a really nice area."

We sat there for an hour. Talking about everything but our problems, our baby, what happened last night, or the fact my best friend leaving was like having my right arm severed. He understood it. He understood *me*. He got that I just wanted a moment of peace, but not necessarily quiet. I didn't want to be with my thoughts. I wanted to feel like I had turned a corner, and life was on its way back to being normal, whatever the hell that was. And in fair dues to him, he let me have it, talking about shit that didn't matter and didn't make a difference.

English tea had never tasted so good.

CHAPTER 19
Marcelo

GABE AND LU COULD ONLY STAY A FEW DAYS, BUT THEIR PRESENCE seemed to have calmed things down and defused a lot of tension. During the time Lu was in London, Paige definitely felt better; and Lu had convinced even Kate to give me the benefit of doubt.

Lu was one of the few people I knew who could confront you with the truth and you wouldn't feel the urge to argue. The way she worded things just put you in a position where you couldn't deny it. She squeezed you gently, but make no mistake, she'd kill you like a bug in between her thumbnails if she had to. I could tell Paige's mood had shifted after they left.

To alleviate the lower tone things had taken, I tried to keep the same pace, suggesting we went for walks, continued sightseeing. The weather didn't help. As soon as Lu left, it was like it was trying to make us pay for the sunny spells we'd had the days prior—gray miserable days with showers that looked harmless, until you realized you were soaked.

"I saw this toy library down the road from here. They have a baby session in the morning and afternoon. Should we take Coffee Bean?"

"I don't think that's a good idea."

I nodded, defeated and deflated. I had tried to suggest different things, and she hadn't agreed to any of them.

"I'm not trying to be difficult. She's not had all her jabs yet. She's still at risk of getting bugs and stuff. So it would be better if she wasn't too close to other children until she has had all her jabs."

"I understand." I tried to approach the subject with caution, but there wasn't really a way I could ease into it. "Paige, you can't lock yourself in this flat again. Staying indoors, the gloomy weather, Lu leaving…" I tried to make my voice as soft as possible. "These things will drag you down if you stop moving."

For a moment she was quiet. My gut telling me that I had overstepped the fine line we were tethering, and she might not have taken what I'd said well.

"I know." I barely heard it, but relief was instantaneous.

"I know the weather is shit, but why don't we go for a walk? We can go to my hotel lobby, it's only a few minutes away, just for some fresh air and a change of scene. They have a garden in the middle. If the weather gives us a break we could walk around it, and duck for cover if the rain comes back."

She said nothing.

"Please? I don't like seeing you like this. It worries me," I admitted, lost for what else to try. My hand automatically reached for her, then dropped when I remembered that touching her might not be welcomed.

She looked at me for a moment. That was one of the improvements. She was now actually looking me in the eyes. "I will get Amber's bag ready. We can take the pram."

I didn't realize I was holding my breath until it came out in a relieved sigh. I nodded.

We walked into the reception, Coffee Bean covered in a plastic dome that made her pram look like a greenhouse, Paige shaking her umbrella to get rid of the excess water, me shaking my jacket.

"I want to introduce you to someone," I said as we settled

at a table and finished ordering our drinks. "She'll be here in a minute."

"She?" Paige stopped adjusting Coffee Bean's clothes to look at me.

"Yeah. I met someone here." I searched for Siobhan. I had told her we were coming to the hotel and invited her to meet Paige.

"You met someone here?"

"Uh-huh."

"Man, you don't waste any time, do you?" She started getting up.

That made me refocus. "What?"

Paige reached for the pram, put Coffee Bean back in it, reached for her coat.

"What're you doing? We just got here."

"Why would I want to meet some random woman you met here? You have some cheek!" She laughed, but it was an angry sarcastic laugh. Realization hitting me a little too late.

"It's not like that." I tried to stop her from putting her coat back on.

She snatched it away from me. "Don't touch me!" The words coming out through gritted teeth.

"You alright, love?" Siobhan appeared out of nowhere. Saved by the fucking bell.

"Paige, this is Siobhan."

Her head lifted, irritated, borderline offended, until her eyes landed on the old lady standing next to me. Her arms froze midway through her coat sleeve, her gaze coming back to me, an adorable pink spreading from her cheeks to her neck. She bit her lower lip, eyes dropping to the floor.

"Is everything ok, my lovelies?" Siobhan's voice broke the awkward silence.

"Yeah, we were just settling in. Should we order you some tea?" I tried not to smile too wide. Paige could deny it all she wanted, but she'd gotten jealous, thinking I had met another woman.

"Don't be daft. It's past midday, it's time for a real bevvy. So, this is your bird?"

I nodded.

"Girl, you're gorgeous! I can see now why he can't stop yapping about you."

Paige's lips stretched into an embarrassed smile. She dropped her coat on the arm of a chair.

"And this must be the famous baba." Siobhan leaned over the pram to peek at Coffee Bean. "Can I pick her up?"

Paige's head bopped up and down. Lip still being bitten. She really needed to stop that. Every time she did it, it distracted me, without fail.

"Oh, my goodness! Ain't you the cutest little thing! Look just like your pa, don't ya? Look at that smile! With them green eyes from your ma, you'll be a little heartbreaker."

"Green eyes?" I looked at Coffee Bean. Her eyes weren't brown but weren't green either.

"Mossy green now, but I reckon they'll go green them."

"You think?" Paige seemed pleased.

"I don't think she likes when everyone keeps saying the baby looks like me." I cocked my chin toward Paige.

Siobhan parked herself on the nearest chair. "Don't blame her, love. Bloody annoying when she did all the hard work, isn't it me baba?" She pulled happy faces at Coffee Bean.

Paige smiled.

Siobhan sat there for a few minutes, cooing and talking to Coffee Bean, melting over baby cuteness like women tend to do.

"You're being a good girl and helping you pa get back in your ma's good graces?" Her head lifted to look at Paige. "Sorry, love. He told me he's been a bellend."

Paige's eyebrows raised, surprised, her lips stretching into a smile that didn't show any teeth, uncomfortable with the subject.

"He also said you're from my neck of the woods. I told him he was lucky if he'd bagged himself a northern girl, but that you'd take none of his nonsense."

Another raise of her eyebrow, small smile, more lip biting.

"Why do I feel like you two are gonna gang up on me?" I pointed a finger at both of them.

"I'm too old to waste time beating around the bush, love." The waiter came over. "One of them glasses of red wine for me, please, my lovely."

"So how did you two meet?" asked Paige.

"At St. George's Garden. He was looking all mopey, and I felt sorry for him."

It made me laugh. "That's not quite right, is it Siobhan? You pulled the old drop the purse trick on me to flirt a little."

"All lies, love. All lies," she said to Paige.

"Oh! You can keep him. I'll pay you to keep him," Paige responded, then chuckled. A genuine laugh this time.

I didn't mention that a moment ago she hadn't been happy to know I had met someone else.

"Like that, is it? In that case, fine, I was flirting a little. But look at him. Your fella is a sight for sore old eyes like mine."

Siobhan's energy and bubbliness lightened the mood, breaking the ice. Like my grandmother, like Lu, she had the ability to pull people out of their funk. I don't know if it was the accent or her personality, but it was her superpower for sure.

We stayed in the hotel lobby all afternoon. Going for walks in the garden when the rain gave us a break, listening to Siobhan's stories and adding to our bar tab when it didn't. And it worked. Paige's mood lifted, even if just for a little while.

♥♥♥

A couple of days of visits came and went. After our close call in the doorway, Paige was still not letting me close, but she wasn't as unfriendly either. Instead, we started talking about small things—how Eight was doing without me, Risa, Freddie, Kate, Ryan, her time in America. Tiptoeing around what we really needed to talk about. I guess I should have been happy there was some progress, but it's hard to see being let out of the doghouse on a one-meter leash as an improvement when I knew we could be so much more.

"Do you think you could…" Paige hesitated, not yet sure if she really wanted to say whatever was playing in her mind. "Do you think you could look after Amber this afternoon for me?" she asked me one morning.

Her eyes sank into me, and I realized I not only hadn't answered but, caught off guard by her request, my face had surprise written all over it. I cleared my throat, tried to readjust my expression. "Of course."

"I need to get some things done."

"Take all the time you need."

"Two-ish ok for you?"

I agreed, while trying my best not to look smug or happy with her request. Gloating about the little space she was giving me would only get me straight back to purgatory prison.

When I came back at two, Paige was dressed in gym gear. Skintight clothes that hugged around her curves like a damn glove. Her thumbs poked through the sleeve holes of a jacket that zipped at the front but stopped before it covered her cleavage. And God help me, pregnancy had accentuated all her curves, and she was damn delicious. I would devour them like a starved man if she let me.

"I left everything ready for you." She brought me back to reality. I tried to look like I wasn't a dog eyeing his favorite treat. "There is a bottle in the fridge too, if you need it. You sure you're ok with her?" She hesitated.

I dipped my chin in a nod that was as confident as I could make it.

She mirrored my nod with another. A hand cupped Coffee Bean's head, the kiss on her chubby cheeks making a louder smack than usual, and she handed the baby to me. Then walked over to the sofa and bent over to pick up a bag.

The pants she was wearing had outer stitches designed to draw the eye and torture me. One horizontally sitting just below her waist like a belt, one vertical down the middle of her ass disappearing in between her legs, and two that curved around her glutes and ran down the back of her thighs. As if I needed a map for where to look.

I ran a hand down my face. This wasn't getting any easier. And the little touches and small moments she had allowed me to have had just knocked everything in me up a notch. Making the hunger even stronger.

"I'll see you both in a couple of hours then."

Another confident dip of my chin. We followed her to the hall. She put on a pair of boots and a long coat that looked like she'd wrapped herself in a duvet. A final look at us, well… at Amber, and the door opened and closed.

I looked at Amber. "Is your momma trying to give me a stroke? She is, isn't she?"

Coffee Bean smiled at me, all gums, dribble, and long blinks.

"You think my suffering is funny?"

More smiles.

"You're in on it, aren't you?"

"Ehh," she cooed back. Toothless and ruthless.

I sighed. There was no winning with these two. "What should we do? Should we watch some TV?"

The following day was more of the same. A short dress

over tights. Everything covered apart from a half-moon of skin in her lower back, on the way down to her ass—creamy, freckled like a tease. Vanilla ice cream with chocolate sprinkles, served with enough ice and distance to give me a brain freeze.

She put on her boots and coat, hesitated at the door before leaving.

It wasn't until the third day—skintight shorts, tights, wraparound top, socks pulled above the knee; striped delight served with a dose of heart attack for me—that I realized they weren't gym clothes, they were dancing ones.

"Celo?"

Something touched my hand. I resurfaced slowly. Slight touches on my shoulder, some more on my hand and arm. My eyes opened to find Paige standing over me in the striped delight with a smile on her face. For a minute I thought I was dreaming.

I smiled back at her.

"Why is Amber inside your hoody?" That woke me up. I rubbed my eyes.

I had fallen asleep on the sofa watching TV. "I didn't want her to fall off."

"So you zipped her in?" Her eyebrows were raised, her lips still grinning.

I looked down at Coffee Bean. Only her head was peeking out of my sweatshirt. I had laid her on my chest to settle her down, and when I started feeling sleepy, I pulled it closed and secured her in place.

"I don't think she minds it." Coffee Bean was still deep asleep.

I unzipped my sweatshirt, and Paige gently picked the baby up.

"Do you need me tomorrow afternoon?" I sat up, willing my brain to focus.

"If that's ok." She lullabied Amber, so she wouldn't wake up.

"Would you mind if I took her to meet Siobhan for a drink?"

Her eyes stayed on Coffee Bean; she bit her lip.

"We'll only be an hour or so."

A deep breath. She was struggling letting me roam with Amber, but after a moment of silence she conceded. "I'll leave the pram for you."

I turned up the next day to find her in skintight pants, a soft fabric top hanging off one shoulder and tied at the side, hair tied in a messy bun. A silhouette of bare skin curved in at the crook of her neck and out at the tip of her shoulder in one smooth creamy line that begged to be kissed. If I could have smelled it, I bet the scent would have been flowers, wood, and oranges—her perfume. Crème caramel served with a stroke for me.

"I made her bag up for you." Her voice made me blink. "There is a bottle in the fridge, ready to go. The pram is in the hallway." A key dangled from her thumb and index. "Spare key. So you can get back in if I'm not back by then."

I took the key from her hand, my fingers running over hers.

She nodded, followed her routine, hesitated by the door like she wanted to say something, and left.

"Should we go throw a party? You, me, and Siobhan, living it large while your momma is doing her thing?" I asked my miniature in Portuguese.

"Ehh."

♥♥♥

At 3.45am my phone rang. Kate, from the business trip she'd told me about a while back. By the time I got to their apartment, I was soaked from the rain, and I could hear Coffee Bean's screams from outside.

My knocks had to get loud before Paige opened the door. She looked as distressed as Amber was.

"Oh great! Just what I need. Why are you here?"

"Your mom called me." I shrugged off my coat and trainers and they stayed on the floor by the door where they fell.

"What??" She looked confused but it only lasted a second before her attention went back to Amber.

"How long has she been like this?" I said, taking Coffee Bean from her arms. Paige was so tired and stressed, she didn't stop me.

"Since 12am. She has cried nonstop for hours." Her voice failed; she looked like she too was going to cry. "I don't know what else to do. I tried everything. Nothing works."

Coffee Bean's face was so red it was almost purple. Her eyes screwed together, tears streaming down her face, chin quivering, little hands in fists, face and hair looking all sweaty.

"She doesn't have a temperature, doesn't want any milk, her nappy is clean. She's sweating like she's hot, but she's barely wearing anything. I don't know what else I can try." Paige's nose was going red, her eyebrows screwed by agony mixed with despair, hands on her forehead.

"It's ok. It's ok." I didn't know who I was trying to comfort. If it was Paige, Amber, or me. Panic started to boil in the pit of my stomach. I was here, but I had no idea if I could actually do anything to make it any better.

I put the purple gremlin down on the sofa and kneeled down, my mind going through everything I had read, everything I remembered from when Freddie was little, trying to find something I could do, something I could tell Paige.

Amber looked like she was in pain. Her legs and arms kicking, body tense like she was about to explode. Her crying rang in my ears, giving me agony as if my eardrums were about to burst.

For a moment Paige and I just stared at her, not sure what to do. Paige started pacing.

Burst… explode… Gas! The pieces of the puzzle slotted into place in my brain.

I pressed her little stomach; it felt rock solid.

"Maybe she has colic. I saw this thing on YouTube about… hmm… about how babies lie down too much and that blocks things in their gut. This dude was doing this massage to help them blow out some gas or something." I pulled out my phone and frantically searched for the video. "I think it's supposed to alleviate the pain in their stomach. Maybe we could try that?"

Paige shrugged at me, her hands slapping her thighs. At this point, if I suggested me kissing her would make Amber stop crying, she'd probably have given it a good try.

The video went on about how to rub your hands on the baby's belly then rotate their legs to release discomfort. I followed the steps. As I was finishing one of the rotations, Coffee Bean let out a loud trumpet-like fart.

"Damn! That reeks! How long have you been brewing that in there, Coffee Bean?" Amber's crying halted then restarted. "I'm going to do it again, maybe she has more in there."

I repeated the massage a good four times. Every time I pushed her legs up and around, more bubbling came out from her rear end. With every release, her crying decreased a little bit more. Eventually, it became just the aftermath of what it was. Almost as if she was relieved, but tired.

"Feeling better?" I asked her in Portuguese. "I have been here two weeks, and you have peed on me, shat, and puked on me, and now farted the whole national reserve of natural gas at me. You're making me look extremely sexy in front of your mom, Coffee Bean."

Paige was hovering over my shoulder, a hand over her

mouth. "How did I not know that? How did you know that, and I didn't even think of it? She has been crying for hours!" She covered her face with both her hands and started crying herself.

I got to my feet. "Hey, hey!" I tried to pull her hands down, but she wouldn't let me. "I know that because I sit for over eight hours a day searching baby shit on YouTube. Do you have the time to do that on top of everything else you do for her during the day?"

I couldn't win. I helped one just to upset the other. The feeling of impotence ate away at my edges.

Paige's hands came down. "She has been in discomfort for hours! Hours! And I didn't know what to do! I should know what to do! I'm such a shit mum!" Her voice was heavy with guilt and tiredness, eyes streaming over.

"Hey, listen to me." I held on to her face with both my hands, her hands holding on to my forearms. "You're a *great* mom. You look after our little girl like a lioness. But this is not a job just for one person. That's why you need two people to make one of these." I jerked my chin toward Amber. "There are tribes across the world that make raising children the business of *the whole tribe*. But here you are, trying to know everything and do everything on your own. It's not fair. It's not fair *on you*. You're a *great* mom. You're just sleep deprived and tired. Ok? That's why you need to let other people help you. You're a great mom, do you hear me?"

I held on to Paige's face and stared into her eyes until she nodded—her sobs getting smaller, her eyes still streaming. Seeing her this upset made me wanna murder somebody. She wiggled herself free from my hands and picked up Amber.

After a couple of minutes, both of them had stopped crying, and I felt I could breathe. The tension left my body, but my ears were still ringing from all the screaming.

"Do you want some peppermint tea?"

Paige nodded.

I headed to the kitchen. While I was making the tea, I texted Kate to let her know everything was under control.

"I guess I should say thank you." Paige's voice came from behind me.

"For what? She's my kid too. I *should* be here. You shouldn't be doing it on your own." I offered her the tea. "Why don't you sit down for a minute and let me take first watch?"

She hesitated for a beat. But then nodded, resigned, spent, and handed me Coffee Bean in exchange for the hot mug. We both walked back into the sitting room. She sat on the sofa facing me.

"Do you mind if I put some music on? Low volume. Marisa used to dance with Freddie when he was struggling to sleep. Maybe it will work with our little madam?"

Paige nodded, sipped her tea, brought her feet up on the sofa, and leaned her head on the backrest, exhausted eyes watching us.

CHAPTER 20
Paige

He pulled the phone out of his pocket, his joggers still wet at the front of the thighs from the rain, and a slower, semi-acoustic version of 'What is Love' started playing. Celo swayed from side to side with Amber's head nestled in the elbow crease of one arm, her breath still catching in staccato fits from all the crying. One of his hands caressed her head, lips dipping to kiss her every so often, his expression full of tenderness.

The answer to the song was standing right in front of me. So much care and love, slow dancing in their bubble of two. His focus and attention all channeled into a single point.

"I think our little girl likes your base-heavy music," he said, but he didn't look at me. He only had eyes for Amber.

"She might not look like me, but *she is* my daughter."

He didn't answer.

I don't know if it was the tiredness, but I felt left out. Jealous of all the comfort she was getting. And God, I wanted some. I wanted to be the center of his attention and affection—put my head on his shoulder, have my head rubbed, feel the warmth of strong arms keeping me safe. Have my face kissed in delicate touches that showed deeper care than any French kiss could.

The song changed to an acoustic version of 'I Wanna Dance with Somebody', and as I watched their moment—his moment as a father—my want got stronger. I noticed everything. The line of his shoulders, long hair falling over his face as he leaned down to kiss her, his arms, big hands, the silhouettes on his joggers. So much power and strength in one body, tamed in complete surrender of a loving moment.

I wanted to cry. To hit him. To kiss him. To fall asleep with him breathing on my neck like he used to.

The birds were announcing the morning outside, the crack in the curtains showing the sky was halfway through changing from its nightgown to morning dress.

He danced with her to another two songs, even though she was already asleep, completely oblivious to my presence. Enjoying being a father to the fullest. Exhaustion was catching up on me; my eyes felt heavy.

The music stopped, and the phone went back into his pocket. Celo walked over to me, grabbed one of my hands and waited for me to stand up, then took us both to my room. He let go of my hand to pull the duvet off the bed, then took it back to move me toward it. I sat down. He placed Amber down in her cot, gently, to not wake her up. He covered her with a blanket, pushed the cot closer to the bed. Then did the same thing to me—pointed for me to lie down, pulling the duvet over me when I did.

He kissed Amber's head, then leaned to touch mine, the nails on his fingers scratching my scalp in a half-moon from my temple to my ear.

"I will let myself out," he whispered.

As his hand retreated, I grabbed it. "Stay until I fall asleep?"

He hesitated for a couple of seconds, my fingers tight around his wrist, then nodded. I wiggled to the other side of the bed to make room, and he lay on top of the duvet next to me but kept his distance even though he was facing me.

We stared at each other for a little while, his head resting on top of his arm. In the silence, I could hear both of us breathing.

I missed him. Missed the moments we shared in bed—his

arms around me, my hair and forehead being kissed, laughing about something that only made sense to both of us.

Before I could think too much about it, I freed myself from the covers, wiggled closer, so I was lying on his elbow, sharing the arm he was using to support his head, my nose almost touching his. He didn't touch me. But, his eyes devoured my face, trying to read me.

I touched the tip of my nose to his.

"Are you sure this is a good idea?" Another whisper. "You're upset."

"I thought you wanted to kiss me."

His answer came after a moment of silence. "I want to do a lot more than just kiss you." His nails ran from the hair at my temple until his hand was cupping my face, thumb running over my lips. My eyes closed, my body relaxing and weakening, leaning into his comfort. "But you will regret this in the morning. Take it from someone who acts like a fool when he's upset." It wasn't a whisper. The words just tumbled out of his mouth with his breathing.

"It's already morning."

He didn't move. Thumb brushing back and forth over my lips.

I rubbed my nose to his. This time not just the tip, side to side. Long, dragged, lazy rubs from one side to another.

He gasped, his eyes closing, his thumb the only thing keeping his lips from mine.

For a moment he didn't respond. Eyes closed, letting me rub my face to his.

Then his palm closed around my neck, index and thumb grabbing my jaw, and he kissed me, his five o'clock shadow stubble rubbing against my skin.

Slow at first. Then wet and deep—his whole body shifting, arms wrapping around me, bringing me in, body flush to mine, my arms pinned to his chest.

The chain reaction in my body, and his, was instantaneous. And I felt calmer, secure, my wants silenced.

But when the kiss got too hungry, he stopped it. Pushed my head under his chin. I tried to wiggle free; he held on tighter, not letting me go anywhere.

"Shhh… You need to sleep."

"Why?" I whispered after a second or two.

He inhaled, sighed. "Because if we do this I would rather you weren't drunk or upset. I need to know you're doing it for the right reasons."

Unable to move much, I rubbed my thigh against the lower part of his body. Everything about him was rock solid.

He groaned, deep in his throat, vibrating against my head. His hand moved to run down his face; he took a really deep breath. "Please don't do that. My good sense only goes so far, and it's hanging by a very thin thread." His hips turned slightly, so one of his legs could block mine.

I wanted more, but I had no energy to struggle. Mind tired, body ringing but comforted. And I stayed where he put me. We both did.

The last thing I remembered was his hand—caressing my hair, down and up my back, down the top of my arm, up to my neck, back to my hair. A routine it danced on repeat until I fell asleep.

♥♥♥

I woke up when Amber started stirring. Checked the clock on the bedside table—8am. She was probably hungry and needed a nappy change. Marcelo was deep asleep, legs tangled with mine, one arm above our heads, his face buried in my neck, the other arm holding me close.

Gently, I tried to untangle our limbs. At first, he tried to hold on, but then let me go, his body barely moving. I picked up Amber and went to breastfeed her in the sitting room, snoozing while she suckled away, nestled in her breastfeeding cushion.

By lunchtime, Marcelo reappeared. He leaned against the doorframe to the kitchen, barefoot, bed head, eyes still swollen from sleep, but face clean.

"Morning."

"Afternoon," I answered, turning my back to him and shoving some clothes in the washing machine.

I heard his steps on the wooden floor. *"Boa tarde, princesinha do pai. Tá se sentindo melhor, meu amor?"* He'd walked to Amber in her rocking chair. His little princess, something better, his love. *"Que sorriso lindo! Mas você acordou toda fresh assim?"* Something beautiful, something fresh. Amber cooed back at him.

I found the cleaning spray and started to clean the worktop. I had hours on my own to think, regret, and feel embarrassed. Think about what I had done. Regret how easily I seemed to forget everything, including how he broke my heart, for a bit of a belly rub like a dog. And feel embarrassed over the fact that had he not stopped me, I would have slept with him. One hundred per cent. I was the one offended, but he had been the one protecting my honor and not for the first time either.

He walked to me. "Everything ok?" His arms reached around my waist, face appearing over my shoulder.

I wiggled out of his embrace. "Everything's fine."

He waited a second. "Doesn't feel like it."

"I don't know what you mean." My scrubbing of the worktop intensified. I didn't turn to face him.

"Are you going to turn around and talk to me?"

"About what? I said everything is fine."

He waited. A particular stain in the worktop wasn't coming off. I scrubbed it harder.

"You trying to scrub the skin off that countertop?"

I turned around to find he had crossed his arms over his chest. All the feelings and confusion swirling in my blood boiled to the surface. "What do you want from me, Marcelo?"

"I want you to talk to me." The calm in his voice annoyed me.

"I *am* talking to you. I already said everything is fine. Stop asking me the same question."

His eyes narrowed, head moving sideways ever so slightly. "Don't you think it's time we talked about this?" His index flicked in between both of us.

"Well… that's easy. There is no *this*." I repeated his gesture.

"Hmm… And I suppose we didn't kiss last night either?"

I stared at him—purposely angry, disapproving of his mention of it—and half turned to go back to scrubbing the unbudging spot.

He inhaled a deep breath, dropped his arms, his head moving, eyes trying to find mine. Textbook adult trying to calm down a child throwing a tantrum—get to their eye level, keep your voice calm. "Paige, I fucked up something chronic, I know. And there are no words I can say that will change what I did. There isn't a single day that goes by that I don't regret it. I will do *anything* to fix it. Please? I love—"

"Get out." I cut him short, sharp, merciless. "Get the fuck out."

"Please, don't do this. I know you're still mad at me but, please, can we—"

"I'm not mad at you. I want you to leave." My words didn't match my tone.

"You *know* we need to talk about this." His tone had all the calm mine didn't.

I laughed, sarcastic, poisonous. "Talk about what? Oh! You thought you'd play nice, come to the rescue, give me one single kiss, and everything would be forgotten?"

"No. But I did think that maybe after last night we could talk about it." His tranquility exasperated me.

"Why? Because you kissed me?"

"Because you asked me for that kiss, Paige."

"And you let me!" My voice raised a level.

"A little hard to resist when you come at me all guns blazing."

"Oh yeah, sorry! I forgot you have no willpower when it comes to women serving themselves to you on a platter."

"No…" The word dragged, a firm correction, his voice still calm. It irritated me even more. "A little hard to resist when you were all I thought about and wanted for ten months."

"Too bad! Cause you're not getting it!" My voice went higher still.

His lips twitched, a cocky smirk threatening to surface before he controlled his expression back to neutral. And he didn't have to say it—he'd already gotten some. Twice. *I* had been the one to give it to him, without him asking. The fleeting, knowing smile tipped me over the edge.

"You know you're being unfair. You can't be mad at me for kissing you when I only gave you what you asked me for." His voice was *still* even.

"And what do you want? A medal?" I half shouted, half angry-laughed. "Let me spell this out for you. There is no *this*." I waved the cloth I was holding angrily between us. "I'm *never* going back to you! I will *never* date someone like you *ever* again!"

His head tilted, eyes narrowed. "*Someone like me*?" His voice went lower.

"A fuck-up. A mistake," I shouted from the top of my lungs.

My scream startled Amber, and she started crying.

For a moment he did nothing—didn't blink, didn't move, didn't say a thing. Frozen on the spot. And I regretted my words as soon as I had vomited them out of my mouth, spat like darts of poison.

His gaze dropped to the floor, lips pressed together. He nodded.

Amber's crying got louder.

He turned his back on me, walked to Amber, gave her a kiss on the head, and headed to the hall. I don't even think he put his shoes and coat on, the door opening and closing almost immediately.

Realization of what I had said, what I had done, made me cover my eyes in shame. And I too started crying. I dropped the cloth on the worktop and braced against it for a minute. Then washed my hands and took Amber out of her chair.

"Shhhhh. It's ok, Poppet. It's ok." I lullabied her up and down.

But it wasn't. I had shoved the knife in up to the hilt and twisted it, to make sure it caused maximum damage. This time, my embarrassment and anger weren't his fault. I had kissed him, given in, because I wanted to. He had tried to talk some sense into me, and I had made it almost impossible for him to say no because I knew he wanted it too. Had it not been for him, I would have a lot more to regret this morning. And in return, I kicked him where *I knew* it would hurt the most. His Achilles' heel. The one thing he had struggled with his whole life. Even though I knew, I knew damn well, that I wasn't really angry at him. I was angry at *myself*. And two wrongs don't make a right.

For the rest of the day he didn't visit, didn't call, didn't text.

The next morning, I got Amber ready for his usual visit. He didn't show. I waited an hour before I texted. No reply. Another hour before I called. No answer. By mid-afternoon remorse was turning into worry, sitting in the pit of my stomach like a stone. So I video called Lu.

"Hello there, flower. How are you?"

"I'm ok."

"Are you sure? Cause it doesn't look like it."

"Marcelo didn't come to see Amber today."

"Ok..." She stopped what she was doing to focus on the call. "Why?"

"I don't know. Well..." I hesitated. "Maybe it's my fault."

"What is your fault?"

"We argued yesterday."

"You argued?"

"I argued."

"*You* argued?" She looked confused.

"Yeah." I couldn't look at her, so I messed with the sleeve of my jumper. "He was trying to apologize; I told him to get out. When he didn't, I said some things I shouldn't have. I don't think he took it well."

She nodded, understanding. "And today he didn't turn up?"

"No."

"He didn't text or call to let you know?"

"No." It took me a moment to organize my thoughts. "It's not like him. I just want to know nothing bad happened to him. That's all."

"Ok. Give me a minute. I'll speak to him."

I nodded.

"Call you right back."

She was gone for what felt like an eternity. And I found myself pacing while I tapped the phone against my fingers. Thinking of what I'd said. How I'd dug up something that had nothing to do with why I was angry because I wanted to draw blood. The daggers I'd thrown and now couldn't take back.

After thirty-five minutes she finally called back. "Sorry it took me so long. He wasn't picking up his mobile. I had to call the hotel."

"And?" My anxiety was making me impatient. The details seeming superfluous, irrelevant, and irritating.

"He's taken some of his meds and is not feeling well. That's why he doesn't like taking them."

"His meds?"

"Antidepressants. They make him nauseous, give him a headache, and he can't sleep, especially when he starts taking them."

"Antidepressants?" The word echoed inside my body like a pinball.

"Yes. He was prescribed some last year."

The stones in my stomach dropped to the floor. I sat down.

"He said he'll try to come tomorrow if he's feeling better."

I nodded.

"What did you say to him, flower?"

I scratched my forehead. Repeating it made it twice as bad. "That we would never get back together..." She waited, knowing there was more. "And that I would never date someone like him."

"*Someone like him*?"

This was uncomfortable. Death by a thousand papercuts. "A fuck-up. A mistake."

"Oh." That's all she said. In a deep, low tone that gave it the hammer of a judge's final sentence.

"You're making me feel worse, Lu."

"You know what that means to him. You know it will sting twice as bad because it came from you—someone he shared his history, his feelings with."

I pressed two fingers deep into my eye sockets. "I know. I was angry."

"Why? What did he do?"

"Nothing." I fidgeted in my seat. "I kissed him."

Her eyebrows shot up. "You kissed him?" Then she smiled. "How was it?"

"Lu!"

She tried to hide her smile, recompose her face. "So let me get this straight… You kissed him, he tried to apologize to you, you argued with him, and told him he was a mistake of a human being?"

I looked up at the ceiling. "I didn't tell him. I shouted it at his face. Even Amber cried."

"Ouch." Her face was serious this time.

"Not helping, Lu."

"I don't know what to say, flower."

"That'd be a first."

"What are you going to do now?"

"I don't know. Hope he doesn't bring it up?"

"It might take him a few days to get over the meds. You might not see him for a day or two. Last time he was on them, he was ill for two weeks when he started taking them."

A feeling of numbness swept through my body. "Ok. Well… I'm glad nothing bad happened. I need to go sort Amber out. I'll keep you posted."

Lu was right. For the next two days we didn't see him, but he texted to say he wasn't coming. The words short, factual, and distant. The gap in the schedule letting me know just how much of a routine his visits had become, and how used I had gotten to seeing him on the daily.

On the fourth day, he turned up. Looking green, as if he was hungover. His beard was longer, clothes not arranged in his normal style. He didn't speak to me, just to Amber, with words I didn't really understand. His gestures, and even his voice, drained of energy. A presence that felt hollow as though his body was here, but his mind wasn't.

By the end of the week, he started to look better but whizzed in and out of the flat like a ghost of himself. If the meds were meant to help, I'm not sure they were working. He behaved like he was numb to everything.

"I can't take this anymore," I said one morning, sitting on the sofa while he held Amber by the window.

He didn't respond.

"This is not you. I don't know what these meds are doing, but this… it's not you."

He looked at me then. His eyes hooded, tired, glassed over. "Isn't it the point? *Not* to *be* me."

"What is that supposed to mean?"

He scoffed, his lips stretching in a smile that showed no joy. His gaze returned to Amber.

"I don't like this."

"You don't like *me* either." His tone was neutral, matter of fact, but the words felt like acid scorching my conscience.

"Look… I'm sorry for what I said." His head turned back to me, eyes on the floor. "I was angry with myself, not you, and I took it out on you. You were right, it wasn't fair. This time you actually did the right thing. And I did give you mixed messages." The apology gushed out of my mouth, loud and forceful, in a flood of words seeking redemption. "I don't like seeing you like this. This is not you." The last sentence was whispered, carrying the disconcert I was feeling.

He took a deep breath, sighed. "I know. This is why I don't like taking the meds. They curb the anxiety, but they also numb everything else. Even when the side effects settle down, my head still feels like it's in cotton wool." He picked up Amber's rocking chair and brought it over to the middle of the living room.

"Do you *have* to take them? Is there something else you can take?" I asked as he kneeled down to place the baby in her chair.

"Depends on who you ask." His voice was devoid of any emotion. Glassed over just like his eyes. This was the first conversation we'd had in a week, and it was like speaking to a stranger.

"I'm asking *you*."

"It calms my thoughts. But it takes weeks to really work. It gets worse before it gets better."

"By better do you mean back to your old self?"

A headshake.

The thought of him permanently in this shadow state upset me, my stomach turning to ice, the guilt tightening the noose around my throat.

"How do you know it gets better?" My voice was small, weak.

"I took it for a big part of last year."

"Why did you stop?"

He started playing with the baby's feet. "I couldn't focus. It was interfering with my work. They wanted to change it to something else, but I just wanted to go back to work. Working is the one thing I'm good at. The one thing I have."

"Who is 'they'?"

"Dr. Fernandes."

"Who's that?"

"My therapist."

He stared at Amber, one of his thumbs rubbing back and forth on her little knee.

"Did you take them because of me? Because of what I said?" It almost didn't make it out of my throat. Rasping, loaded, half whisper, half guilt.

For a moment he was quiet. "There is a lot going on in my head, Paige. Things I need to resolve, decisions I need to make, things I need to come to terms with, things I need to get over. And the clock is ticking, you know. I'm running out of time. My thoughts started to spin, and I didn't want to go down a rabbit hole."

Another long stretch of silence. He seemed to stare at Amber without really seeing her.

"I've already regretted taking them. I only have another

two weeks before I go home. I don't want to spend them like this—feeling like a zombie. But I'm not sure what will be worse, taking them or coming off them."

"What are you going to do then?"

"I want to stop taking them. But it will make me feel rough as a cob. I will probably lose the next two weeks anyway."

"Should you really be doing it like that? Don't you need to taper it off or something?"

"I'm going now."

This was one of the changes in his behavior. Before, I had to kick him out of the door. Now, he wanted to leave fifteen to thirty minutes earlier.

Celo leaned down to kiss Amber. *"Até amanhã,* Coffee Bean." And without any further comments or goodbyes, he took himself to the hallway. I followed.

"Are you going to be ok?"

"Peachy," he answered, without looking at me, voice in monotone, as he zipped his boots and grabbed his coat.

His disassociated state broke something in me. He was like this, and he was on his own for most of the day. When it had been me feeling low, and nowhere near as low as this, he had tried his best to get me out of the house, to move, to get some fresh air. And I couldn't take it. I walked to him and hugged him—tight, long. He didn't hug me back.

Left on her own in the sitting room, Amber started crying. She did that whenever she felt she was being forgotten or left behind. Must be some cave baby instinct to ensure survival or something.

I let go of him.

He nodded, once, head and eyelids heavy, the door opening before his coat was on.

CHAPTER 21

Paige

Saturday came and Marcelo didn't turn up.

"Is everything ok with him? He has been here every day at 10am like a Swiss clock, no?" Apparently, even my mother had gotten used to his daily visits.

"Yeah. Do you mind looking after Amber for a minute? I'm going to check he's ok."

"How are you going to do that?"

"I know where he's staying."

"Are you sure you want to go over there? What if you come across something you don't want to see?" I could see what she was thinking. It was Saturday morning. Maybe he went out last night, maybe he's with someone.

"I don't think it's that, Mum. I think he's not well."

I handed Amber to her; she followed me to the hall.

"If I need to stay for a little while, would you be able to look after her for me? There are bottles ready in the fridge."

"Of course. But are you sure you want to go over there? Won't this give him mixed messages?"

I straightened up after pulling my boots on. "Mum, when I wasn't feeling a hundred per cent, he was here. Annoying the crap out of me to go for walks and get out of the house. He didn't let me wallow in my own misery even though I was being a bitch to him. If something is wrong, he has no family here apart from a two-month-old baby. There is no one here to check on him and make sure he's ok. I'm still mad at him, but I'm not going to let him wallow if he's not well."

She nodded.

"I'll text you when I know what I'm dealing with."

The first and second knocks went unanswered. The third one was a police knock—closed fist giving the door a good battering. A neighbor's head or two peering into the corridor to see what was happening. Mid second obnoxious knock, the door burst open.

Celo was in his boxers, no top, bare feet, messy hair. He shielded his eyes from the light coming from the corridor, the room behind him in semi-darkness. Without a word, he turned, crossed the expanse of the room, and disappeared into an opening on the opposite wall.

I let my eyes adjust before I closed the door fully. The flat was open-plan—sitting room with a sofa, armchair, and coffee table to my right; kitchen with a small dining table to my left. All the blackout blinds were closed, the slivers of light coming through the bottom and sides of them painting incomplete rectangles on the wall. I dropped my coat on the arm of the sofa as I stepped in and followed him into the flat's inner sanctum.

Lines of thin light escaped the blinds to my right. I had to wait another minute before my eyes could take in the rest of the room—a hand dragging along the wall, tripping over the stuff he had all over the floor.

Celo was lying on the bed face down. The scene was familiar. I had found him like this in his house, after the fight with Felipe.

I took a seat next to him. "Celo?" The skin on his shoulder felt clammy. "Why are all the blinds shut?"

"I have a migraine." His voice had the raspiness of someone who had not spoken for a while.

"Have you taken anything for it?"

He shook his head, but the movement was wrong—too short, too minimal, too tired for someone who had had a lie-in.

I remembered his antidepressants. "Can you take painkillers with your meds?"

"I stopped taking them."

That made me pause. After his last visit I had googled the side effects of antidepressants and what would happen if he stopped taking them. I tried to remember what I'd found. The list wasn't short: dizziness, vertigo, headaches, nausea, cold sweats, fatigue, and a worsening of anxiety or depression were the ones I could remember.

"Does your doctor know you stopped?"

His eyelids closed in an exaggerated blink, as if he was too exhausted to nod.

"Did he agree to you doing it?"

His hand moved sideways twice, coming and returning, the bed sheets making a rasping sound under his palm. And I realized he was trying to keep his head still.

This wasn't good. He was withdrawing. "Do you have any painkillers for the headache?"

More rasping.

"Can the concierge not bring you some?"

"There is a pharmacy downstairs in the shopping arcade."

"Why didn't you get some?"

"I feel dizzy. Everything is spinning."

I didn't really know what to do. I had felt low after having Amber, but nothing like this. I had never taken meds that made me this ill either. But I knew one thing: sitting alone in the dark wasn't going to make him feel any better.

"Celo…" I caressed his head. "You're covered in this weird sweat, maybe taking a shower will make you feel better? Do you think you could shower while I go downstairs to get you some paracetamol?"

"Why are you here, Paige? You don't have to babysit me.

This is not your problem." He sounded irritated, as if I was getting in his way.

"Yeah. I say I'm fine too, then I go and do something dumb." I quoted his words.

His smile came with a scoff and no teeth. "You and your quotes, Lewis." But he started to get himself up and sat at the edge of the bed—elbows leaning on his knees, head lowered, hair covering his face. Breathing like he was trying to curb dizziness and nausea.

"This is incredibly sexy, isn't it? Ain't you glad I'm the father of your baby?" His voice was disdainful, bitter.

"Come on. Let's get you in the shower. Can you stand up?"

His head looked away from me when he nodded. It took him a minute before he stood up. He took two steps and swayed. I grabbed his arm to steady him.

"I can do it my damn self." He pulled his arm away from me, swaying even more. He had never spoken to me in this tone. It took me a second to remember mood swings were also part of the withdrawal symptoms. On the videos I had watched, a lot of people mentioned they felt constantly angry.

He stumbled through the door to the bathroom, squinted at the light coming through the window.

"If you're still feeling dizzy, maybe it's better you sit down rather than stand up. Are you ok to undress on your own?"

"Why? Are you gonna help me?" He was being sarcastic. "Tsk, tsk, tsk." His index finger moved from side to side in front of his face. "You're not allowed to see me naked, Lewis."

"Sorry to break it to you, but I've already seen you naked. Are you going to be ok in the shower? If you are, I'm going to go downstairs and get you some painkillers."

"Peachy," he said but he didn't sound or look like it.

"Don't go falling and cracking your head open."

"That's not a bad idea."

"Don't joke about that. Where is your key to the door?"

"Kitchen table, I think." The words were mumbled rather than spoken.

On the small table, he had left his laptop, phone, keys, and two baby books. Several pages had their corners folded. The second book made me laugh—*The New Dad's Survival Guide: What to expect in the first year and beyond.* At least he was right about one thing: it was survival alright.

By the time I came back with painkillers and a bottle of water, he was sitting under the shower, still in his boxers, arms resting on his knees, head bowed.

"Hey, you ok in there?" I stood in the open doorway.

No response.

I walked in, switched the water off. "You ok?"

"Does it look like I'm ok?" Voice sour, sarcastic, but his head didn't raise.

Trying to decide what to do, I walked back into the bedroom. He needed to take the painkillers, and I needed to get him out of the shower, but he would get me soaked. With a lack of any other ideas, I stripped out of my boots, jumper, and jeans, then stepped back into the bathroom in my underwear and T-shirt.

"Celo, you need to take these." I pushed the paracetamol tablets into one of his hands.

"Great. Now, it's a party." Still with the sarcasm.

"Just take them."

He shoved the tablets in his mouth, his hand reaching out for the bottle of water. I handed it to him.

"You're going to stand up and turn around. Hold on to the wall, ok?"

"Just go away, Paige. Leave me alone." His words were unfriendly but labored by nausea; his eyes were shut.

"Nice try. Get up." We struggled to our feet. His body was heavy, using mine for support. "You're still in your boxers, and you're all sticky. So, you're going to turn around and hold on to the wall, and I'm going to take them off and help you, ok?"

"Are you going to ask me to pick up the soap as well?" he muttered, eyes still shut.

"Funny. Turn around. Hands on the wall." I pushed his shoulder so he would turn.

"Is this some weird police officer kinky shit? Because I'm really not feeling up for it," he grumbled into his chest, forehead rather than his hands on the wall.

"Sorry to disappoint you, but Lu does this too. When she's uncomfortable, she starts being crass to make me blush and drop it. So this doesn't work with me anymore."

Saying that was a mistake, because he upped the ante.

"She can only make you blush. But I can kiss every centimeter of your skin, fuck you deep and slow, and make you come until your whole body is trembling."

I didn't know if it was his low tone, the way he said it—matter of fact, like a promise—or the fact we were both semi-naked in the shower, but a ghost of something touched the back of my neck.

"Lost for wise words, Lewis?"

"Don't be a prick. I'm trying to help you."

"I didn't ask for your help."

"I didn't ask for yours either, but here we are."

His boxers were soaked and sticking to his skin, hard to remove without using my full palms to push them down.

"Definitely a police kink," he mumbled.

"Oh do shut up." I turned the shower back on and was grateful I had chosen to strip off most of my clothes, because the spray hit him and cascaded down to me. "Lean your head back, I'm going to wash your hair."

At first he didn't do it, but as I rubbed on his head, he slowly leaned backward.

"What part of 'I have a migraine' don't you understand? Stop pulling my hair. It hurts."

"What? You're not enjoying my fetish?" This time I was the one being sarcastic.

He let me rinse his hair without complaining. His head stayed facing upwards, eyes continued to be shut.

"I'm going to soap you, ok? We need to get this weird sweat off your skin."

"Is that what you're calling it? Cause it feels distinctly like you're just feeling me up."

"You wish," I said, rubbing soap down his back.

"I do. You're rubbing the wrong end. A little lower and around the front would be nicer."

"You're asking the wrong person. You should ask Angela," I snapped back, growing annoyed by his obnoxious mood.

His head moved to facing forward.

My hands stopped moving.

He turned around. Hooded, heavy eyes stared me down. "You don't wanna talk about it, but you're more than happy to throw it back at my face, huh?"

I didn't respond. We stared at each other. He was irritated by my words, and I by his foul mood.

"Thanks for the help, but I got it from here. It'd be best if you leave." His tone took a distance and formality he hadn't used the whole time he'd been here.

I didn't move.

He kept his stare, his breathing still that of a person who was feeling nauseated, body swaying a little. "Go, Paige." A hand sent me away.

I stepped out of the shower and walked into the bedroom. Took me a minute to find the switch to turn the lights on. The water ran for another fifteen minutes, while I found a towel, dried myself, put my dry clothes back on, and walked back into the bathroom to wring my tee in the sink.

He didn't seem to do much in there, but eventually he came out. The paracetamol must have kicked in because he looked steadier on his feet. He stood in the doorway to the bedroom, completely naked, squinting at the bright ceiling lights. It was hard not to stare, while he walked to the switch and hammer fisted the lights off. The natural light from the bathroom prevented the room from being in total darkness, our eyes taking a minute to adjust before he walked to me and grabbed the towel out of my hands.

"Why are you still here?" He dried his hair, his body, and rummaged in the chest of drawers. His movements still off, tired, a little uncoordinated.

"Do you feel better after your shower?"

His hands stilled, his head turning sideways toward me. He was quiet for a moment.

"Some," he said, putting a pair of boxers and joggers on, clearly deciding not to continue the argument. Then he walked to the bed and lay back down—face turned away from me.

"Move over a bit."

He did, and I sat down next to him, back propped by the headboard. For a while neither of us talked, the silence diffusing the tension. Both of us more comfortable with the quiet than speaking.

"You don't have to stay here, Paige. Go home."

I lay down, facing him. Tapped his shoulder with my nail until his head turned to me. "Sorry. No can do."

He looked at me for a moment. "Your mom has Amber?" He never called her by her name.

"Yeah."

"Does she have enough milk?"

"I will have to go back at some point." I thought for a minute. "When you feel better, you should come back with me."

"I don't think that's a good idea. I'm not good company."

"I wasn't asking."

I heard him smile. "Bossy."

Another long spell of silence. "We didn't really know much about each other, did we? You didn't know about all this." He waved a hand toward his body. "I didn't know your name was Paige Marie, that you were from Manchester, or that you drive."

"We didn't have much time. Knowing someone takes time."

A nod. "I have never done this, you know."

"This what?"

"Have a woman in my room, in my shower, in my bed, that I wasn't sleeping with. There's a first for everything. Ironic." He mumbled, then snorted and moved to lie on his back staring at the ceiling.

The statement hit a nerve. I couldn't figure out if he was being thoughtless or still trying to push my buttons in the haze of his mood swing. "What is ironic?"

"That that woman is you. The one I want the most." He said it as a matter of fact. No flirting, no eye contact once or ever, hands resting on top of each other, staring at the ceiling like he was deep in thought.

He didn't have to take the meds. He didn't have to be here. He could've gone home, ran like I did. Maybe I wasn't good for him either. "Also the one that drives you to antidepressants, huh?"

His smile came with a snort. "Ironic."

"But you're still here when you could go home."

He nodded.

"Why?"

"Would everyone just quit telling me to leave already? I'm not leaving. I'm not giving up on my family. My daughter is not growing up without a father, even if we never see eye-to-eye again."

I had to give him some respect. For all my anger and upset, he was trying to do the right thing by our daughter and by me, even when that cost him dearly.

"Funny how in the last three weeks we have learned more about each other than the three months back home." Celo turned on his side, head lying on his arm. "Why are you here, Paige? Doing all this. Sitting in the dark with me. I'm sure you have better things to do."

I wiggled myself closer. "Because you were there for me when I wasn't in a good place. Dragging me out of the house, calling Lu. So unfortunately for you, you're stuck with me."

"You're gonna regret saying that when I find a way to be ill every week."

His phone started ringing in the other room. He didn't move. It rang again. Still no movement.

"Should I get that for you?"

"Knock yourself out."

CHAPTER 22
Marcelo

I STILL FELT HUNGOVER, BUT AT LEAST MY HEAD HAD STOPPED throbbing like a woodpecker was trying to make a nest in it.

"Hi Risa." I could hear Paige on the phone in the lounge. "Yeah. No, everything is fine." A gap. "He stopped taking the meds… Yes, I know about them… No, the doctor didn't agree… I know, I didn't think he could stop them cold turkey either… He had a migraine when I got here. Said he felt dizzy, looked nauseous, was all sweaty. But he had a shower, took some painkillers, and drank some water. He seems a little better, is talking more… Yeah, I'm going to make him have some food, don't worry… I'm sure he wants to talk to you, but he's still lying down in the dark. I'll ask him to call back once he's up… No problem, Risa. I'll keep an eye on him, yeah. Don't worry… Ok. Ok. Bye."

She stayed in the lounge for a beat. Then came back and lay next to me where she'd been before.

"Risa wants you to eat something."

"She *always* wants me to eat."

"How is your head?"

"Better."

"Mum is making lasagna. It's already going dark outside. Why don't you come back with me?"

I still felt off. But staying closer to her was better than staying here soaking in misery. So I nodded.

"Can you take a little light?"

"Sure, but you'll have to ignore the mess in the room."

She reached over and put the side lamp on, then turned around and lay back down where she was. My eyes stung with the brightness, watering and blinking on repeat. But for the first time since she got here, I could actually see her face properly. For a minute, we lay there. Not saying anything, just looking at each other. Her presence making me calmer, silencing my thoughts. It made me think of the day I left the hospital after the fight with Felipe. She had hugged me and stayed with me in silence. Like now. No words, no need for thinking. Her skin, dusted with faint freckles. Green eyes as hypnotic as ever.

"If I'm coming with you, I'd better get dressed. I don't think your mom will appreciate me turning up topless."

"Again." She smiled.

She continued lying down while I got changed, her eyes watching my every move. She wasn't mine. Might never be. But she was here. And for today, that was enough.

I hadn't realized how much time had passed. When we stepped outside, the evening was well and truly on its way. And as soon as we stepped into her flat, I could smell the food. I was still nauseous, but my stomach growled. Happy to have something after a day of nothing.

Paige went straight to Coffee Bean. "Hey, Poppet." Her tiny face lit up. She was happy to get some food too. "That smells amazing, Mum. I'm so hungry."

"It will be ready in a minute."

I hovered by the door, not quite sure what to do. I had never been here at this hour.

"I'm glad to see you're feeling better, Marcelo."

I nodded.

"Do I have time to feed Amber?"

Shit.

"Yeah. It will be nuclear hot when it comes out anyway, so we can let it cool for a second."

"Great. I will be back in a bit." She turned to me. One nod, a question. I nodded back, an answer. And she disappeared into the hallway with Coffee Bean.

A blessing that. Even though the meds normally knocked everything right out of me, I still wouldn't know what to do with myself if she decided to breastfeed in front of me. After the first time I'd seen it, I'd avoided it like the plague, worried it would make me feel the same again.

"Would you like a coffee, Marcelo?"

"Just water, please."

"Don't stand there. Take a seat." Kate waved toward the table she had set, including a place for me. "Paige tells me you have suffered with a migraine for most of the day today."

I wished it was only a migraine. I didn't want to explain, so I just nodded. Her voice was still a little off, but at least she was being friendly.

"I get those sometimes too. Debilitating. I hope you like lasagna."

"Smells great."

Dinner was uneventful. Kate reminisced about Paige's dance competitions when she was little. Both of them the most approachable I had seen them since I got here, but I felt detached, out of my body, like things weren't happening right in front of me but at a distance. As if my consciousness was floating above me, watching my life like a spectator waiting to be entertained.

I bathed Coffee Bean, under Paige's watchful guidance, and she gave me a bottle to give her her last feed. And the irony wasn't lost on me. The two things I wanted most were to have my two girls back with me. To be Coffee Bean's father—a real dad, properly involved in looking after her—and to have Paige by my side, sharing a bed with me. Now, when everything felt so hopeless, that was exactly what I got. For one day at least. I honestly couldn't figure out if it was a kindness or the ultimate torture.

My mind was at war with itself. Blaming me for the mess I was in; angry at life for the cruelty of dangling what I wanted most right in front of my nose then shutting the door in my face. Feeling better being here with them; wanting to leave because I couldn't stand to look at what I was losing. Glad to have come; angry at the impotence of not being able to change anything. Feeling utterly alone, when I was with the woman I loved and my baby. Hopeless, even though everyone was being nice. Marveling at how catastrophically I had fucked myself over; despairing at how screwed I was.

"Are you feeling better?" Paige asked midway through setting up the sofa with a duvet and pillows for me.

"Some. Paige, I don't have to stay here. I'm only down the street. This is really not necessary."

"I'm still not asking."

"Good night, guys." Kate appeared in the doorway.

"Night, Mum."

"Night, Kate. Thanks for dinner. And for letting me stay."

She nodded, her eyes hopping between me and Paige before she vanished down the hall.

"I don't think your mom likes that I'm here."

"She's fine. I spoke to her."

"Paige, really, I'm not comfortable with this. I'm going back to the hotel."

She stopped fluffing the pillows. Picked on one of the corners for a beat. "Would you feel better if you stayed in my room?"

"I wouldn't make you sleep on the sofa."

"I wasn't planning on it." My face must have looked surprised, because she added, "Don't worry. I won't make a move on you. We can put Amber in the middle of the bed for your protection."

At that I had to laugh. "You already putting our daughter to work, earning her keep?"

"She's not as good a bodyguard as she's a magnet. It might not work in your favor."

I probably should've said no. She had been very clear that there would be no turning back from where we were, and she was probably only doing this out of some twisted sense of guilt. But I found myself nodding and agreeing. Torture or kindness, if one night of getting the two things I wanted was all the cards I had left, then I was playing my hand.

She grabbed the pillows, I grabbed the duvet, and we headed to her room. Coffee Bean was already asleep in her cot. Standing by it, I watched her breathing. The sleep of the innocent—peaceful, deep. My fingers ran over her little head.

"You're out of luck. Your bodyguard has clocked out for the night."

"Sleeping on the job already. We're gonna have to talk about this in the morning."

Paige smiled, then picked something from one of the drawers and walked out of the room. When she came back, she had different clothes on—shorts and T-shirt—and a couple of glasses of water.

She picked the side closest to the cot, placed one glass at each of the bedside tables, and got herself under the duvet.

"You gonna stand in the corner all night?" she called back to me, head already on the pillow.

I stripped to my sweatpants and lay opposite her, facing each other like we had done in my hotel room.

"Are you sure you want me here?"

"You'd have done the same for me."

After a moment, she switched the light off, my vision taking a second to adjust. And I watched her. I watched her watch me. I watched her eyelids get heavy, then close. I watched her breathe deep, peaceful. And I couldn't sleep, my brain keeping me awake. But even if I could, I didn't want to close my eyes on this—the life I could've had. The family that was supposed to be mine. The gifts I had lost in one moment of stupidity. A normal person would have lain here and cried. But I felt so sunk, so numb, I did nothing.

When it started to get light, I got up, got dressed, and showed myself out.

♥♥♥

After lying in bed staring at the ceiling for hours, I called Marisa.

"Finally! Are you trying to give me a heart attack?"

"Sorry, Risa."

"Risa?" Her head dipped to the side. "I like my other name better."

She meant Mom. I smiled at her but didn't answer. The smile feeling like a performance that took some effort.

"What is going on, son? How are you feeling?"

She wasn't asking about my migraine. I thought for a minute, wondering if I should lie or tell her the truth, but I've never been a good liar, and Marisa knew me like the palm of her hand. Truth it was.

I took a deep breath. "Angry… empty."

She tried to keep her face still, but her frown and eyes showed her worry. Her pity bugging me.

"Why did you stop taking the meds?"

"I hate how they make me feel."

"Why did you start taking them?"

"I panicked. Thought I had started to spiral."

"Why? Did anything happen?" Her voice was gentle, but she was trying to get to the bottom of it.

"Paige doesn't want anything to do with me."

Both her eyebrows raised, surprised. "Wasn't she there yesterday?"

"Probably out of guilt."

"I'm so sorry, son." She went quiet for a moment. "Did you speak to Dr. Fernandes?"

"Tomorrow."

Her concern was making me mad. I don't know why, there was no reason for it to, but it did anyway. I rubbed a hand back and forth over my face. Cracked my neck trying to disperse the energy.

"So what is your plan? Are you going to stay there?"

"Yes. I'm not leaving. I don't know how many times I have to say this. I'd appreciate if people would quit telling me to leave." I snapped at her. And realizing the sharpness of my tongue, instantly regretted it. "Sorry, Risa. I didn't mean to snap at you." Another deep breath, roll of the shoulders. "I was going to ask her to come back to Brazil with me, even if just for a while, but there isn't much point now. I'm pretty sure she won't come. So I need to prepare to move here."

"What? Why?"

"Because I have a daughter, Risa. Isn't it obvious? My daughter is not growing up without me. I know everyone wants me to disappear out of her life, but I'm not doing it. I'm not my mother." Another sharp snap. I was starting to sound like a cornered dog, growling and showing my teeth.

"I never said you were, son." Her voice was soft, trying to pacify me.

This was going from bad to worse. "I'm sorry, Risa. I didn't mean…"

"I know." She waited. "If you feel you need to be there for your daughter, then you should do that. I was just wondering how you're going to do that with a new bar opening, Eight in full swing, and everything you have here."

"I don't know. I still need to figure it out." My patience was standing on thin ice. "Risa, I need to get off the phone. I need to go see Amber."

"Ok..." She sounded uncertain, concerned, the tone making me even more mad. "Call me later?"

I nodded. Even though I had no intention of doing it.

"Celo, I know you. I know you say you'll call, then you don't when you're like this. But you'll call me, you hear?"

I smiled at her, full of sarcasm.

"Marcelo Rissi Costa, I don't care how you're feeling, you *do not* give me that attitude."

"Sure, Risa. I will call. Why not?" I conceded. It wasn't her fault I felt like my bottom had dropped off. It was nobody's fault but my own. All of it.

CHAPTER 23

Paige

"Marcelo has left already?" Mum asked as she came into the kitchen.

"Yeah… I think he left first thing in the morning. I didn't see him go." I didn't mean it to, but my voice sounded disappointed.

"He'll probably be back at ten. Anyway… I actually have something to tell you. Well… to ask you."

That got my attention.

She placed two slices of bread in the toaster. "Ryan has asked if we can go over to visit in the next few weeks. He wants me to have a look at a big project he's building, and he's looking for a designer to consult."

"He finally found an excuse to get you over there then, huh?" I smiled at her.

"It's not like that."

"Sure it isn't."

"Anyway, I was thinking that you, Amber, and I could go. Ryan is desperate to spend some time with you and the baby while she's still little."

"Just me and the baby, right?" I giggled.

The toaster popped, a cupboard door clicked open, the ceramic of a plate chimed against the worktop, the butter dish top clinked as she removed it from its home.

"He wants to catch up on some lost time or something," she

continued, as if she hadn't heard me. "So? What do you think? Should we go?"

I smiled at her. "Of course, Mum. It'll be nice to see everyone."

"Oh!" She seemed to be taken aback. "That was easier than I thought."

"Who am I to stand on the way of love?" I dramatized.

"Stop it." Her butter knife was pointed at me, but she was smiling.

♥♥♥

At ten, Celo came over. He seemed tired and was recovering from a bad night, but the weather was better, so we went for a walk, had lunch in one of the cafés.

Over the next few visits we fell into a rhythm. He came at ten, then again at two. His side effects appeared to clear a little every day, but his mood still volatile, shifting from calm to white anger and frustration with the most mundane things in the blink of an eye. He tried to keep it under wraps, apologized when it spilled over. We found interesting places to visit, went for lunches together, had tea with Siobhan regularly. And although we never talked about the kiss, or the night in my room, or the day in his, things seemed to have shifted.

Days came and went, we co-parented, took Amber to doctors' appointments; we were good together. It actually gave me pleasure watching him with our baby, all his doting and devotion even though he wasn't fully himself.

We developed this weird friendship—too close, too charged, with too much history to be friends; not close enough to be more. It was pleasant but, if I'm honest, it left me wanting. I could see glimpses of us, of what we could be. Sometimes he would look at me for that little bit too long, make a loaded comment, or touch me in the middle of a conversation and my whole body would sizzle. But he kept his distance from me. Didn't cross the line, didn't try to fix things. It was like he'd given up trying.

Days passed before he was something close to his old self, but he was subdued, and the countdown had started for when he had to go home. As his last day approached, an undercurrent of sadness seemed to run underneath everything. Every gesture taking an extra meaning, tainted by a level of desperation.

He was more pensive, quieter, showing a degree of introversion that was too much even for him. He held and kissed Amber for long stretches of time. Caressing her face, talking to her. The whole thing taking the finality of someone who was on death row and knew the execution day was coming.

Five weeks ago, I didn't want him here and would have enjoyed knowing he was leaving. Now, I wasn't so sure.

On the penultimate day, I found myself going through the photos we had taken when Lu was here. She had shared them all in a group she'd labeled 'Fantastic Five'. She and Gabe kissing under Big Ben; Marcelo smiling and carrying Amber like a kangaroo; Gabe next to the mounted guard; Gabe being bitten by one of the guard horses; Marcelo, Amber, and I standing at a respectable distance from the mounted guard. Gabe carrying Amber; the Westminster Bridge penises with Big Ben in the background; views from the river bus; Marcelo and Gabe standing outside our old uni. The heart bunting at Greenwich Market; Lu and Gabe smiling at each other over the Greenwich Meridian. Marcelo and I looking at each other, standing toe to toe over the same line.

It wasn't the photo Lu had shown me on the day, but if one picture symbolized where we were, it was this one. Celo and I face to face, standing to either side of a line, something else keeping us close together. Tied by an invisible force, neither of us able to walk away or let go.

When I raised my head, the first thing I saw was the teddy bear at the corner of Amber's cot. The one Celo had given her. Over the last five weeks he'd literally thrown himself on the floor so we could walk over him. Silently helping me when I needed without me having to ask. Looking after me even when I treated him with distance and distaste. Staying near, holding on to us with everything he had, even when it cost him his mind.

I walked to the chest of drawers, opened one, and dug through the million baby clothes to find the boxes. I hadn't looked at them since he had given me the second one. Couldn't bear to look at what was inside the big one ever since I'd left Brazil.

I opened it. Memories coming back to me. Different memories. After I left, whenever I looked at this box, all I saw was him with Angela. But today, what I saw was him smiling at me. Our conversations in the pool in Ilhabela. *Are you ok back there?* He had squeezed my hand and looked back at me the first time I rode on his bike. How he looked at me like I was the most beautiful thing he'd ever seen. Lying in bed, laughing, whispering, his hand caressing my hair, my face, lips exploring every inch of my skin. His arms always around me tight. Laughing while we danced *sertanejo.* The way he put his forehead to mine every time he couldn't express his feelings in words. Sleeping with his face on my neck, arms wrapped around me as if I was a tank of oxygen. His respect for my anger when I used my drunkenness and upset to enjoy his comfort and affection without granting him forgiveness.

After the things I'd said, he had stopped trying. But he was still here. Still turning up every day. Silent, but constant even when he wasn't well and his mind had pulled him under water.

I picked the bracelet up from the box, opened the latch, added the baby pram charm to its siblings. Each one of them telling a story. *One for every place you'll find me—a cocktail for what I do, the São Paulo charm for my city, a diamanté snake for where I live,* he had told me when he wrapped it around my wrist. And now, one for the new life we'd brought into being.

If there was nothing left, then why did his absence for a few days leave such an empty space in my day? If everything was truly over, why couldn't I let go of this piece of silver? Why couldn't I let go of him, of the memories? If we weren't meant to be, then why did him leaving feel like a death sentence? If it was so wrong to forgive him, if I shouldn't forgive him, then why did I feel like he was in my blood?

♥♥♥

"I need to ask you something," he blurted out during his visit on the last day. Amber was in her play gym; I was sitting in my regular chair.

"Ok… sounds ominous." Suspicion made me cautious.

"Can you promise me you'll think about it?" There was a level of desperation to his voice.

"I don't know what it is yet."

"Just promise me you'll keep an open mind, ok? I wasn't going to ask, but I can't leave without asking."

"Ok…"

"I've decided to come and live here." I started to speak, but he waved me off. "Please, just hear me out."

He moved to kneel next to my chair, one hand on each arm, caging me in.

"I want to be here because I want to be present when Amber is growing up. I have, at most, eighteen years before she's doing her own thing or even moves away for college like we both did. And I don't want to miss it. She is growing so fast, you know? Since I've been here, she's learned to smile, she laughs, she's started to recognize people. I don't want to miss when she has her first tooth, or walks. But it's going to take me a little while to get things organized back home. I need to clear the house and find someone to run the business for me—both of them, it's not a straightforward thing. I have to look after all the people that work for me. I also need to sort a visa to stay here, register Amber's birth in Brazil so I can make her my next of kin; and I would like to introduce her to Risa, Rô, and Freddie before I come back here permanently. So, I wanted to ask you, if you would be willing to come to Brazil for a while, just while I get things organized. You won't have to do a thing, bring a thing. I will sort and pay for everything. I know it's a lot to ask. But I won't be able to come back here for a while, and by then she'll be a different baby. I don't want to miss anything. You don't have to answer straight away, but please think about it, ok?"

He stared at me. On his knees, heart on his sleeve, face anxious, eyes hinting at the panic he was feeling knowing he had to leave.

"I can't," I responded too quickly. "I can't go back to Brazil."

"You didn't even think about it."

"My exit was a tad… dramatic. You made a fool out of me in front of everyone. It would be beyond embarrassing to come back with my tail in between my legs like I didn't learn my lesson." My voice dropped to a whisper, and I couldn't look at him as I said it.

He sighed, head dropping. "Nobody thinks that of you, Paige. If anything, they think I'm the idiot." He was fighting my argument but already sounded defeated.

"I can't either way. Ryan asked Mum to come over to the States for a couple of weeks. He wants to see Amber too. I was thinking of staying over there for a little while."

Celo let go of my chair and got to his feet, eyes fixed on the fireplace. He rubbed a hand down his face, itched his neck, and looked at Amber, his jaw muscle clenching tight under skin.

"So you decided to go to Denver." He was upset, but his tone had an undercurrent of anger. His mood was still swinging.

"I'm not moving there permanently, but we would be there for a month or more. I don't know yet. Maybe you could come to visit."

"This means she will be five or six months old next time I see her."

"I know. But we have video call. And we could organize a couple of visits? I'm sure we can work something out."

He nodded, but his eyes dropped.

I stood up. "Hey, I'm not trying to keep her from you. I have no intention of doing that. It's just that my dad asked, you were going home—I didn't know when you would be back. So I figured that there wouldn't be any harm, you know? And I honestly thought that if I'm in America, at least we're on the same side of the pond. I'm sure we can figure something out."

Another nod, a quick raise of his eyebrows. "I have to go. I need to pack." He moved toward the hall. I followed.

"Are you mad at me?"

"I'm not mad at you. I'm mad at myself," he said as he put on his high tops.

"You wanna talk about it?"

"What is there to talk about? You've already decided you're taking our kid to Denver for a month or more." He snatched his coat from the peg.

"I thought I was making things easier for us."

His temper boiled to the surface, his voice raised. "No, Paige. You're making it easier for you, but you didn't think about me when you made your decision. You didn't even ask me if I mind you taking my kid to another fucking country. But what rights do I have, right? Who the fuck am I to have a say on where my kid goes? I suppose, I should count myself lucky I even know I have one."

And with that he was gone.

Three hours. For three hours I sat with what he'd said and the million other questions that had been floating in my mind like icebergs threatening to sink me.

I should be happy he was leaving. For weeks all I'd wanted was for him to leave. But right now, that was not how I felt. The deadline giving me a sense of impending doom. Every minute that ticked by making me feel closer to sinking. The words we had exchanged, the words he was leaving with, giving it an even sourer taste. At one point I even wondered if he was going to come back to say goodbye. The idea that he might not was agony.

Confused and conflicted, I called Lu.

"Hey, flower. How are you?"

"He asked me to come to Brazil." I didn't have time for pleasantries. In fact, time was the one thing I didn't have.

"Ok... And what did you say?" Lu smiled, half excited at the prospect.

"That I can't."

Her smile dropped. "Why?"

"Because he made a fool out of me in front of everyone. How am going to show my face there? Everyone will think I'm an idiot. What is that word you use?" My unease was making me agitated. I paced the room.

"What word?"

"For people that are cheated on and stupid enough to stay."

"Corna?"

"Yeah, that."

"You're not a *corna. Cornos* are the people whose partners are serial, unashamed cheaters. They know they are being cheated on, they know it will never stop, but they pretend to be blind. That's not what you are."

"How is that not what I am if I come back? He cheated on me in front of everyone."

"He cheated on you *once*. With Angela, who everyone knows is a viper. Nobody thinks you're a *corna;* everyone knows she's a homewrecker."

"Which makes me look even more stupid." My voice raised enough to make Amber jump in her seat, her eyes going big, her body tensing.

"No. If anything, it makes Celo look stupid."

"Potato, pot*a*to."

"Flower, since when do you care what people think? Plus, you guys have a baby together. Do you really think people don't expect you to turn up here at some point? Half of that little cutie's family is here."

"Lu, did he tell you he was planning to move over here permanently?"

"He said he would talk to you about it, yeah. But that he was prepared to rent the house, have someone else run the bars, and start again in the UK. He said he wanted to be close to you and Amber."

"Why didn't you say anything?" My temper was approaching borderline panic.

"Because he said he wanted to talk to you."

"Well, he did. And I told him I'm going to Denver."

"What?" Lu frowned. "To live?"

"No. Well… I don't know yet."

"Is that a possibility or a done deal?"

"Kind of a done deal."

"So you decided to relocate your baby without running it past him?" Her face changed into an expression that told me I was missing something obvious.

"I thought it would make it easier, you know, if we were at least on the same side of the Atlantic."

"Well… not quite. Denver is fourteen hours' flight from São Paulo. It's twelve to London. But I don't think he's upset with the distance or you going to see your family. I think he's upset with you making a decision about your mutual child without involving him. He already feels like a second-class citizen in her life. You might have just cemented that."

"Not helping, Lu!" My tone startled Amber. She started to complain. "It's ok, Poppet. It's ok. Where is your dummy?" I picked her up from her chair, trying to keep her from crying.

"The other day you were complaining he'd stopped trying with you. Don't tell him you don't want him, push him aside, then be surprised he stopped trying."

"I didn't push him aside."

"You tell me, flower. How would you feel if he came in and announced he was taking Amber back to Brazil with him without talking to you?" She waited a minute. When I didn't respond, she continued. "By now you must know what runs behind everything he does. He's prepared to quit his whole life here, everything he worked for to come live in London. You're not stupid, flower. Surely you can see what he's trying to do. He wants to stay close to you and your little girl, even if he has to put up with this weird friendship you guys have got going on."

"It's not a weird friendship. We are co-parenting." I was too defensive. Even I could hear the lie in my tone.

"Oh, really? How is this co-parenting when he doesn't have a say on anything to do with his baby? And how is it not weird when you have kissed, slept in the same bed, and have this stupidly intense chemistry?"

"Lu! I'm not calling for a bollocking! He's leaving at 5pm. You were supposed to be helping me!"

"Flower, I'm going to ask you a question. Answer me

honestly, ok? Why are you panicking that he's leaving? You know he'll come back."

Her question made me halt on the spot.

"Paige…" She never called me by my name. "I'm your friend, and I'm going to tell you the truth. You're not allowed to be mad at me."

I groaned. "Don't, Lu."

"You need to stop this nonsense and talk to him. Really, talk to him. It's time, flower. You guys need to talk about what happened and where your relationship is going. You need to stop running. Because, flower, as far as men go, Celo is actually quite reasonable. A bit messed up in the head and full of demons, granted, but if you talk to him, he's a fairly straight shooter, and his heart is in the right place. You know he's terrified of losing you or the baby. Don't you think you've punished him enough?"

She was starting to annoy me. I wasn't annoyed with her tone or even her directness. She was annoying me because she was right.

"I love how everyone is expecting me to forgive him. It's like you guys have forgotten what happened. He cheated on me, Lu! I caught him naked between Angela's legs having a right good time! He made a fool out of me in front of your whole family! But he comes over here for a hand full of weeks and it's all forgiven and forgotten? Why? Because he's playing nice?"

I could hear her sigh on the other end of the line. "No, flower. Because he's heartbroken about what happened just as much as you are. And because he loves you and you love him. What do you want to be: happy or bitter?"

The deadbolt hit the latch, my anger morphing into sadness. "I don't know if I can forgive him."

"I think you already have. You just don't want to admit to it."

Despite being lullabied up and down the room, Amber started to cry. The more agitated I got, the tenser her little body had become. It was like she could sense the heaviness.

"Amber is crying. I need to go, Lu. I'll call you later."

♥♥♥

Five o'clock came and went with no sign of Celo. The anguish I was feeling manifested itself as agitation, and I rocked Amber up and down the sitting room like I was trying to dig a trench with my feet. Until a taxi stopped on the curb right outside the window at quarter past five, and he got out.

I threw the door open before he even knocked, and Celo came into the hall but didn't remove his coat or his shoes. He wasn't staying.

He looked at me for a moment, one of his hands busy—flipping and rotating his lighter. Expression blank, but eyes resigned, defeated, hurt. His gaze dropped to the floor and stayed there for a while. He said nothing.

But after what felt like minutes, he sighed. The lighter went in his pocket and his hands asked for Amber. I handed her over.

He held her suspended, much like the first day he came to visit. He spoke to her in Portuguese, making promises to see her soon, telling her he loved her, kissing her repeatedly. She smiled back at him, cooed, responded to every single word he said. Little arms and legs kicking with excitement. My eyes started to sting, my throat closing.

When the words weren't enough, he hugged her for a long moment. Lips permanently on her head. Then handed her back to me.

"I need to go," he said, voice low, more of a whisper than properly spoken. But he stood there not moving, looking at me like he was waiting for something.

I couldn't respond. If I did, I risked crying. Pinned to the spot by a sadness that made no sense. He wasn't going to war, he wasn't dying, we were going to see him again, but it somehow felt like we weren't.

He came closer, his hand caressing Amber's head over and over again, refusing to let go of her. He lowered his head to kiss hers one last time. On the way back to standing he touched his forehead to mine, hand cupping the back of my head.

And his veneer broke.

His eyes squeezed shut, his face twisting into pain, mouth quivering and stretching into a thin line. He tapped his head onto mine, once, twice, then pressed them together with so much force I would have moved backward if his hand hadn't been at the back of my head. Tears spilled over, heartbroken, devastated. He hugged us—tight, grabbing fists full of my clothes, my hair. His breath faltering in silent sobs right next to my ear.

Amber complained about being squeezed in between us, and she too started crying.

Celo let go. Stepped away and turned his back to me, head lowered. He wiped at his face, sniffled, took a couple of deep breaths, hands on his waist. And I tried to comfort Amber and stop her from crying. After a couple of minutes, she did.

His arms dropped from his waist. He half turned to me, but his eyes stayed on the floor. He nodded, letting me know he was done and going.

And I couldn't take it. I couldn't take this. I couldn't let him leave like this. As his hand reached for the door latch and the door opened, I grabbed at his sleeve.

"We'll come."

His head turned my way, but he didn't look at me.

"We'll come to Brazil."

His eyes rose to mine, eyelashes wet, sockets still red from all his rubbing. Face confused.

"I have to wait for her final jabs in a couple of weeks, and I need to go to Denver for a week or two, but we will come."

His whole body turned to me, the door left half open. "You will?" He looked shocked.

I nodded.

He lunged forward, hands holding my face, wiping away the tears I didn't know I was crying. "Please, don't say that to me if you don't mean it." The words tumbled out of his mouth like he was running out of air.

"We'll come."

For a moment he stood there, hunched over me, my face in his hands, eyes searching mine for any signs that I hadn't meant what I'd said or would change my mind. Unbelieving, frozen, not breathing.

"We'll come to Brazil. After the jabs and Denver, we'll come."

And he hugged me. Tight, but different. Full of relief.

Amber started crying again. The taxi honked its horn outside. Celo let go to peek through the door and signal to the driver—one finger in the air, one minute.

I smiled at him, rocking Amber to settle her down. "Go. Call me when you land."

He nodded, gazed at me for a second longer, but didn't smile. He marched to us, kissed Amber's head, then my forehead, and walked out of the door.

CHAPTER 24
Marcelo

So much happened in such a short amount of time, it wasn't until the taxi turned the corner that it hit me. Relief so immense that I had to lean on my elbows and take a minute.

I had always hated crying. Not because men shouldn't do it, but because in my life it had never changed a damn thing. It didn't make the blows stop coming, it made them increase and hit harder. It didn't bring my grandparents back; it didn't rewind the clock and erase any of my mistakes. But right now, I didn't mind it, and I didn't care. Because this was relief. Unfiltered and concentrated utter relief.

I had come to Paige's apartment feeling as though I had been dumped in quicksand, slowly sinking, trapped with no way out. Anger mixed with regret so deep, it tied around my neck like a suffocating ball and chain. I hadn't been able to keep my composure, bawling my damn eyes out like a kid. Cracking and caving under the weight of saying goodbye as if I was a lump of scrap metal on a crusher. I had no idea how I'd make it through the twelve-hour flight, sitting in confined space, festering in the way I was feeling.

Then Paige had thrown me a lifeline.

I leaned back into the seat, staring at the ceiling of the cab, taking deep breaths, half laughing, half crying to myself. Looking completely unhinged to the driver eyeballing me through the rearview mirror. The current of electricity coursing through my veins made me want to run a marathon.

For weeks, I hadn't slept for more than a handful of hours. The whole thing with the meds had either stolen my sleep or turned it into nightmares. But on the flight, I slept like a baby. Don't think I even saw the safety announcements, because for the first time in my life I felt my luck had finally turned, and life was giving me an opportunity I didn't have to bleed for.

Marisa picked me up from the airport. Big smiles, hugs that made me feel I was home. She straightened my clothes, and asked me if I'd eaten, smelling of Anaïs Anaïs like she always did.

We had stayed in touch throughout the time I'd been away, but I could tell she was worried about me more than she'd let it show. She'd known leaving was going to be hard, so she'd made sure she was the first person I saw coming off the plane.

I hated this. I hated that I made her worry. That I was such a burden to her, someone she was always concerned about, like I was made of porcelain and would break at any minute. I wasn't. But I was happy to see her.

Risa was one of the few people that truly knew me. She read my face, saw right through my shit, and told me straight whenever I stepped out of line. If she pitied me, she never treated me different or rubbed my head. I received the same treatment and care as her real children. That's what made me believe she loved me like she loved them. She hadn't given birth to me, but she was my mother in every other sense of the word. And trust me when I tell you, even at twenty-eight, she could still whoop my ass with a single look.

"Are you going to see Dr. Fernandes this week? I think you need to after the mess with the meds." She maneuvered out of the car park. I don't think she really cared about the pills. She just wanted to make sure that stopping taking them hadn't made me feel worse.

"I am. But I'm not looking forward to it. I'm sure he will chew me out about it, don't worry."

"Good." She glanced at me sideways, smiled. We both knew he would just tell me something I knew already—that I shouldn't have done it cold turkey. "So… how did you leave things in London?" She checked her mirrors as if she was asking just to make conversation, playing it down.

"Still touch and go. Some things came out in the wash."

"Like what?" Risa sounded tense, but she kept her eyes on the road.

"It turns out we didn't really know much about each other."

She peeked at me sideways while trying to keep her attention on the road at the same time. "That's kind of normal. In any relationship you have the honeymoon phase; then around the six-month mark, you start to get to know the other person better and see their flaws. The problem is that your relationship has never followed a regular, linear path. You're doing it cross-Atlantic, with a year's lag, and a baby."

I snorted and nodded. When you're as lucky as I am nothing in your life is 'regular'. 'Normal' is almost an unachievable ideal. If what Paige wanted was an easy life, I was definitely not the right person for her.

"The important thing is: do you still feel the same way about her, now that you know her better?" Risa was serious, her voice a little tense, unsure if what I was saying was a good or bad thing.

"No." I didn't mean it to, but my voice took a lower tone. "I respect her more. I want her more. I don't know how to explain it, Risa. But despite the fact I messed things up and she's upset and angry with me, we were still both there, you know. Does that make sense? When she was armed and throwing knives at me, or feeling low, I was still turning up. And when it all became too much for me, she was there. Sitting with me in the dark, making me eat, making me get out of the apartment. It didn't seem to scare her, you know?" I thought for a second.

"She saw me, Risa. She saw me on the meds, coming off them, in bad shape. She didn't run. And I didn't run either."

"You talk about it like being human and having bad days is a deal breaker."

"No. But realizing someone is a hot mess might be." I looked out of the window. It gave me a weird sense of comfort looking at the familiar landscape. "People look at me and they see one thing, Risa. But if I let them close, what they find is something that isn't as sexy or well put together."

"Who is? I told you before. Nobody is as collected and put together as they appear on the surface."

"Some less than others," I mumbled.

"Yes. But it didn't stop you crossing the Atlantic to try and get your family back, did it?"

I didn't answer.

"You know, I saw this quote on Instagram recently. It was by some Canadian psychologist. I think he's called Jordan Peterson or Patterson. I don't know his work, but I liked what he said: 'A harmless man is not a good man. A good man is a very dangerous man who knows how to control himself'. That's what matters: being a good man, Celo. Someone who fights for and does the right thing for the people he loves. Your heart is in the right place. *That's* what matters."

I nodded, smiled. Marisa never let me play the feel-sorry-for-myself card.

We hit a spot of traffic and Risa's attention diverted. She indicated, focused on getting in the right lane.

"Did you two talk about what happened?"

I thought back to the morning after Paige and I kissed. That kiss had lit me up like Vegas. It had taken every milligram of self-control and good sense I had not to turn it into something more. But the next morning it was as if I had walked too close to the sun. High and hopeful one minute, incinerated the next. "Some. But not much."

"Ok…" The word dragged, and she hesitated, trying to understand. "So how did you leave things with her?"

"We still need to iron things out. Like you said, it's going to take time."

"I'm not surprised. I didn't think Paige was going to forgive you just because you turned up. She's going to make you work for it. She's a smart woman." Risa said it as she focused on her driving, almost as if she was mumbling at something while her attention was elsewhere.

I waited until she got to the lights. I knew she would want to look at me once I spilled it. "They might be coming to Brazil in a few weeks, Mom." I looked at her then, and I couldn't help but smile.

Her head whipped toward me, eyes wide. "Oh, my God! Why didn't you say that to start with!" She slapped my leg. "Do I really have to squeeze everything out of you?" She was also smiling. "So I'm going to meet Amber Marisa?" Her glee and excitement were contagious, and it enabled me to bask in my own.

The lights turned green, and the traffic started moving.

"That's a good sign. A really good sign," she said as we moved forward. I still didn't know if she was talking to me or herself, but she sounded relieved.

"Everything is still hinging, and I'm still walking a really fine line, Risa. So keep it to yourself until she gets here, ok? Just for you, me, Lu, and Gabe to know. I don't want to pin too much on it either. When I asked her originally, she said she wouldn't come. She changed her mind just before I left. A few weeks is a long time; she could change her mind again. So I don't wanna make a big deal about it." I didn't need people talking to Paige and making her feel under pressure. Or for my head to swell full of hope so I crashed and burned if she changed her mind.

"Sure. It's still good news, though!" She smiled wide, full of teeth. And I could feel my smile getting wider too, despite wanting to keep my expectations under control.

But of course, relief doesn't last long for the damned. Being in London had made me live in a state of suspension—away from some of my problems and responsibilities. Coming home threw me back right in the middle of it.

"How has Felipe been with the news?" My voice was serious.

"At first, he was annoyed of course." Marisa's eyes stayed on the road. "But the most he said about it is that he hopes Paige isn't stupid enough to take you back. Which, let's be honest, he was always going to say." She was editing. Keeping to well-known facts to avoid creating any more friction.

"You know… that was one of the reasons she quoted for not wanting to come back here originally." The thought rattled my cage, making me angry. In a confined space and without options to burn the energy, my knee bopped up and down at speed. "She was worried people would think she's a fool if she gave me a second chance. That's why I don't want anyone to know she's coming. The last thing I need is someone filling her head with this crap."

"I see." Marisa glanced at me sideways.

"I have done my best to give Felipe time to adjust, Risa. And I have kept my mouth shut and taken his anger like a good sport. But he'd better not get in the way of me getting my family back. The same goes for Angela and anybody else with an opinion."

"I understand." She sighed, hands squeezing the steering wheel. "But right now, while we drive home, can we allow ourselves to be happy that your little girl and Paige might be coming? Let's focus on the positive and enjoy the moment. We'll deal with the problems when we need to cross that bridge. Focus on the good news, ok?" She tapped my leg, diverting the subject to something we could both feel good about.

♥♥♥

It was nice to be back home. Great to go back to work. The warm weather and home food shifted my mood and made me feel better. If I ever thought routine was taxing, I had gained a whole new level of appreciation for it.

For the days that followed, Paige video called every day at pre-agreed times so I could see and speak to Amber. I got regular pictures, videos of her doing her exercises or smiling. But at the end of the first week, just as I had finished showering, my phone rang out of the blue.

"Paige? Is everything ok?" It was 1am here, 5am there, and she was video calling me.

"No. I mean, yes, but not really."

I leaned the phone against some stuff on a shelf so I could wrap myself in a towel. "Why? What's wrong?

Her head leaned to the side. "What are you doing?"

"I was in the shower. What's wrong?"

"Oh." She leaned forward, looking sideways like she could see what was to one side of me. Suspicious, questioning.

It took me a second to understand what she was thinking—that I had company. Her distrust was a reminder that things weren't resolved between us and I might never live down what I'd done. Realization made me lean against the basin countertop and sigh. "I just came back from work, Paige. You know I always shower before I get into bed."

She looked at me blankly.

I picked the phone up, flipped the camera around and showed her my empty bathroom and bedroom, then flipped it back to me. "Satisfied?"

"I don't know what you mean." She didn't look at me when she said it.

"Hmm..." I reminded myself that I had given her reason to distrust me, trying not to let it annoy me. "Why are you calling me at 5am, Paige? Are *you* with someone?" But the irritation came through anyway.

"Actually, I am."

Cold ran through me. And I noticed she was sitting against a headboard I couldn't tell was hers or not.

She moved her phone and showed me Amber—awake. Wide-eyed and alert.

I braced myself against the countertop as I laughed at how my jealousy had escalated from zero to one hundred in seconds, not sure I'd ever get used to feeling this possessive over anyone.

"Can you talk to your daughter in Portuguese and tell her to let me sleep? I tried in English—several times—and she's ignoring me. Maybe you can work your magic? Blame Lu. She told me to make you suffer with me."

I smiled at the phone, ironic but relieved. "Sure. Put her on." Amber's chubby cheeks filled the screen. "Coffee Bean, you need to let your mom sleep," I told her in Portuguese as I was asked. "But before we talk about that, do me a favor? If any man gets near your momma, scream your head off, puke, pee, and poo on him. Full attack mode. Can you hold the fort for your daddy?"

Amber didn't seem to know where to look, but she smiled, cooed, and squeaked.

"Good girl."

Paige put the phone down somewhere so I could see both of them. "She doesn't seem to be taking your pep talk very seriously."

"She is. We are still negotiating the sleeping terms, but she has just reminded me she is half British and shall never surrender. Right, baby girl?"

More squeaking.

"So the two-and-a-half-month-old is a fan of Churchill, huh?" Her eyebrows were raised, skeptical.

"Powerful brain, I told you." I unraveled the towel from around my waist to dry my face, hair, torso, and arms so I would stop dripping all over the floor. When I looked back at the phone, Paige was staring at me. I knew that look, knew it damn well. It made me smile and tipped the balance in my favor, making me brazen. "Liking what you see, Lewis?"

She blinked, pretended to adjust Amber's clothing. "Cocky as ever, I see."

"Ah… So you do remember it." I smiled at the phone.

Her head tilted, face unimpressed, eyebrows raising. "Focus." She pointed at Coffee Bean. "Baby. Awake. Mother not sleeping."

"Sorry, couldn't resist." Sorry my ass. "Give me a sec. Father. Wet. Naked." I pointed at myself.

"Really? Hadn't noticed." She played it down.

"Hadn't noticed, huh? Ok."

I took the phone into the bedroom with me and leaned it on top of the dresser while I put my underpants on, giving her a full view of my chest, abs, and V-line but nothing else. I worked hard to have the suckers, might as well use it to my advantage. And I'm not gonna lie, I wanted a little revenge. I had spent five weeks feeling hot under the collar every time she breastfed Amber or leaned over something. It was her turn to feel bothered. She could deny it all she wanted, but she wasn't immune to me.

"You're doing this on purpose," she said before I picked the phone back up.

"I don't know what you mean. I'm just getting dressed so I can focus, like you asked me to."

She rolled her eyes at me, and I tried to keep a straight face.

"Now… Coffee Bean…" I went back into Portuguese as I leaned against my headboard. "Here is the plan. I like that your mom called me, and I'm enjoying talking to her. So you can stay awake for a little while longer, then you fall asleep and give us a minute, ok? But do me another favor and do it again tomorrow. Deal?"

"Ehh," she babbled back at me.

"I'm starting to think this was a mistake."

"No. She has just agreed to go to sleep."

"Has she now?"

"She has, but it's best I stay on the line, just in case she doesn't follow through on our deal."

"Is that so?" Paige smiled at me. She knew damn well what I was doing.

I smiled back. "How are you?"

"Tired. Awake."

I nodded. "Hmm… Me too."

She shook her head, but the smile stayed on her face. "Was Eight busy?" Her voice was semi-sarcastic, semi-joking. Humoring my wanting to talk to her.

"Uh-huh. Still sorting things out after a long time away. We entered a competition for the best cocktail in the city."

"Do you think you can win?"

"We'll see. Depends on who we are competing against."

"How is the other bar coming along?"

"Currently a wreck. They're still ripping the old stuff out of it. We started training the new managers at Eight. It's costing me a damn fortune at the minute. But at least we're on schedule." I flipped the phone and propped it on a cushion so I could lie sideways while talking to her.

Paige followed suit with her device so our screens would match. It took her only a second to realize I had given her a full view all the way down to the waist of my boxers. She raised an eyebrow, rolled her eyes, and shook her head. But after her display of disapproval, her eyes scanned down the screen. I tried not to grin.

"Look what I found in my photos…"

A few taps and a pic came through: me holding Amber suspended in front of me, pulling a ridiculous face because of the poonami she had unleashed on me out of nowhere.

I laughed. "Are you trying to put me in my place?"

"If the shoe fits."

We smiled at each other for a beat.

"Did you apply for her passport?"

"Uh-huh. Did you see her passport picture?" She smiled at me, the image clearly fresh in her memory.

I smiled back. "Very sweet. How long will it take to come through?"

"A few days. Depends how busy they are."

"She's still going for her jabs this week?" I was making conversation, but I also wanted to know she was preparing to travel. The knowledge she was sorting things to make it possible gave me hope that she hadn't changed her mind.

"Yes. If she feels unwell after it, you might get another phone call in the middle of the night."

"Lucky me." I grinned.

She rolled her eyes.

Within thirty minutes Coffee Bean had fallen asleep.

"I don't know if it was you speaking to her in Portuguese or if she thinks our conversation is boring."

"Does it matter if it works?"

"I suppose not."

Paige placed her in her cot, but kept on speaking to me, lying in bed, for another forty minutes. Talking about everything and nothing, shooting the breeze.

After that, she called me every time Amber was awake late. Then I started calling when I had finished work for no reason at all but to hear her voice and see her face before I fell asleep. The tone of the conversation changing from things to do with Coffee Bean to chatting, joking, and flirting. What she wore also started changing. From T-shirts to lace things that drove me to distraction and made me not sleep until I'd sorted myself out. I thought it would stop when she went to Denver, but it didn't—the time zone difference working in my favor.

It never crossed the line, though. We flirted and teased each other, but it never evolved into anything more. Whether this was a negative or positive, I wasn't quite sure. But at least it was me she saw every night, and she knew the only woman talking to me in bed was her. It didn't really change where we were, but I hoped it would rebuild her trust that I wasn't fooling around and was serious about her and our family.

CHAPTER 25

Paige

The time he normally called me came and went, and he didn't call. By the end of an hour, the delay started to annoy me. What the hell was he doing?

> **Me**
> Going to bed now. x

The answer came back in minutes.

> **Celo**
> It's band night. Had 2 take them 4 food. Home in 1 hr. Can I call you then? Bjos.

The message came with a photo: the usual place he took bands for a late meal. Gabe's band were all sitting around a table. Lu was there too. I hadn't asked, but every time he was doing something out of routine, he would send me pictures of where he was, who he was with. Like he was trying to prove a point.

I sent him a picture back. Amber and I in bed. Amber asleep, nestled to the side of me.

He sent me a voice note, unusual for him. "I'm leaving now. Will get home, shower, and call you. Don't go to sleep. Please? I really, really want to see you. Wait for me?" He must have stepped outside somewhere because the background wasn't as noisy as I would've expected. I could hear his voice clear as day—deep, raspy, sexy.

I listened to the message twice. Three times. Amber twitched next to me. She recognized his voice too. There was something about it. The accent, the timbre, I don't know. But it vibrated right through me, echoing in the quiet, sending chills down my spine.

> **Me**
> Hurry up. Tired mum here. 😴

> **Celo**
> Trying. Hard-working dad here. 😉

He called me an hour and a half later. Fresh out of the shower. Doing his little 'I'm not aware I'm showing you my fit body' routine.

Two could play this game. I had lost some of the baby weight, so had finally gone shopping and bought a selection of pretty things. The lacy halter-neck nightgown I was wearing gave me a killer cleavage, showing *the two birth marks I liked to torture him with* as he'd said once.

"What is that?" I pointed at the screen. A piece of plastic was covering part of his left peck.

"New tattoo."

"What is it?"

"You'll see it when you get here. Coffee Bean in her cot?"

"Yeah."

"Is that new?" He pointed at what I was wearing.

It was. "No. You've seen it before."

He shook his head. "I would remember."

"Hmm, how do you know?"

"Because I like it." He smiled, devilish, unrepentant. His eyes danced side to side, up and down the screen, top eyelids appearing and disappearing. He readjusted the way he was sitting and mumbled something in Portuguese I didn't quite understand.

"What did you say?"

"Did you get the tickets? I emailed them today."

"I did. It didn't need to be business class."

"Yes, it did. Fourteen hours in a plane with a baby on your own is no joke."

I flipped the phone and propped it against a pillow so I could lie on my back and pull my knees up. It caught a wider angle, all the way down to the top of my thighs. He flipped his phone to match mine.

"O negócio é de renda e curto. Cê vai mesmo acabar com a minha raça, né?" He scratched his neck.

"What did you say?"

"I said it looks nice, that thing you're wearing."

"Thanks." I pulled the hem down, only for it to roll back down my legs and gather in the fold between my middle and my thighs.

Celo grunted, closed his eyes, and started poking a thumb to his forehead.

"Are you ok? Do you have a headache or something?"

"Or something."

"We can talk tomorrow if you need to sleep."

"No, that's not what I need." Voice husky, he stopped poking, and his arm disappeared from view.

"What do you need then?"

He looked at me for a long minute but didn't respond. Hooded, heavy eyes like pinballs, all over the screen and back to my face.

"What are you doing?"

"Looking at you."

"I noticed. I thought you wanted to talk to me."

He shook his head.

"You wanted to see me?" I repeated his voice message, joining the dots.

A nod.

"Dressed in the thing you liked in the photo."

Another nod, lazy blinks.

From anyone else this would sound weird, but not him. This last month on video calls he had talked more than usual, but Celo wasn't really a talker. He was more comfortable with silence than most.

"Sounds like you had a long day."

"Yeah. Tired now." His gaze lingered, head tilting. He was remembering, as was I, that when we were together and he had days like this, he liked to lie on my shoulder and let me run my fingers through his hair. He would say he was tired, but within minutes of me running my nails on his skin, he would start kissing my neck, rubbing himself on my thigh. The tiredness turning the sex into something mellower, slower, but hot all the same.

A hand ran down his face, rubbed his neck, then was placed behind his head, a tattooed arm taking over one side of the screen. The tip of his fingers appearing and disappearing behind his neck—rubbing, self-soothing.

I lay there, staring at the ceiling, letting him look at me. My mind elsewhere, lost in memories that made me run my nails over my own skin, self-soothing just like he was.

CHAPTER 26
Marcelo

I STOOD OUTSIDE ARRIVALS AT GUARULHOS AIRPORT, PACING. THE fourteen longest hours of my life were almost over. Paige had messaged me to let me know they were at Denver airport, then again to say they were ready for take-off, and her phone would be off, but the pit of my stomach was still twisting, the voice at the back of my head telling me that she could still have changed her mind at the last minute.

Over the last month we had video called daily. I called her when I got home from work, and we talked for long hours on the phone about nothing and everything. Making plans for when she came. Playing teasing games neither of us admitted being aware of.

And still, my mind kept telling me that I would crash and burn, and she would change her mind.

Waves of people came through the gates and a sea of people waited outside. Drivers held placards with surnames written by hand. Two little kids held a sign they'd painted for their grandma. An old man held a big bouquet of red roses. I'd considered bringing flowers, but that wouldn't have been practical with the baby.

The board at the top of the gate announced which planes had landed, which ones were waiting for luggage. Paige's plane was still in the air, just to add to my torture.

The airport was busy, which meant immigration and

luggage belt queues would be busy too. It could take over an hour, and I would be a ball of tension for the duration.

Grandma arrived, the kids dodging passersby to run to her, screaming with excitement. Businesspeople nodded at drivers who jumped straight into serving and helping with luggage. A young couple celebrated their reunion with the girl jumping to straddle the dude's waist, their PDA verging on obnoxious even by Brazilian standards. The old boy handed the bouquet of flowers to, who I assumed was, his wife with a peck on the lips and a long hug—a lot more restrained and refined than the young couple but probably more loving.

Who was I kidding? Given the option, I would've loved for Paige to give me a PDA welcome any day. Fuck restrain and refinement. But that wasn't what I was going to get.

The board changed to 'landed'.

What *was* I going to get? Truth be told, I had no clue. We'd been talking and even flirting on the phone, but we hadn't talked about us or defined where we were. We were more than friends, but not really lovers; what was the etiquette for that? How did you airport greet the love of your life that you cheated on, had a baby with, and don't know if she'll ever forgive you?

I gave my brain something else to worry about. Paige had fourteen hours marinating in a flying can with a baby. If Coffee Bean had given her a hard time, she might land wanting to murder me for asking her to do this. There was no way of knowing if they'd had a good flight or not, even though I had booked them into business class.

I reached for my phone to stop my brain from overheating.

Lu
Anything yet?

Me
Plane landed, but nothing yet.

Risa
Your girls landed?

Me
Yeah, not out yet.

Nothing from Paige. The last message I'd sent was still unread.

The board changed to 'disembarking'.

Man, this is when I missed smoking. Cigarettes are not good for you but in situations like these they actually give you something to do. I pulled the lighter out of my pocket and sat down. I'd been flipping it between my fingers for a few minutes when I realized a little boy holding a blue teddy rabbit was watching me. I smiled at him; he hid behind his mother's legs, looked up to her for reassurance. She was busy talking to airport staff.

I showed him my lighter. Moved it from one hand to another while he watched me, then made it disappear and showed him my empty hands. His eyes grew big, marveling. Freddie also loved this trick. He was bigger now, but it still got him. I waved at the kid. He waved back with his teddy. I showed him the lighter again, his expression surprised. He really thought it had disappeared. From one hand to another, and… gone. Empty hands. He smiled this time, slapped his mother's legs to show her, but she was busy and told him to wait.

I leaned into my elbows, rested my forehead on my knuckles. All this waiting was going to be the death of me. While I was staring at the floor, two small shoes appeared in my field of vision. The little boy had walked toward me, his mother watching him from a distance.

I smiled at him. Showed him my lighter, his eyes focused on my hands as if he could figure it out now that he was up close. From one hand to another, and… gone. He smiled at me. I reached behind his ear and made the lighter reappear as though I had pulled it from inside his head. He looked surprised, little hand reaching for the side of his head to check there weren't any more lighters in there. I looked at his mother, just to check she was still ok with me playing with her kid; she was smiling.

"Is this your rabbit?" I asked him.

He showed me the teddy.

"Is it the rabbit from the cartoon?"

He nodded. Then set off running back to his mother, almost getting run over by luggage trolleys. That was when I caught sight of caramel hair, peeking through the gaps in between the heads of people waiting.

I jumped to my feet.

Paige was pushing a luggage trolley in front of her, Coffee Bean strapped to her in the baby carrier sling. She maneuvered the trolley left, following the corded path designated for arrivals; then stopped, both her hands wrapping around Amber in the carrier. She couldn't see me; her eyes scanned behind her, to her side, looking for me. Her head turned one hundred and eighty and landed on me, standing at the end of the arrivals path.

For a beat, her face told me nothing and the knot in my stomach got tighter.

Then she broke into the most beautiful smile.

TO BE CONTINUED.

PORTUGUESE TRANSLATIONS

Pg. 5
Cacete! Merda! Porra! Desgraça!
Damn it! Shit! Fuck! Fucking disaster!

Pg. 37
Oi vovó, vovô, Freddie, Tia Lu.
Hi grandma, grandpa, Freddie, Auntie Lu.

Meu pai veio me ver hoje. Eu bati uma real nele, sabe? Colocamos todos os pingos nos i-s.
My dad came to see me today. I gave him a real talking-to, you know? We dotted all the i's and crossed all the t's.

Pg. 55
Minas Gerais – Belo Horizonte; DF – Brasilia; Goiás – Goiânia
Three Brazilian states/counties and their capitals
Fun fact: Paola Santana is personally connected to all three states

Pg. 88
Vovó
Grandma

Pg. 104

Oi, princesinha. Mas que linda! De laço no cabelo. Você sentiu saudade do papai?

Hello, little princess. You look so beautiful! With a bow in your hair. Did you miss your daddy?

Pg. 136

Sampa

Affectionate nickname for the city of São Paulo in Brazil

Pg. 144

Ficantes

Ficante (singular), *ficantes* (plural)

Brazilian slang for a hookup – someone you are romantically or physically involved with but without any commitment

Pg. 147

Guaraná

Brazilian pop / fizzy drink made from the guarana berry

Pg. 147 and 151

Pão de queijo

Brazilian cheese dough balls made with tapioca flour or cassava starch

Pg. 148

Mercearia

Grocery store

Pg. 191

Boa tarde, princesinha do pai. Tá se sentindo melhor, meu amor?

Good afternoon, daddy's little princess. Are you feeling better, my love?

Que sorriso linda! Mas você acordou toda fresh assim?
What a gorgeous smile! Did you wake up looking this fresh?

Pg. 200
Até amanhã
See you tomorrow

Pg. 222
Sertanejo
Brazilian country music

Pg. 247
O negócio é de renda e curto. Cê vai mesmo acabar com a minha raça, né?
The thing is made of lace and short. You're really trying to end me, aren't you?

ACKNOWLEDGMENTS

I could not have written *Glowing Embers* without the support of some very special people.

My daughter, **Natalha**, who has always supported—and continues to support—my writing adventures, and who gave me **Sienna**, the inspiration behind Amber Marisa.

Janine, the voice behind Siobhan Williams, who made sure my Scouse accent was pure and real.

Tai and **Maria**, my amazing beta readers, who were tortured with the first draft of both *Playing with Fire* and *Glowing Embers*.

Helen Hawkins, a fellow romance writer and my editor. She is the reason you can read this novel without thinking I butchered the English language—even as a foreigner. And if you find any mistakes, they are mine. As per usual, I edited her edits. Sorry, Helen, again!

Abbie Rutherford, the typesetter who has made the inner pages of both *Playing with Fire* and *Glowing Embers* look so good.

And last but definitely not least, **God.** Yes, The Almighty. For continuing to indulge the desires of my heart to write, and for sprinkling me with the grit and creativity to chase my dream. I still don't deserve such a blessing, but He has given it to me anyway. If you're looking for real, unconditional love... Seek Him out.

ABOUT THE AUTHOR

Paola Santana is Brazilian but lives in Liverpool, England. Like her main character, she came to visit and had her heart stolen by a local. When she's not reading or writing, you can find her talking about books on her social channels. *Glowing Embers* is her second published novel and the second instalment in the *Playing with Fire* series.

CONNECT WITH PAOLA

WWW.PAOLASANTANABOOKS.COM

instagram.com/paolasantanabooks

tiktok.com/@paolasantanabooks

facebook.com/paolasantanabooks

www.ingramcontent.com/pod-product-compliance
Ingram Content Group UK Ltd.
Pitfield, Milton Keynes, MK11 3LW, UK
UKHW042345220426
470291UK00002B/61